The Manningtree Witches

A. K. BLAKEMORE

GRANTA

Granta Publications, 12 Addison Avenue, London W11 4QR

First published in Great Britain by Granta Books, 2021

A CIP catalogue record for this book is
available from the British Library.

2 4 6 8 9 7 5 3 1

ISBN 978 1 78378 643 5
eISBN 978 1 78378 645 9

www.granta.com

Typeset in Garamond by Patty Rennie

Printed and bound by CPI Group (UK) Ltd,
Croydon, CR0 4YY

THE MANNINGTREE WITCHES

for Paul Blakemore

'. . . then they all consult with *Satan* to save themselves, and *Satan* stands ready prepared, with a *What will you have me do for you, my near and dearest children, covenanted and compacted with me in my hellish league, and sealed with your blood, my delicate firebrand-darlings.*'

Matthew Hopkins, *The Discovery of Witches*, 1647

1643

'If our witches' phantasies were not corrupted, nor their wits confounded with this humour, they would not so voluntarilie and readilie confesseth that which calleth their life into question.'

Reginald Scot, *The Discovery of Witchcraft*, 1584

I

Mother

A hill wet with brume of morning, one hawberry bush squalid with browning flowers. I have woken and put on my work dress, which is near enough my only dress, and yet she remains asleep. *Jade. Pot-companion. Mother.* I stand at the end of the cot and consider her face. A beam of morning sun from the window slices over the left cheek. Dark hair spread about the pillow, matted and greasy and greying in places.

There is a smell to my mother, when she is sleeping. It is a complicated, I think mannish smell. I smelled a like smell when I was sent, as a little girl, to fetch my father away from the Red Lion and to supper. The inn would be clattery with men's voices and small-beer sour, and my father would be very jolly indeed, sweeping me up and kissing me on my forehead, his coat crisp from the rain in the big fields. Then we would walk from the alehouse back up the Lawford hill together, my tiny hand in his much larger. That was fifteen years ago, Father long dead.

So my mother – who is at present snoring fit to wake the Devil, as they say – and I sleep together, side by side, in this one chamber in the house the fifteen-year-dead man built for us. A house of three rooms, meanly furnished; two beds, one window, plaster blue with mildew. Things being born in the walls, I suspect. I know all the noises of her flesh, and all her complicated, mannish smells. I was in her flesh once, strange to think. Flesh of it, her flesh.

I force myself to look at her face for a very long time, and to consider it closely. It is so still that at first it might seem like a death-mask, or a statue's face. But even motionless, it is not so serene as any monument I have ever had the pleasure to see, be it by chapel or church, in Manningtree nor Mistley (not that there are many such images left in Essex at all, now Dowsing and his rooters have done their work, peeling the blithe martyrs down off St Mary's and hold-ing a bonfire for them over on the village green). Even in repose, my mother's character seems to shape every plane and furrow of that dry face like a maker's stamp on a horrid little pat of butter. Her Christian name is Anne, but she is called *the Beldam West*. It suits her, because it sounds wide and wicked; the sound of it is like the name of some dusty place in the book that God might drop big meteors upon. *Beldam*. 'Belle' is a French word, meaning beautiful (which my mother is not, though they say she was, once). And 'dam' like 'damned'. Over which I suppose it is not my place right to speculate.

I take her apart now, while her repose affords me the opportu-nity, and consider her piece by piece. Her nose is long and set in a crooked shape, having been broken. It was broken at least once, to my knowledge – four years ago, by a most wonderful right hook from Goody Rawbood as the two of them quarrelled in the herb garden on a late-spring afternoon. I do not remember what the sub-stance of their falling out was, on that occasion, but I do remember the hooting of the men gathered at the fence to watch. I remember the blow was struck. I remember how my mother tottered back into a rosemary bush with a hand clapped over her face, blood leaking sticky between her fingers, and raised a sweet fragrance as she tum-bled down onto her cules amid the little blue flowers. I can barely keep myself from laughing aloud when I smell rosemary, to this very day. Goody Rawbood is dead, of course – as people who wrong my mother have a way of ending up. See how the smell and look of her leads me to other things, other places. Or else my understanding of other things and other places comes through the smell and look of her, and that is what it is to have a mother.

But no more digressions. My mother's cheeks are hollowed out, the skin stretched over them tight and brown. The unwary blade of sunshine from the window whitens the down on her chin and her temple, and refines the thin lines age has lain at the corners of her eyes and around her mouth, like a cat's whiskers. Her forehead is pink with sunburn. The skin around her neck is loose, as though those folds are easing into their good fortune at having been spared proximity to the cruel eyes and sharp tongue that so disfavour her among our neighbours; a neck like a fat hog's wattles, baggy and discoloured and appalling.

The mouth is the worst thing. She holds her thin lips slightly open as she sleeps, and they are raw and dry at the corners, where a sediment has gathered. Looking in through this red opening you can perceive her mouth's interior satin, and see how her teeth are stained from chewing tobacco, how the wet root of her tongue jostles, as though she is dreaming a conversation. Or, more likely, a row.

Here is my very unchristian thought: I wish I had something horrible to hand to put into her mouth. I imagine I am lowering a wriggling mouse between her lips by its pink tail, then clamping my hand down over it. Or no. A jar of hot horses' piss, a fistful of rabbit droppings, blood – pig's blood – hot from the slice—

My mother's eyes open, and she says my name, quietly: 'Rebecca? Beck?'

'It is I.'

She mutters something I do not hear, and presses her hand to her temple. She groans. 'Never get old, Rebecca,' she says. 'Mind me, girl. I am all filled up with aches and pains before the work of the day is so much as thought of.'

I answer that her aches and pains might have more to do with the Edwards' small-beer than anticipation of honest labour. She is a very great drinker, and often says that drink does more than God in the way of comforting the poor man (*or woman, for that matter,* she will add, with a wink of her black eye).

'Mind thy tongue', she snaps back, wetting up her lips. 'And utter not that name in my house,' she adds, sleep-fuddled and haughty in even measure. *Utter* is the very word she uses, thinking herself Moses.

I ask her if the name 'Hobday' is still quite well to the ears of God and man. 'Because I've some linens to take to the Hobdays up the hill.'

Mother has risen from her bed now, and gropes for the chamber-pot. She squats down by the side of the bed and draws her wrinkled smock up over her knees, relieving herself. Her piss is a dark yolk-yellow colour in the mornings after she has been out drinking, and it smells yeasty, causes the whole room to smell yeasty. This is the smell of Friday – and Saturday, too, most usually. When she has finished she shakes herself off with a few jerks of her haunches and clambers back into the cot. Hot little room, the sun coming in from the east. *Layabout.* 'Take some milk-pottage for Bess,' she says, yawning. She lowers herself down and draws the coverlet over her breast, closing her eyes again. I wait there at the end of the cot for any further order or imprecation, but none comes.

Vinegar Tom bolts in through the door as it is opened, and leaps up onto Mother's bed. He mews a dismissal over his shoulder at me, and settles down by the Beldam's hip to lick the summer night off his fur. She lowers her hand to scratch at him between the ears. 'Impudent girl,' my mother murmurs, 'thou backward paw, thou whelk.'

I am very grateful to close the door behind, to shut away the creature that made me.

It is early in the morning. A nice big cream of cloud settles on the horizon. Out in the yard, one of the hens takes a considered step, her head held askew, like a woman in marvellous skirts stopping to check the tread of her boot for a stone.

2

Crone

Manningtree and Mistley are two villages that together add up to something like a town, fitted tidy as pattens, left and right, tucked neatly by the waters of Holbrook Bay on the crook of the Stour. When the tide is in, the blue slice of water jostles with little fishing boats and the hoys of merchantmen, and their rigging makes a marvellous cutwork of the sky. By night, they say smugglers make use of the waterway to go inland, carrying braces of French pistols and pyxes and gilded prayerbooks in Latin, which is the black speech of the Pope. When the water draws out, it leaves behind wide beds of soft silver mud where sandpipers, curlews and godwits scratch slender trails in their digging about for worms. It smells good or bad, depending on your point of smell – of sea-scum, bird shit and wrack drying up in the sun. There is one long, narrow road that runs alongside the riverbank, from the little port of Manningtree and the white Market Cross to old St Mary's Church in Mistley. Along this road is where the people live, for the most part, in some few dozen houses hunched along in various states of disrepair and flake, all mouldy thatch and tide-marked, half-tended gardens and smalls drying on lines that hang window to window across the muddy street. Smaller ways and alleys lead up away from the river from this one road, and into the rolling hills, and the fields where the true wealth of Essex chews cud in the fields: cows, warm golden and with fat udders so full with milk it makes your own tits ache just to look at them. Up in the fields is the world of the herds, as the valley and water is the place of birds. And the herds mill about the neat manor houses of the yeomen and petty gentry to whom they belong (and those yeomen, from their vantage point at the top of the valley, can look down their noses very well at those simple folk who live by nothing but the river and their wits at the bottom).

The old Widow Clarke also lives among these rolling hills and fields. Masters Richard Edwards and John Stearne – who is the second-richest man in Manningtree – must climb out of bed in the morning, throw open their damascene curtains, and have their vista of plenty, otherwise sweet and green as a good pea soup, ruined by the sight of her little hovel stuck in the middle of it all like a hard nub of gristle, with the jutting gables and baggy thatch, and a meagre garden choked with brambles and vetch.

There is a fine blue sky, and I might make enough work to keep me far away from my mother until sundown, so I am quite cheerful, and do cheerful-person things, like whistling while I walk, and swinging my basket of pottage quite carelessly. The heifers in the fields are warming their sides in the morning sun, and pay me little mind. Once I am done at the Widow's I will go directly to the Hobdays', further up, to deliver their nice linens and mended shirts. The Goodwife Hobday is a kindly woman – no doubt she will slip me a few extra coins for my trouble. Perhaps a slice of plum cake, too. Maybe we will sit by the hearth a while and talk of Manningtree's comings and goings: what strapping lad has joined up with – or been pressed into – the militia, what the dark young man recently come from Suffolk might want with the lease to the Thorn Inn over in Mistley.

When I reach the Widow Clarke's house, I stop at the gate. The front door stands wide open, and there, by the worn stone of the entryway, sits a rabbit, milk-white. He is looking at me askance with a red cabochon eye. Rabbits are a common enough sight in these fields, scramming into the long grasses from the herdsmen's heavy trampings, but I have never seen one like this before, a rabbit white-all-over. It has no obvious business being there – so brazen and unblemished – by Bess Clarke's dirty stoop. His nose twitches, but the creature is otherwise wholly still, with that peculiar blood-drop of eye trained directly on the gate where I stand. The whiteness of it makes it quite an eerie sight, as if there were no real shape nor weight to it, and we consider each other for the best part of a minute before I push at the gate and call a wary good morning to the Widow Clarke. A bustle comes from within, and the white rabbit at last jerks to attention and absconds into the undergrowth. Elizabeth Clarke appears at her front step, rubbing one hand on a sordid apron and grasping at the lintel with the other. 'Rebecca West,' she says, screwing up her eyes against the wholesome sun, 'good morrow, sweetheart.'

I have asked the Widow Clarke how old she is before, but she was not exactly certain. One need not look at her for long to conclude *very*. Old enough that time now seems beneath her notice, and she'll spend a good deal of it doing whatever nonsense she pleases. She is in possession of the full complement of ailments that afflict the elder folk of Manningtree, though usually discretely: her little paw-like hands shake with a palsy, her runny eyes are clouded, and her mouth nearly toothless. She has even lost a leg, somewhere, somehow, someway. I have seen men crippled like that – those who went away to fight in France or the war in Scotland – but never a woman. I suppose that once a woman reaches a certain level of excessive superannuation her critical limbs might simply begin to give out and fall off, much as the teeth do, and as does the hair.

Perhaps the Widow Clarke's left leg is buried unmarked beneath a patch of scrub right there in that disorderly garden. Perhaps she simply stood up one evening to find the connective gristle that attached it to the rest of her worn to a thread, and threw it on the fire with the chicken bones, a *hey-ho* and a shrug. This is what I see, looking at the Widow Clarke – a withered and slatternly old woman. Other people must see her differently, though, because they think her cunning. The town maids go to Mother Clarke for tongues, charms and scratchings, to cast the shears and sieve and beg Saint Paul for the name of her husband, or know if the first babe she gets by him will be girl or boy. I think it is the Widow's web-in-the-eye that makes people believe in her cunning. Beyond the uncanny way it makes her look – like a fairy came along and scrubbed the meats clean of spots – people get terribly superstitious about such things as cataracts, and choose to believe that God would not be so cruel as to rob an old woman of her earthly gaze without equipping her with a spectral one, to say sorry. You would think them unacquainted with Job. There is a rumour that tells that she was struck by lightning, once, on All Saints' Day, and lived.

'The Beldam sent thee,' says the Widow Clarke, as though this were special knowledge given her by God, and not an occurrence common to every Saturday.

'There was a rabbit by your door just now,' I tell her. 'It was the queerest thing.'

'Oh. Aye?' The Widow Clarke scratches her face incuriously.

'White as snow it was. And with red eyes.'

She shrugs. I follow her into the house. One room with the windows all boarded. The only light within comes from the open door and a low fire chuckling in the grate. I begin to set out the pottage and clear away as best I can the remnants of the last evening's repast, tossing a few dry crusts out over the threshold and into the garden.

The tiny house smells dank as a burrow. The Widow lowers herself down into a stool, indifferent to my busywork. She has a peg leg of old, deeply scored wood, but she is not wearing it now, and she moves around the cottage by handing herself from one outcrop of battered furniture to another.

'Many years ago,' says Mother Clarke – and I can tell it is not a 'says' so much as a 'begins' – 'Many years ago,' she begins, 'not much after my James was born, we were living up in East Bergholt. Well. It must have been about noontime, for the sun was very high, and casting tall shadows in the yard. I had put the babe down and was going to take some feed for the chickens, when I saw the strangest thing. A leveret, black and brown, sat not a yard from the threshold. She played and flitted there for some minutes, as I recall. All long shanks and ears pointed and black at the ends – black as soot. In the middle of the day and in the middle of my yard.' I half-listen to the Widow Clarke as I set to sweeping the stoop as best as I can with the bundle of rushes that serves her for a broom.

'Like she was dancing there. Not a yard from my threshold,' she repeats, idly plucking at the strings of her little stained cap. 'I did wonder at it.'

'I'll bet you did,' I say.

'They say there was a great queen who lived in these parts once, and that she went to fight the pagan invaders who came from o'er in France. They say the morning of—'

As soon as the pagan invaders get to be involved I think it time to look to my own leaving. I straighten up at the stoop and give the old woman my best huff, pushing my cap back. 'Really, madam,' and, setting my hands on my hips, 'what nonsense is this?'

But on she goes as if she hasn't heard me. 'They say the morning of a great battle, as she was riding out into the fields in her golden greaves and mantle, there, a hare, a little leveret just the same, ran out before her horse. And that—' Here she raises her head to look at me with a mysterious smile '—the queen died that very same day, slain by pagans. An omen, see,' she adds, for my better understanding. 'Hares.'

I put down my broom of rushes to take the Widow Clarke to table, a bowl of lukewarm pottage in front of her. 'Well, a rabbit is no hare and you are no queen, madam,' I say, loud, so that I know she will mark me, 'and you shan't be dying today neither. Not by starvation, at least. Here, look.' I press a spoon into her vague fingers. 'Pottage! And perhaps the Beldam will bring you some eggs later, as well.'

She blinks at me a few times, sidelong and sad, then lowers her spoon to the pottage and takes a mouthful. 'It's cold,' she murmurs, grinding her grey corpsey gums.

'You're most welcome.' I dip to her in an ironical curtsey, and move to shake her sour bedlinens.

'She's a good woman, your mother,' Bess goes on mumbling, through a mouthful of pottage. A wet oat glisters at the corner of her wrinkled mouth.

'So you say.'

'She is,' Mother Clarke insists, a dripping spoonful held before her pursed lips. 'Soft on the inside and hard without, like a crab. We first met when I was out on the field over yonder, at the spinney. I was picking up sticks for the fire, and there she was leaning at the fence post in her liver-spotted dress. She said she had watched me and knew of my poverty and my lameness, and pitied me for it. She said that she knew ways and means for me to live better.'

'Might those "ways" and "means" go by the names "Rebecca" and "West", perchance?' I ask, folding the counterpane. I look over my shoulder to flash a grin to the old woman, and find that her pale gaze is fixed on my back through the half-darkness and that a strange, smug look has come over her face. Old Mother Clarke may be rounding blindness, but in that moment it feels as if her cloudy eyes are boring through my very skin. Very strongly, then, I want to leave that tumbledown hovel.

'Master John Edes, is it?' Elizabeth asks, her thin lip curling.

And I am caught off guard and so reply my 'What?' with an abruptitude that can only be suspect.

'Master John Edes,' Mother Clarke repeats, patting at the pottage with the belly of her spoon. 'The clerk. Word is you have taken quite a fancy to him.' She makes a dry, indulgent noise.

I set the counterpane back and smooth it down with my hands, feeling the colour rise in my cheeks. White, pink. In this moment I find myself twisting inside, caught between a deep-held shame and a sort of resentment. Resentment that Bess Clarke, this flake, this cripple – whose only relation to my mother and me is geographic, whose only sympathetic features, helplessness and drowsiness, are those she shares with every baby or drunk – would look to know my innermost thoughts and desires. It is a feeling of invasion, except glossed with understanding of that invasion's essential triviality, like when a gnat crawls into your tear duct to die of a May morning.

And then there is the shame, because the old woman is not wrong, all told. I have indeed 'taken a fancy' to the clerk, John Edes. I have had most passionate thoughts of his small blond moustaches, which curl up at the corners of his mouth and make him look like a happy tomcat. I have thought at length about what it would be like to kiss him there, where the whiskers meet his lips, and feel the roughness and the softness together. I have enjoyed the shapeliness of his large hands against the clean print of Matthew's Gospel, enjoyed watching him moisten a finger to turn a page. And all these thoughts I have again now, all in a rush, prompted by the intimation of their existence and with Bess Clarke's sclerotic gaze fixed on the back of my cap. So I say 'What?' all over again, blushing and incredulous. And I call her a mad old bat.

The Widow knows enough to know that I am lying, damn her, and simply bunches her shoulders, with a grin. Can she see me? Can she see me where I stand in my head, with Master John Edes loosening my imaginary stays with those nice big hands of his? I must leave, just in case.

'Mother will be over later, no doubt,' I say all at once, and fix my cap, and seize up my basket, and blunder back out into the morning sunshine and the wholesome smells of wet grass and herds, smells that Old Mother Clarke might live among, but is certainly not *of*. Those good things, gold wheat and cattle, God's things.

As I go about my day, it becomes harder to keep faith in Old Bess Clarke's ingenuity as a diviner, and easier to believe that my mother has been prattling off to her. When we sit down that evening in the little parlour to work, I am in a state of high dudgeon, for rumours, once begun, are wont to take on a life of their own.

To call either my mother or myself a 'seamstress' would perhaps be excessive – but I have a quick hand and a light touch with the needle, as well as a good eye for the tiny sprigs and scrolls that might prettily ornament the flat collars of white Holland now in fashion, or the ribboned babies' caps. My mother's mending is capable, though rough: but none who have seen her down by the fleet, at the part we call the Judas Gap for its deep and secret swelling in the winter months, dress bound up around her hips and bodice loosened, lustily flogging a creamy froth of lacy underskirt against the rocks like a cat o' nine tails against the back of a New England scold, could deny that laundry is her true calling. *She'd probably do the whole town's washing for no more than a pat on the head, she enjoys it so much*, is one thing I have heard a woman say of my mother.

That rock over there knows how I feel when George comes back late from the Lion, is another. Work has been slower of late than it ever was – the goodwives of Manningtree find they have more time on their hands for the comparative frivolity of needlework, with so many husbands and sons and brothers taken off of them by the Eastern Association – but we find ways to make ends meet. Though barely, some weeks.

So we sit down to our work in the little parlour, as it ever was, the door open ajar on a cloudless night in some futile hope of a draught, and I sulk.

Somewhere close at hand, an owl pipes at the thick summer stars.

'Finally,' Mother rumbles, biting off a thread and waving her needle toward the door. 'A little conversation.'

I keep my gaze in my lap, where the branch of a fruit tree takes shape on the sleeve of Mr Redmond's undershirt, and make a *hm* or *yes* or some lumpen sound.

'My daughter,' she sighs. 'Mute as a manikin in her brown study. It is well indeed I've the night-birds for company.'

I raise my head to look at her. 'And what might we possibly have,' I ask, pricking in a tight stick of forget-me-not-blue with each word, 'to talk about, pray tell, Mother?'

And then. And then she says – with a glister of insinuation in her eyes – 'All that time you have been spending at the good Master Edes', I would have hoped to find thee a woman of learning by now. A regular slanderer.'

I cast down my embroidery and give her my fiercest look. 'Salonnière, Mother, is what they call Queen Mary, and is the word you will be wanting here,' I say. 'Slanderer means something else entirely. And John Edes – now, there's a topic. Tell me, exactly, what is it you've been wagging your tongue over to old Bess Clarke, regarding Master Edes and myself?'

Mother is a piece of work. You can see the choice deceptions jostling in her eyes like trout under the bright top of a stream. First, she raises a hand to her stomacher and parts her lips with a false, persecuted look. 'My honour,' she says, all well-I-never-thought-I-would-see-the-day-such-slander-would-pass-your-lips, voice and face wheedling and wounded respectively, and then she thinks to change tack and both voice and face harden immediately. 'As if I have nothing better to do than prattle over John Edes,' she snaps. 'A man like that,' she slips her tongue to the corner of her mouth, moistening a thread, 'a man like that'd stick his Thing up a haddock if a Bishop told him not to.'

'Mother!' My cheeks burn. And my loins flip.

'It's true,' she sniffs. 'What is John Edes to me? I know a coward when I see one, bending and genuflecting hisself to any fat old arse with a fat old purse. A regular hill-digger.'

I feel a great smoke of wrath rise in me then, a hatefulness. I resent that I am allowed to have nothing of my own, nothing that doesn't bear the grub prints of her opinion. 'Shame,' I mutter through my teeth. 'You know not the first thing concerning—'

'Mind thyself, girl,' she interrupts, wagging her finger in a warning way and fixing me with her eyes, 'I know cowards, and I know men. And there's many say once you know the former you know the latter just as well.'

'Aye,' I say, with a private smile, passing my needle back through the fruit tree branch, 'and enough of them have known thee, too, so they say.'

Too far. Vinegar Tom yowls and spits as the candlestick crashes across the parlour, spraying sparks. I upend my chair as I take to heel, flying up and out through the open door just as she grabs at the heavy jug, which bursts against the lintel just behind me, bursts with a terrible noise.

A good day for John Banks. He sold his old grey mare, that morning, to a cooper down from Ipswich, though not without shaving a few years off of her. Then he went to the Red Lion and promptly drank away a tenth of her price in cider, which he must remember to adjust for when telling the abstemious Goody Banks what the beast fetched. He lopes hazy up the Lawford hill toward farm and homestead, scratching at the seat of his britches and feeling everything to be intensely beautiful. A fulsome belch allows him to taste the mingled sharpness of apples and bile on his palate, a contrary flavour he finds perversely pleasant. The moon and stars shimmer colloidally above as he stops by a fence post to piss, a short way from the Beldam West's.

A shout and a smash move him from his drunken reverie. In his haste to stuff himself into his trousers he trips backward over his own walking stick, fumbling with the buttons of his fly. Some spectral thing in white streaks down the path in front of him, the path from the West's cottage, making a terrible noise of sobbing and hewing, before it slips away into the darkness of the wood that fringes the top of town. He will tell his wife about this later, when he climbs into bed. She will be less convinced of the phantom's alleged post-mortem provenance. Friday night, after all, is when the Devil hosts his Mass.

Soon John Banks tells his story to others, and so does Goody Banks. Naturally, it grows in the telling, beginning with a warp at the level of the hour. Soon a lake spools from its right place, and a specious dawn peers over the horizon of his fiction, paring tender moonlight away. Soon the one white thing he saw has become four black, and 'seeing', for that matter, has become 'wrestling as Jacob did the angel'. His own part expands, and takes on the dimensions of heroism. The Beldam West's solidifies, leaning sultry in a doorway, stripped to her underthings. Whispering – forespeaking – a scar-like cloud on her brow. It is a much better story that way, and Lord knows John Banks has little else to recommend his company.

The testimony of Sir Thomas Bowes, Knight,
which he spake upon the Bench, concerning the aforesaid Anne West,
she being then at the Bar upon her trial, 1645

That a very honest man of Manningtree, whom he knew would not speak an untruth, affirmed unto him, that very early one morning as he passed by the said Anne West's door, about four o'clock, it being a moon-light night, and perceiving her door to be open so early in the morning, looked into the house, and presently there came three or four little things in the shape of black rabbits, leaping and skipping about him, who having a good stick in his hand, struck at them, thinking to kill them, but could not, but at last caught one of them in his hand, and holding it by the body of it, he beat the head of it against his stick, intending to beat out the brains of it; but when he could not kill it that way, he took the body of it in one hand, and the head of it in another, and endeavoured to wring off the head; and as he wrung and stretched the neck of it, it came out between his hands like a lock of wool; yet he would not give over his intended purpose, but knowing of a spring not far off, he went to drown it; but still as he went he fell down, and could not go but down he fell again, so that he at last crept upon his hands and knees till he came at the water, and holding it fast in his hand, he put his hand down into the water up to his elbow, and held it under water a good space, till he conceived it was drowned, and then letting go his hand, it sprung out of the water up into the air, and so vanished away: and then coming back to the said Anne West's door, he saw her standing there in her smock, and asked her why she did set her Imps to molest and trouble him? To whom she made answer, that they were not sent to trouble him, but were sent out as Scouts upon another design.

3

Maiden

On Sundays we go to church, my mother and I, along with the rest of them. Them being the town. The high windows of painted glass in St Mary's Church, Mistley, were smashed last Christmastide, then glazed again by Lent, then smashed again by Mayday, like the whole town was engaged in some mad dance of window-smashing and patching in the place of clapping and leaping. And now they stand boarded. At the nave was Caritas, with her lovely sky-blue wings, and a blindfolded Justice, and also Gabriel with his jewelled sword and a little lamb on his yellow sandals. They say Minister Long will not seek to restore this divine retinue again, reasoning that if the community will not consent to windows that reflect the glory of the Heavenly Kingdom, then the bare, hard boards that stand in stead of painted glass might serve as an ironical tribute to the dedicated Puritan asceticism of his congregation. Yet regardless of his ironical disposition, I think the Minister must dislike that even now, on a stifling late-summer morning, he must perform his service in the flickering glow of candlelight and what little sunshine leaks in between the slats. Public opinion is mixed. Some abhor Romish images, some just like to look at coloured glass. Some do both and prefer not to discuss the matter at all.

St Mary's is a small church, but serves Mistley and Manningtree both, in a single congregation. From his pulpit, the Minister sees serried rows of faces, arranged along the pews in more or less accurate embodiment of our general significance as ordained by God. Left of the aisle the women sit, heads covered with starched caps, and right of the aisle are the men (those that remain), sombre in their wide-brimmed hats. In the front pews, the faces of the substantial folk are pale and still. Faces as scrimshaw, fine silks sleek and dark as a Spaniard's dog. The Godly men like to take notes through the sermons, scratching down queries and points of contention to raise with the Minister once his preaching is done. As his eye moves further back from the pulpit, the faces of the men and women it lights on seem to crumble, showing the marks of hard weather, poor victuals, and accustomed brawl; the caps become ragged shawls, the gowns thin stuff of French green or a faded sand colour, with deep-baked stains. There, from the poor folk in the back pews, come whispers and surreptitious tittering at the salacious parts, the circumcisions and the whores and all of that, and occasionally projectiles – walnuts or thimbles thrown by sticky-faced children, who are naturally sceptical and will not be made to sit still for nigh on two hours of homily.

My mother and I sit at the back, on the left side, in the last pew but one. Here and there I see a ribbon of emerald satin, or a seditious scarlet trim, curling from between the tightly pinned plaits of a Prudence or Rachel or Esther, and down over a bare white neck like a rivule of blood. It is close and hot inside the church, and the women fan themselves with their handkerchiefs, churning up bemingled emanations of rosewater perfume, womb-clot, sweat and cinders. Above all is the round face of Minister Long, who is but very recently installed at St Mary's, having been sent from London to replace Minister Caldwell, whom the ague took, suggesting he was not as favoured by God as he would have had us think. Minister

Long is quite young, and I think he has difficulty obscuring his feelings from people in the way that a man – and especially a minister – ought. Sometimes his pale eyes flick hopelessly up from his lectern to the wriggling Puritan quills, and he wipes his sweaty upper lip on his sleeve, wondering what fresh spiritual controversy they might frame from his mild sermonising. I think 'Long' an unfortunate name for a Minister. The joke suggests itself.

In the last pew but one from the door, I am poorly placed for a view of Master Edes, but I know where he is: two rows ahead on the men's side, between the Yeoman John Stearne – his sometime employer – and a dark-haired gentleman whom I do not recognise, and who might therefore be our newcomer, Mister Hopkins. I see him turn to talk hush-hush to the dark-haired man while Minister Long expounds upon Elijah and the pagan king, and enjoy the slope of his nose in profile. Mister Hopkins, if that is who he is, also has a nose – sharp, unbroken, flared and red at the nostrils, which he dabs at with a laced kerchief.

When the sermon is done we step out from the dim church into the September sunshine all blinking and fluffing, like newly hatched chicks. Greetings and how-ye-dos and Lord's blessings – the blessings of God upon you good Sirs – are exchanged all round, routine and accustomed as the creaking of an old step. The Godly men will linger in the churchyard all afternoon discussing the finer points of Minister Long's homily, and the Godly women will glide between the graves like funeral barges so that we might all get a better look at the fine Flanders lace of their underskirts. But most of us have better things to do.

The road back into Manningtree has baked dry in the heat, and a fine brown dust hovers about our languid processional as we make our way down the incline. The Stour at high tide is a wrinkling blue over the bankside line of scrub and sea thrift. It is a windless day, and the church bells can be heard from as far away as Felixstowe, sounding across the waters of the bay. Mother, very tall and robust in her tight-laced church frock of murray worsted, walks up ahead in the company of Liz Godwin and the widows Anne Leech and Margaret Moone. I hang back with Margaret Moone's eldest daughter, Judith.

Judith is a sluttish, pale girl, two years my junior and a good part imp, I think. Her mouth is a startling red spotted all about with pimples, causing her to appear always as though she has just come from a messy repast of blackberries. Judith's livid mouth is a thoughtful, explanatory flourish in the Lord's design – like the yellow bands of a hornet – for she is very free with words indeed. I am pleased our mothers' affinity has made a friendship between us, for I do not think I would have the fortitude to withstand her bad side. We are walking arm in arm down the long hot road toward town, when Judith throws back her head and declares, 'Lor',' lightly blaspheming, 'Lor', I was so bored I could have eaten a baby. The Edwards' new one, perhaps. He is a very fat little thing.'

I say that it wasn't so bad, and that I liked the bit about feet.

'I have washed – my – feet—' Judith says, in mimicry of Minister Long's mourning drawl '—now, how might I defile them?' And she claps her hands together and I laugh, with an *amen to that*.

Judith squints her eyes up narrow and leans in close. 'I am not the only one who found it tiresome. Have you noticed—' and she here shoots a look at our mothers walking ahead '—how the Dames always come from service with faces like slapped arses?' And we are laughing between ourselves at that when Prudence Hart sinks into step beside us, with a smile some-sweet some-wicked. She chirrups us a *good morrow* and knits her fingers below her swelling belly as though we might fail to notice it. She will be delivered when winter has set in, most likely – a risky business.

'What ho, Goody Hart,' grins Judith, her foxy brows rising. 'And look at you, stout as a Harwich seal.'

Prudence laughs. 'My Thomas says it quite becomes me.' She pats at her paunch. "Tis a shame so many of the young men have gone off to do battle with the Antichrist. Now you shall have no one but the puddles to remind you of your plainness.'

The rivalry of Prudence Hart and Judith Moone – neighbours and barely six months apart in age, who were raised up making cat's cradle by the fire together – is now largely a matter of display, an exercise mildly diverting for themselves and for others. The origin of their enmity, if any existed at all, is now lost to the mist of the plenty years before the fighting started, when men ate beefsteak every night and effectively bridled their women's conniptions (or thought that they did).

'Oh,' says Judith, reaching over me to pat at Prudence's arm, 'worry not, Goody Hart. We know we can trust to thy friendship in that regard. 'Tis a shame,' she pouts, "tis a shame the Holy warriors could find no use for thy dear Thomas. Tell me: was it his age as disqualified him from service? Or his blubber?'

Prudence ejects another nasty laugh and hangs back, at last, smile pickling on her face, to wait for her own mother. Judith grins triumphantly. 'The skirmish is mine, I think,' she says, chewing at her dirty thumbnail as though to reward herself. 'That little arseworm,' she adds, with a thoughtful backward look.

Market Street is excitement of a sort, after the doldrums of the service. Judith and I go along quite happily in the sun, peering at the wagons unloading outside the ordinary and into the dirty windows of the mercer's shop. It is hot. I feel the sweat prick beneath the frill of my cap. Ragged children play in the dust, and a few women, having families too large to count it a heresy to work on the Lord's Day, make quiet effort toward the scrubbing of their stoops. The air is sour with the smack of horse-dung and sweet with the smells of cooking lard and onions, and suddenly Judith spins and nips at my cheeks with her fingertips, saying *ah, ah – let me pinch some roses into your face, Beck!* But when I realise why, my own embarrassment equips me with a deeper flush than all the pinching in the world might have, as I see that Master John Edes has emerged from the bakery and is approaching us, with the dark-haired stranger from the church in tow.

Edes bows deep, and presses his hat back from his very good face. 'Miss West, Miss Moone,' he beams, 'a good morrow to you.'

'Master Edes,' and we ourselves dip, dark skirts rippling, eyes dropping modest.

'The Lord has blessed us with another fine day. It might still be midsummer,' Master Edes smiles, squinting up into the cloudless blue afternoon. The sun glints off the buckle on his hat, as if it cannot quite believe its luck in getting to touch him, and who can blame it.

'It is too hot, to my mind,' Judith replies, disagreeably. I keep my own eyes lowered to the baking dirt, but I can see that Judith has raised hers square to the dark-haired stranger, curiosity overcoming modesty. I feel the film of sweat on my skin, the hair loosening from my cap.

'Well . . . God might favour us with a little rain. It would bring a pleasing freshness to the air,' Master Edes answers, diplomatically, scratching at his moustaches.

Beneath my skirts, my stocking sags loose around my left knee. Intently I look at the uneven lacing of my bodice, the stomacher a little askew, and feel more shame. I wish I might own myself, as Judith does. Judith the hoyden girl with the crusted pimples at the corners of her lips and her short chin raised in small rebellion eight times a day. I feel her standing there, stiff as a bramble, solid as a rampike, thoroughly committed to the project of casual moral delinquency. I envy her and could kiss her both.

'Miss West?' Master Edes repeats.

I realise I have been wound too tight about myself to be listening to a word that has been said, and am reluctantly forced to acknowledge that, yes, Miss West is myself, with another surreptitious bend at the waist and an 'I – my apologies, sir.'

He smiles – hallelujah. 'Your lesson,' he says. 'On Thursday?'

'Yes. I shall come 'round noon, sir.'

'It is well.'

I lift my eyes then to the smiling Master Edes in a manner that could be – and that I know will be, by the dawdling Market Street goodwives who are pinning out their laundry and half spying on this fortuitous meeting – spoken of as coquettish. I meet with John Edes once weekly in his quarters above the White Hart, for the learning of my letters. I think in times more ordinary, or company more thoroughly Godly, such an arrangement would no doubt be considered scandalous. But as it is Manningtree and the Year of Our Lord 1643 – in which many educated men have it that civil society might be ravaged to bits very soon indeed – people do more or less whatever it is they wish, provided they can stand to be the subject of all the town's gossip the next day. So I learn from Master Edes what a girl like me might ordinarily glean from her own father – to read the gospel and understand its lessons, to sign my name, to perform basic arithmetic of the kind useful for the management of a household, and for knowing when I am being welched on. I am a quick study and already know how to do these things, and more. But I am not yet ready to abandon Master Edes' gentle sciolism, the two hours of the week when I sound out syllables with that marvellous face bent low beside mine. *Cal-um-ny. For-bear-ance.*

'Allow me to introduce Mister Matthew Hopkins,' Edes continues, gesturing sidelong at his companion, who tips his hat indifferently.

'Oh!' Judith exclaims. 'You are the gentleman from Suffolk as has taken the lease on the Thorn.'

Mister Hopkins shifts uneasily under Judith's gaze, evidently discomposed by his reputation's newfound independence from his person. 'I—' he says. That is all he says, with a needy sidelong look at Master Edes. He dabs at his temple with a kerchief crumpled in his left hand.

Edes laughs. 'News travels fast in Manningtree, Matthew. Too many women,' he says, 'too short on employment.'

'Indeed,' Hopkins replies.

'Sirrah,' Judith interjects. 'Men coming is rarer and more welcome news than men leaving.'

'Ah.' Hopkins presses his fingertips to his mouth. His eyes, shadowed by the wide brim of his hat, are fixed somewhat above our heads. 'Alas,' he continues, lackadaisically, 'my poor health prevents me from joining the cause of the righteous. But it brings me joy at last to be among such ... God-fearing people.' He sounds less than convinced, staring off into the blue skies over the butcher's shop. I think he looks like nothing has ever brought him joy in his life. He presses his lacy kerchief to his temple as though it might whisper to him instructions for the congenial navigation of our meeting. I feel a peculiar sympathy – he looks like I must, this Mister Hopkins – not knowing where to put himself, or what to do with all this cumbersome *existing*.

'Mister Hopkins,' Edes interjects, by way of explanation, 'is not long from Cambridge.'

Matthew Hopkins, the Gentleman and Cambridge scholar. Carefully, I take the measure of him. He is young enough, and handsome. Handsome in that way that might prompt women to say *he'd be handsome, if*—, dark and with a grace that seems near-womanish. A neatly combed moustache and a thin, skittish mouth. His apparel is as fine as one is likely to see in Manningtree, and bespeaks a restrained good taste: high boots polished to a gleam, hair in ringlets almost to his chest. But there is something about him slant and insubstantial, as though all the dramatic outfitting houses none of the usual human meat. Black boots, black gloves, black doublet, black cloak, black ringlets and then a white face floating lost in the midst of this funereal confection. Over his shoulder, I see my mother waiting at the turning to the market square, her hands planted on her hips and her face puckered in a look of suspicion.

I make my apologies to the two gentlemen and explain that my mother waits on me. Both Hopkins and Edes follow my eyes and look to where she stands, all sunburned, by the white Market Cross. John Edes tips his hat to her. No reciprocal gesture of politesse is forthcoming from my mother.

'And mine,' adds Judith, with a sighing look toward the Widow Moone, who taps her foot by the grocer's. 'Farewell, and good fortune at the Thorn!' she adds, with a brazen smile at Hopkins.

Mother walks ahead of me up the Lawford hill, her strides long and purposeful. We climb and the sticky, layered smells of the town are replaced by the freshness of the meadows and a trembling breeze. On my right side are the fields stretching amply to the blue of the horizon, to Kent and the sea and beyond, knotted over with herds. On my left, the thatched roofs of the town are bathed in the yellow angel-light of the early evening, and the smokes rise from Felixstowe. It would be a pleasant walk, I think, to take of an afternoon with someone you loved.

'So—' says Mother, peering back over her shoulder '—will you tell me, then, who Master Edes' friend was, with whom Judith and yourself were conversing so cosily?' There is a note of abjection in her voice because I know something that she does not, and she hates it, and now she must pretend she has no real interest and merely enquires out of politeness.

'Mister Matthew Hopkins,' I oblige her. 'Him who took the lease on the Thorn.'

'Fellow looks like a milksop. All that sable get-up.'

'Certainly don't look like any innkeeper that I've ever seen.' I whisk my walking stick in a haulm of long grass by the curving path, causing a cloud of gadflies to rise madly heavenward.

'Aye, and how many innkeepers would that be, Becky?' Mother chortles, and looks over her shoulder to see that I am suitably chastened by this reminder of the narrowness of my existence. 'Changeling girl,' she sighs. 'Perhaps it would do you some good to get in your cups some. Put a little colour in thy cheeks, hey?' And then she stops and she turns toward me, and she raises a roughened hand to the side of my face, a queer expression in her eyes. I flinch – but it seems she means only to touch with tenderness. 'You're all that remains to me now, Becky,' she says, quiet.

In this light, and with the wind stirring at a bit of hair that has fallen from her cap, I think there is a certain ruined handsomeness to her after all. Tall as nightmares in her frilled Sunday frock. I cannot think of what to say, so I say only, 'I do not want to be all that remains to you,' and push her hand away and move past her to carry on up the hill path, whacking my stick side to side.

'It is to your benefit I work, Beck,' Mother calls after me. 'Lord knows, no one else does! I see you, girl! I tilled what you grew in!'

But I walk, and I keep to walking, and eventually her whickering is lost to the breeze. I walk on past our front yard where the chickens scratch at themselves, past the gate rotting off its hinges. I walk past the long-empty house that stands across the path from our own, the old sty collapsing against the west wall. I walk over the hill and then down the other side, and the sunset flares hard like a jewel against my face. Alone now, I think, *my God.* The indignity of it all. The hopelessness. I could cry, because nothing has ever really begun, and nothing is ever likely to. My Sunday stays are tight, and stopping by the fence at the bottom of the Hobdays' low field I loose them, and breathe the tart smell of cows, and see someone has carved a cross into the post there.

I am poor. But what is worse, I am poor and *peculiar.* In the Hobdays' field there are patches of lusher grass in the parched field, thriving where the cows have dropped their guts, and this takes me to thinking of the dead, as I lean up against the fence post, loosening my stays. The dead, who are under the ground, poor and peculiar and otherwise. And that gets me to thinking of my father, whom I do not think of often, and who we find no time in our days to honour. Would things have been better if he were still here, still alive? Probably not. He was a scoundrel and a drunk, as far as I remember and rumour suggests. We would still be poor – and perhaps poorer still – with a wastrel of no account sleeping through church and falling asleep by the fire with his hand down his breeches. Poor, yes. But man, wife and child – father, mother and daughter – as a situation, it is inarguably less *peculiar.*

My mother is right. She does see me. How could she not, it being that we work, sleep, wake and piss together, side by side, stifling? We are like two trees that have grown entangled in the denseness of the wood and find their roots interlocked, ripping at each other's branches in the wind. And I can see no other way out. No way out but him.

4

A Discourse

Matthew Hopkins watches the girls trip away, then the two white caps of the Wests bobbing up the hill in the distance. He asks if the girl is simple-minded. 'The dark one,' he clarifies. She has a weird look to her, he thinks, as though she'd be more comfortable up in the sky, perched on a ragged limb of cloud, than in a provincial church pew. Eyes wide-set and all the colour of pupil.

'Rebecca? No,' replies Master Edes. 'Timid, I suppose. Her mother, mind . . .' Edes chuckles as the two men continue up the street toward the Market Cross. 'The Beldam West is a formidable old scold. She did time in gaol, some years ago, for killing a neighbour's pig.'

'A pig, sir?' Hopkins blinks at his companion, mouth set in a firm line beneath his black moustache. 'Mercy. How?'

'I am not right sure – this was before I came up from London. Some genteel scrap in the front yard, and in the middle of it all the Beldam West marches into her house, comes back out with a butcher's blade, and slices the poor hog right across the wattles before anyone can think to stop her. And the pig wasn't even the primary point of contention.'

Edes laughs, but Hopkins remains mirthless. 'Women,' he exhales, weary.

'A woman? Lilith, more like. No . . . If you have come by Manningtree looking for a wife, your search may be long indeed, sir.'

'Not a wife,' Hopkins replies.

Parliament secures a victory over the King in Berkshire against long odds, prompting a confused atmosphere of dog-days carnival across the villages and hamlets of Essex, the men drinking and firing their muskets off into the lilac dusk, for God's judgement is surely passed upon the unrighteous. They massage the spare accounts of the battle to increasingly extravagant divinity, and soon the Archangel Michael is manifesting over the field of engagement, and white horses gallop through their fuddled cider dreams. September becomes October becomes November. The harvest is brought in as the languid summer finally exhausts itself, and a painted effigy of the Pope is set to blaze on the village green.

Matthew Hopkins reopens the Thorn Inn with little ceremony. As the year turns, his taste for dismal costuming provokes less astonishment, and even begins to make a sort of sense. While others rush about their outdoor business as quickly as they might through the autumn drizzle in an effort to repair to the comfort of their hearths, Matthew Hopkins struts about the town like a dour long-legged crow, with John Edes and John Stearne and the most learned company he is able to find in so backward a place as Manningtree, all the Nehemiahs too, happy as a Puritan might be. Some call him a backward man, a coaltit. Others admire him – no family to speak of, but plenty of money, it seems.

Matthew Hopkins rides his horse through a field at dawn and notices a black feather lying in the grass, glossy and ideal. Matthew Hopkins hosts. Matthew Hopkins expounds. Matthew Hopkins discourses, the town's foremost autodidacts groping for each morsel of his exultant theology.

'For he is, of course, a Prince of Air,' says Hopkins, lifting the edge of his riding cloak in such a way that his learned companions might better appreciate the broidery of the hem, the sleekness of the sable. And it makes sense to them then, when he puts it like that, how the Devil might thicken like butter and slide under the pantry door to cover a man all over. A man, or a woman.

They can imagine the Devil there, some great thing in the sky, or as a mist rolling in off the river, gathering the smoke of scullery fires to himself. For later use. Or as the miasma that hovers over the marshes and flats, bringing the ague. A dark head crowned in slender red leaves of narrowdock, a moth with mouths both front and back. Cavorting in the autumn clouds that are like strips of flayed skin. The Devil minces and the Devil dances. He dances like a girl might, slender-hipped, hair falling wild around her shoulders. Inflamed. Now the nights grow longer, he might go from door to door of an evening in the guise of a swarthy pedlar, opening his coat to the wide-eyed goodwives and maids, and where there ought to be bobbins of silk ribbon and little pearl buttons, he shows to them his merchandise of sootkin and smooth-newt: *this one here's Prickeare, and this one Prettyman.* And all the while a grey cat watches from the strawberry patch.

The Devil is in the moist places of the forest, under fallen logs. He speaks to the centipedes and the toads, and they drag their soft bellies out over the rocks and mulch to lame the horse of a gentleman passing by on his way to Ipswich, or find a place to nestle warm between the parted thighs of some country lass, whereon she dreams of marriage to a Turk who uses his tongue down there. He spits rainbow. He slides a rainbow up inside you.

'The power of creation, of course,' Hopkins says, smiling indulgently at John Stearne as the pair of them sit together by the fire, 'rightly belongs only to God.'

Can hate or desire or hunger heave islands from the sea, or speckle an empty sky full of stars? No. And yet they are as real as you or I, and no man might dispute it. And such is his power, gnawing at you like an empty belly until you'll take any horrid thing in your mouth, stroking softly and expertly at the pink points of the breasts and secret parts until you beg to have the power inside, filling you up. The anger that billows when you look at the smiling face of one who has wronged you, making you want to take that face into your hands and tear it up like damp paper.

Satiety. If we could ever meet it, perhaps we would know something close to peace. We chase it. This is the illusion he promiseth, an overflowing without end, a darkness that toucheth every part of you, every organ of you at once, to feel the roots stretching down down and away into the earth and into everything, through the green bones of dead men, their dreams shifting beneath your feet like an underground river.

'This the malevolent inverse of the oneness promised to the virtuous at the white gates of Heaven. As moon is to sun, as woman is to man.' Hopkins says all this, and the men listen intently, their eyes glowing in the firelight, the shadows undulating on the parlour walls.

5

Boy

Gunpowder Treason day has passed, and the painted pope is sizzling black-cheeked up on the village green. A bright but frigid morning, the line of the coast brindled with the purple of sea aster, brittly salted. The Stour is at its lowest ebb, and the sheen of the flats makes it difficult to tell where ground ends and water begins, out in the bay. By the quay wall stands a strange company of women, bundled up in ragged coats and cheap fur muffs to keep away the cold.

'Oh, I could do with a little snifter of something,' says the Beldam West, shivering in her coat. 'Just to keep the cold off. A little cupful of something.'

Margaret Moone clicks her tongue. 'It's not yet noon even, you slattern.'

Principal among the assembled women by age is Old Mother Clarke, bent over her stick, and appearing to take a reptile enjoyment in the feeling of the sun on her face. Her ragged shawl is pulled back over her liver-spotted scalp. Principal by height is the Beldam West, knotty and vigorous, with a purloined cloak wrapping her shoulders. Beside the skin-and-bone Beldam, the Widow Moone looks especially soft, her white face beneath her lacy white cap just like a sugared bun in crinkly paper wrappings, her body straining at the cheap stuff of her dress. Then there is the Widow

Leech, who looks as much like a leech as the Widow Moone resembles her own, astral namesake. The Widow Leech: having gone from maiden to Leech, it seems she is likely to die one. A busy, black-eyed little woman with a pinched mouth well attuned to the heat of local controversy. She finds it out and then on she latches, having three grown daughters who have left home, and thus little better to do than interfere in the lives of others. Completing the party is Liz Godwin, who is a slender, well-formed woman with the empty, docile eyes of a desirable horse. Liz Godwin is liberal in the disbursement of her chewing tobacco, which is fortunate, because she has no wit to share.

The women speak of names. Babies' names. All are themselves past breeding, but they are seasoned critics of their neighbour's offerings.

'*Free-love*, the Edwards have named their new one,' scoffs the Widow Leech. 'Have you ever heard the like of it?'

'Free-love sounds more of a girl's name, if you ask me,' muses Godwin, who does not understand their jokes.

'Doesn't sound like any kind of name at all,' the Beldam West declares, definitively.

'I *have* heard the like,' Margaret Moore reports. 'And worse. Did you hear what the Cates up Bergholt way called their own little one? *Continence*,' she breathes, to the delight of all, 'Continence Cate.'

There is a flurry of head-shakes and well-I-nevers and not-in-my-days. Then Anne Leech adds that there's a girl as is called 'Silence', down in Thorpe, and she can only assume her parents sought to draw attention to her virtue by it, given the Devil gifted her a hare-lip.

'So I should have named Becky,' the Beldam sighs.

Margaret Moone declares Rebecca West a *right little Madam*, and wonders that there is no man who seems ready to have her as a wife, considering that any man that did marry her would never hear a cross word in all the days of his life. Or any word at all, for that matter.

'Oh, that's what you think is it, Mag?' the Beldam counters, incredulous. 'By God,' she whistles, 'sweet is the face my Becky shows to the world, but the girl spits poison when she has a mind to.' Only Liz Godwin cringes at the casual blasphemy.

Old Mother Clarke stirs, opening her cloudy eyes. 'Aye,' she says, 'and so it should be. There's enough mules and moppets among the women of the world. If she has clout, and the good sense to keep it hidden, sounds to me like she is well ready to be wed.' She closes out her contribution with a short, cracking laugh.

'At least she does as she's bidden. My Judith,' begins Margaret, 'not three nights hence, I tell her to fetch me a bundle of wood from the stack out in the yard. And there she's sitting, doing no more than warming her corns by the fire and drinking my beer, and flatly, *I will not*, she says.' This elicits a murmur of communal displeasure. 'And I says, it is best you had fetch it, girl—' Margaret stops here to check the little knot of women are paying her story sufficient attention '—*or else*. And she says back, *else what? Will you fetch a stick and beat me with it, Mother?*'

The other women crowd in toward the intimation of violence, like it is a fire, but the Widow Moone is silent. 'And did you,' the Beldam asks, impatiently, eventually, 'fetch the stick, and whisk the little jade?'

'No,' replies Widow Moone, with a shrug. 'I put my shawl on and fetched the wood myself. Such is the widow's lot.'

Mother Clarke sighs. 'A girl of that age,' she says, 'just wants to see what power she might have. Break apart something in her hands and smile at it while she does. And a man won't do. A man ain't human, to a girl of twenty. He's a bit of God. Or so she is taught. So he seems to her. A man has no blood to splash about in.'

There is silence for a few moments as the women reflect on Mother Clarke's argument, allow it to soak in. 'Aye,' Leech sighs, 'I have said it many a time before. There's people, and then there's men.'

At that moment Misters Matthew Hopkins and John Stearne emerge from the dock office across the way, lovely furs frothing at their collars in the spry wind, and begin to pick their way along the road. They pass by the women with a reluctant tipping of their hats, like crows' sharp heads to a wound. Conversation is resumed once the men are out of earshot. 'Mister Hopkins has been up to Cambridge,' the Beldam notes, authoritatively.

Liz Godwin narrows her eyes. 'That isn't so impressive,' she says. 'My Thomas's been up to Cambridge.' Thomas is her husband. There is barely a woman alive in Manningtree in the autumn of 1643 without a husband or son named Thomas.

'I'm not talking about market day, you lack-wit,' the Beldam spits back at Liz. 'There is a school in Cambridge. A school of philosophy. If your Thomas has been there he conducts himself with a remarkable humbleness.'

'I thought Hopkins a lawyer,' sniffs Leech.

'Those black moustaches,' mutters Margaret Moone. 'I think he looks like the Devil hisself.'

Her remark ushers in an ominous lull to their conversation. The low tide has littered the flats with stinking knots of bladder wrack and kelp, a detritus of fraying rope and broken traps. Two boys – Thomas Briggs and Elias Frost – play at crabbing a short way off among the pools, barefoot, under the greedy watch of the gulls. The boys are skipping back and forth to a bucket set in the wet mud between them, ankles streaked with silt.

'Master Thomas Briggs,' the Beldam calls, 'why do you waste good bacon on those crabs, hey?'

Briggs stops in his tracks and casts a hesitant look at the Beldam, winding in his crabbing line. He wipes his nose on his shirt sleeve, and says nothing.

His silence irritates her. She calls out again: 'Did you hear me, Master Briggs? Besides – is it not a little cold to be japing on the flats, this morn? You'll catch a death of chill.'

Briggs remains still and silent, jutting his lower lip in a truculent manner. The other boy has paused to watch the exchange unfold now, too. The Widow Moone screws her pink face up to gaze across the luminised mud at the shy youths. 'Answer the Beldam, Thomas Briggs,' she says. 'And where be thy mother?'

Thomas Briggs lifts his head defiantly, and shouts back: 'My mother says I am not to speak with thee, nor any of thy like!'

With near-supernatural alacrity, before her companions' gasps of disapproval at the child's audacity are even half-spent, the Beldam leaps over the quay wall and bounds onto the mucky flats, leather sailor's jacket flapping in the wind behind her like the wings of a great bat. Thomas Briggs and his companion make to bolt, but it is too late, and Master Briggs yelps and wriggles as the Beldam seizes him by the ear and begins to pull him back toward the bank, calling him a disrespectful little whelp, an uppity lad, and all manner of thing. The tugging and jostling continue as Briggs' young companion escapes unpursued into the town, forgetting his little boots at the foreshore.

The Beldam hauls the boy over to the bank. Thomas grabs at the Beldam's cap, tugging it half off her grizzled head before he tumbles and falls, with a smack, on the rough stone of the walkway. He is bawling now, all audacity forgotten, as she seizes him by the shoulders and sets him back on his feet, chin scraped and bloodied. She gives him a hard shake: 'Shame! A crying shame,' she chides him. 'What might thy father think, if he heard thee address thy elders so saucily?'

This mention of the Yeoman Briggs – late of the Eastern Association – is unwise, prompting, as it does, renewed wails from young Thomas. The Beldam draws her hand back to strike the child, and the other women, stilled by shock until now, move to intercede. 'Now, Nan,' breathes Margaret Moone, grabbing her back by her shoulders, 'that's quite enough.' And not before time, for Priscilla Briggs – mother to Thomas – now stands at the end of Market Street, a basket of cakes fallen from her grasp and slopping in the mud as she points a trembling, accusatory finger at the five male-factors gathered by the riverbank. She lets out a shriek, then rushes toward the commotion.

The women stand back as Priscilla Briggs kneels to clasp her shaking son in her arms, then turns her livid face up toward the Beldam West. 'Wench!' she cries. 'Laying thy hands on him – a boy of eleven!' And she locks one arm around her son's shoulders and waves the other at the Beldam in a sort of erratic threat.

For a fleeting moment, the Beldam looks nervous. She did not mean for this to happen, and it is doubtless embarrassing for all concerned. She hides her nervousness with a laugh, looking down at Goody Briggs' tear-streaked face. The laugh is anarchic and comes from deep in her throat. Raising her hands in submission, she tells Goody Briggs that they have striplings much Thomas's junior loading dragons up North, so she would hope the lad could stand a little honest chiding for his sins. 'But if you look to raise up a saucy rascal, Goody Briggs,' she sallies, planting her hands on her hips, 'then I shall interfere no further.'

Others have come now, drawn by the racket of women, Leech-like: a few dockhands who stand dumbfounded on the pier, chewing their clay pipes, the baker at the doorway wiping down his floury hands on his apron. Misters Hopkins and Stearne.

'See to it you do not!' Goody Briggs cries, climbing back up to her feet. 'Slattern!' she adds, again, for good measure.

Hopkins strides forward at this juncture, flicking back his cloak and offering Priscilla his arm, a true underworld gallant. 'Madam,' he murmurs to Priscilla, softly, like he is soothing a spooked horse. 'Goodwife.'

Rather than take the offered arm, Priscilla Briggs seizes at his shoulder and throws herself tearfully into his dark curls. 'Naughty women,' she sobs into his velvets, 'they're all naughty women.' Thomas Briggs watches red-eyed and mouth agape, all injury apparently quite forgotten. Hopkins, gracefully discomfited, offers Priscilla a perfunctory pat between the shoulders.

Now Mister Stearne clears his throat and blinks his watery eyes against the frigid wind. 'May I enquire, my good ladies,' he begins, 'what has occurred here, to raise such tumult?'

Liz Godwin is relieved that somebody has finally posed a question she feels she can answer, and so she does answer, and her answer runs something like this: 'Well, sire. The Beldam West asked as to why the Master Briggs was wasting good bacon on the crabs – for see, sir, he was crab-fishing – and said that he would catch his death of chill, but the Master Briggs made no reply. So she asked again, and then Master Briggs says, sir, cocky as you please, that his mother had instructed him he is not to speak with the Beldam West nor any of her like. Those were his words, sir. Though what he meant by them I can scarce tell, for young Rebecca is not among our company, and—'

Hopkins raises his hand for silence. The Beldam's face is pinched as though she still suppresses laughter, her cap askew. Then Godwin gulps once, and peevishly summarises: '—so she caught at him by the ear'ole, the Beldam West. Then the young Sir took a tumble and scraped his chin up. And then Goody Briggs arrived.'

Glances are exchanged and measures taken throughout the taut assemblage as silence falls, punctured only by the hiccupping sobs of Mistress Briggs.

'Well,' says Hopkins. 'I am a single man, and as such it ill behooves me to make recommendation with regard to the most sacred feminine duties that pertain to the raising of children. But as a humble servant of God, and as your neighbour, perhaps I well might remind you all of the virtues of modesty, obedience, cleanliness' – here, his eyes drop to the Beldam's mud-spattered skirts. Her eyes are downcast, but her lip trembles with private mirth. Margaret Moone and Widow Leech, as well, have their lips screwed down tight over giggling – 'and continence, that—'

Widow Leech is the first to crack, clapping her hand over her mouth too late to stifle a fulsome cackle. Then Widow Moone, then the Beldam, then even wheezing Mother Clarke fall to laughing.

'—that might make you *exempla* to all the daughters of our town . . .' Hopkins' brow darkens as his exhortation concludes unheeded. He folds his arm about Mistress Briggs. 'Come, Goodwife,' he sighs. 'Let us sit you down at the inn.'

Misters Hopkins and Stearne go to the White Hart, with Goody Briggs and little Thomas in tow. The women stand and laugh for a long time by the quay wall. Then they go home, and make supper, and comb out their hair, and forget *continence*, and their laughter. But Hopkins does not.

6

Divination

We lie side by side in our smocks on Judith's bed.

'Listen to her in there.' Judith peers toward the closed door, behind which the Widow Moone sleeps in the adjoining chamber. 'Listen to that.'

We listen to Widow Moone's snoring. She inhales majestically, hugely, and then there is a pause of two, three, or even four heartbeats before an equally sumptuous exhalation follows. 'Threescore times a night I convince myself Madam's finally croaked it,' Judith sighs, bereft. 'But nay.'

The fire has burnt down to a mess of glowing embers, and there is a fine-spun frost at the windowpane. 'What would you do, if she did?' I ask her. 'Croak it, as you say.'

Judith bites her lip, thoughtful. 'Bind my breast and become a sailor,' she answers.

I give her a look.

'Ah, I know not,' she says, with a prone shrug, gazing up at the cracked plaster of the ceiling. 'Go into service, maybe. In Colchester, or Ipswich. Somewhere with a halfway decent haberdasher's shop. Somewhere they sell proper blues. Would a true cobalt not become me, with my colouring?'

'You'd not last a week in service,' I tell her, correctly. 'Not got the temperament for it. Pretty red hair though, which is probably preferable.' I reach my hand out across the pillow to touch her pretty red hair, which is fine and soft. I tell her again of my time bound out as a servant in Rivenhall, and how my master would beat me with a walnut cane when he came home drunk and found some petty thing I had done that was not to his liking. Judith smiles. She enjoys outrageous tales. The more bloodthirsty the better. As girls, we would sit up late with her father's old *Acts and Monuments*, marvelling over the pierced flesh of martyrs, our breath warm and shallow.

Judith turns her head to look at me. 'And have relations with the Old Beldam West improved,' she asks, 'while we're on the subject of beatings?'

'Why do you think I'm spending the night here?'

She shows her small teeth in a grin, face wan in the firelight. 'On account of my pretty red hair?'

'Don't be wanton.'

'Oh!' Judith suddenly exclaims, propping herself on her elbows. 'Did you hear of the falling-out at the quay, morning after bonfire? Master Briggs and your mother?'

'How could I not? The whole town is ablaze with it. *Naughty women.*'

'They say Mister Hopkins interceded, all gentlemanly carriage,' Judith sniffs, after a short silence. 'I think I would have liked to have seen that. The Grand Beldam facing down the Cambridge Puritan.'

I wait the course of one of Widow Moone's snores, two of them, knitting my hands over my breast. And then I ask it, voice whisked aery with a false indifference, 'Was Master Edes there, know you?'

'Devil take John Edes, woman,' says Judith, dropping back to the bed with a huff of exasperation. 'Do you never think of anything else?'

I consider the question for a moment, drawing the blanket up to my chin. 'Not really, no.'

'All right then.' Judith's mouth sets into a thin, determined line as she clambers over me and rises up out of bed, fetching her shawl and fussing about to light a candle.

'What are you plotting?' I ask.

'Back in two shakes,' she says, and her tongue wets her lips and a bit of wickedness wets her eyes, God love her.

I settle on my side and follow the sound of Judith's footsteps around the house. Down the stairs, patting across the flagstones, the squeal of the pantry door. Soon she reappears, a cabbage on her hip, triumphant as Salome with the Baptist's dripping head. With mock reverence, Judith sets the cabbage down on the boards before the fire, along with a stick of charcoal and a wad of crumpled paper. 'There,' she says, returning to the bedside and throwing the covers off me, 'come on now!'

The night is cold. I whine as Judith wrangles me from beneath the blankets, hauls me up by the sleeves of my smock, and sets me scowling before the paper and the cabbage. 'We shall warm thee with lustful thoughts soon enough,' she grins. 'Now. Take up the charcoal in one hand and put the other there, upon the cabbage.'

I do as I am bidden. 'Now,' Judith says, 'I shall blindfold you. Feel your hand about the cabbage, there. Set down the image of it on the paper.' Her breath is warm on the back of my ear, and stale and beery. A shawl is placed before my eyes and tightened and fastened there. I know what game she is proposing. It is just on the edge of what might be permitted. A superstitious business.

'If your mother learns of this . . . some would call it divination,' I mutter, and yet excitement clings to my protestation like a burr on floss, I cannot help it. Judith can hear this excitement, and she laughs.

'And they would be oafs,' she says, patting at my shoulder. 'It is not divination. It is a cabbage.'

The glow of the candle leaks through the shawl. I feel the leaves beneath my fingers, cool and fibrous and ridged and veined and carven. I press my tongue against the roof of my mouth, think of sap-flood, bitter on each bite. My fingertips move across the upper curves, which feel like a brow furrowed in thought or creased in the effort of concentration, to find the cabbage's centre, which holds the point of a ring-finger like pursed lips, a raw green kiss. Then the dimples and frills follow outward in a circular motion, the leaves sometimes clinging reticent to each other, sometimes yielding, moist beneath each wing. Here, an overhanging rimple is the corner of a bearded mouth. Above, a tissue of veins like the blue lacework of an upturned wrist, a temple. I draw what I feel – until I also feel Judith's breath on the nape of my neck, and shove the blindfold up and off my eyes, unaware of how much time has passed, unnerved by my own raptness. Charm-drunk.

Down with the charcoal pen, away with the cabbage. It looks so innocent, now, sitting at the edge of the hearthrug, so banal, so inoffensive. I feel something that is like the cool, flat side of a blade pressing between my legs, and I laugh, and the room is cold but my cheeks are hot. One of those queer, out-of-the-ordinary moments you catch falling into your life like a flake of fire.

Judith shuffles forward on her haunches to snatch up the smudgy drawing. 'Now then,' she says, officiously, 'let's see.'

She holds the sketch up to the embers and yellow light floods the paper, and dark lines and powdery smears seem flush, almost, with the silent motion of fire. Judith begins to attribute a succession of winsome qualities to the drawing – strong arms to hold me with, good white teeth, etc. – but I can't see it, can't see any of the things she sees there. What I do see is like an armful of laughing bones. I see, perhaps, the semblance of a red spot leopard-eye, a roiling hole that swallows and swallows itself, like the glint of light on the water at the bottom of a well by which one knows the depth of what might otherwise be thought a darkness infinite, but is not comforted thereby. This is the moment that I realise my life will never again be an ordinary one. Something is begun, and I am tangled in it.

'Rebecca?'

Judith's voice draws me back to the room, where she holds up the drawing before the flame. I tell her to throw it on the grate, overtaken by a sudden chill. I feel like something is there in the chamber with us, or very near to the room – as though something lingers just beneath the lip of the tiny window, brushing at the glass with weird fingers. Judith does as I say, and we watch as the drowsy cinders flare and eat the paper up.

'*Divination*, indeed,' Judith says, clicking her tongue. 'You would think *heresy* would be useful, at least.'

I look down at my hands clasped over my knees and see that they are blackened with coal dust. I rise, and go to the washstand. I pour the water from the jug, and it is good and icy cold. I slide my hands into the basin, draw them out, wipe them on my smock, and there I see it – my own bowed head and the curve of my neck reflected, and another, darker shape besides. Like a hand, a hand reaching for my throat. There is a metallic taste in my mouth, now, like the taste of blood.

I must flinch, for Judith looks, a crease forming on her brow. 'Becky?'

I tell her it is nothing, and that I'm only weary. I press the backs of my wet hands to my cheeks.

'I didn't mean to frighten you, Beck,' Judith says, carefully. She is worried I will tell. Where did she learn it? Mother Clarke, most likely. Seems very much like one of her kitchen spellings. But what would Judith need from a cunning woman? She has no sweetheart to chant over.

'Don't fret over it,' I tell her, and get back into bed, and roll on my side, and press the musty sheets to my mouth. She watches me for a short time, piqued, but eventually follows, blowing out the candle and drawing the coverlet up over us.

I lie awake for a long time in the darkness, and I consider what it is I have seen, or think I have seen – and what the practical difference between seeing something and *thinking* you have seen something really is. I am not superstitious – I am useful. I have taught myself to watch and listen. I have seen enough suffering in my life to know that the diseased mind is prone to invent all manner of phantoms that might hover over a person. Better to blame a sprite or a puck for the souring of the milk or the tangles in the horse's mane than to concede that one's own slovenly habits may have contributed to the situation. I think it is a vanity, in fact: all these Jezebels who think their beauty so great it might attract even the Devil's notice, fabulating courts-full of demons to suck on their pretty tits, and all because their husbands never raise eyes from their beer mugs to look at them. No. Do not fancy yourself a witch. Do not fancy yourself at all. A little pain and next to nothing of joy, wet stockings and cold beds, but your body works, Rebecca, your eyes are sharp, a man will have you in time, or will not, at least, say 'no'—

I dream that night, curled beside Judith. A lance of sunlight clatters down into this dream. My smock melts from my body beneath the rays.

I lie in a glade. Alone, beside a mirror-like pool. The pool is fringed with rushes and minuscule flowers of blue and white, and there are willow trees that bend to soak their bladed leaves in the water. It is such a beautiful place, and I feel contented there, although I am naked. That I find myself naked, in this dream, only compounds my joy: I am in my prone body but also seeming to look down upon it from above, as though I am both body and sun, and find myself pleased by my own body, sleek and narrow and pink like the inner parts of a shell, and just as pleased to be the sun and have so pretty a garden and girl to look upon. The heat pools on my skin.

A rasping sound comes from somewhere nearby. I lift myself to look out over the pool toward this strange sound. Beyond the water there is an orchard, lush and dense, dissolving at last into the shimmer of pale heat. On the far bank of the pool stands Margaret Moone. She wears a white gown. She lifts her arm to reach for an apple that quivers on a low branch above her head. She is laughing. Her fingertips brush careless at the fruit's tight red skin. Up, up, a wonderful stretch, and then she jumps. Slowly, she sails through the air, like a bubble rising through oil, her toes pointed. In the joy of this majestic flight she seems to quite forget the apple, and cuts a way through the air with her arms. Her cap falls from her head as she flies, as though torn off by a gust, but there is no wind – the branches of the fruit trees are still – and her yellow hair streams out behind her. Then, gently, she descends, and where she lands the grass dimples beneath the touch of her feet, like a muslin stretched out over a pudding. A strange, soft garden. She bounces again, and again, each arc is accompanied by the rasping sound. She looks like she is laughing, merrily and ceaselessly, but that laughter I cannot hear. Nonetheless, to watch her sail so regally, so jubilantly, through the warm air of this dream-orchard fills my dream-heart with joy, and so I begin to laugh as well, and fall back against the grass, which leaks its heady odour all around.

There are two butterflies dancing against the relentless sun.

They are huge and black, and come to rest on my belly, where the movements of their tiny feet tickle at me. I watch them. Their thin, compact bodies seem to labour unduly beneath the weight of those extravagant wings, black but painted in places with transparencies of purple and deep burgundy. Bashful, sightless eyes of lilac powder at the tip of each great fluttering pinion. *How beautiful they are*, I think. How difficult they make their beauty look. They flicker their wings open and closed, sunning themselves, and move to nestle in the dark curls of hair just above my loins. There they pause, attentive, as though my secret parts were a flower of rare sweetness.

Tiny shudders move all over my skin. Shocking, pure feelings of a rain falling all over me as the butterflies jostle between my thighs with their caressing flickers. There is a third butterfly, and this falls on my breast, and then – then – the front of my body cools, thrown abruptly under shadow. I open my eyes and there are no more butterflies. I open my eyes and I am looking up into the face of Mister Matthew Hopkins.

He says nothing. He puts his gloved hand on my body and the feeling of pleasure surges again, and it is shameful, and my happiness in the orchard is horribly spoiled. I grasp at his wrist as he touches my hip and I tell him we cannot, and look to the far bank, where Margaret Moone is reaching the high point of another lazy flight through the darkening sky above the crowns of the apple trees. He follows my look. 'Ah,' he says. 'We need not concern ourselves with her.' And he is right, because Margaret Moone stops mid-air and sheds her legs and arms like a moult, and rounds out into a cold hard rock, a true moon at last.

And then he puts his arm firmly about my waist, and he drops his mouth to my throat and kisses me hungrily there. I warm, I relent, my eyes begin to close. The last thing I see is the mirror-like water of the pool, and the boughs reflected within it. And I see there is a noose hanging empty from the low branches of one silver, invert tree.

When I wake my mouth is sour with sleep, and it aches, as though bitten. Judith's weasel eyes are on my face over her crumpled handful of blanket. Morning chill in the little chamber, a little periwinkle-coloured slice of sky. 'Do I dare ask what it is you dreamed?' she asks.

I tell her she may but I'll be damned before I tell it.

'An answer which suggests you are already,' she says.

Her lips twist at the corner of the coverlet, and we fall to giggling.

7

Catechism

The catechism. 'God is a spirit. God's infinite perfection is implied in these and suchlike phrases: I am that I am. I am the beginning and the ending...' My fingers are knitted in my lap, demurely. Skirts and stockings, but below, legs and loins. What is next? 'God is light, and in him is no darkness.' *No darkness* – none. One can hardly imagine.

I sit across from Master Edes. He nods encouragement at me. I like to think he is proud. 'And – how many Gods are there?' he asks.

'Only one – but distinguished into three persons: the Father, the Son, and the Holy Ghost. There is none other God but one. Teach all nations, baptising them in the name of the Father, and the Son, and the Holy Ghost.'

John Edes wets his thumb at the corner of his mouth and turns the page. *A Short Catechism, containing the fundamental Principles of Christian Religion*, by Doctor William Gouge: there is a frontispiece depicting Doctor Gouge himself, the celebrated minister, with his hair cropped close in the Roundhead style, and one eye rather bigger than the other. When Master Edes first showed me it, I said that the Doctor looked a little like the Widow Leech, 'meaning no disrespect to the venerable preacher' – and that made him laugh, his cheeks flushed very adorably. Everything that passes between us

I commit carefully to memory, like a child pressing violets between the pages of a prayerbook.

'Good, very good, Miss West,' he says. 'And – furthermore – how is God made known unto us?'

I repeat the words of the catechism, feeling myself to be a dirty, impious girl. It is early afternoon. The bright bell-like morning has been muffled over by grey cloud that the sun breaks through only in fitful winces. I like Edes' modest accommodations above the White Hart. I like to see how a man lives, how men might live, without women. I feel more reverence when I enter there, and find myself among John Edes' simple and beautiful and unadorned possessions, than I do when I cross the threshold of St Mary's. Here there is a holy emptiness, a wonderful austerity. It is so different from the poky disorder of my own home, where Vinegar Tom drags around his ragged blanket and scratches at his sores with mysterious determination, where mother's bundled herbs hang drying from the crossbeams and shed their intricate little burrs. When I picture heaven in my mind, what I see is something like this: Edes' table of unvarnished hardwood boards, the sunlight finding not a single crumb to glare on, his clean shirt spread before the fire to dry, the blue glazed jug in his washing stand. Even the smells of bacon grease and tobacco smoke drifting up from the inn below are those good and wholesome, fat baby sort of smells. Late at night, when I am alone in my bed, I imagine Master Edes in this lovely clean place, in his lovely clean shirt, reading. Perhaps the *Sayings* of John Dod.

I reach the twenty-third proposition. This is: 'I was shaken in iniquity, and in sin did my mother conceive.' Some nasty thing previously a-doze within me stirs, rears its black nose. I feel my hands squeeze into fists against my skirts.

'Shape,' Edes interjects.

I look up, and our eyes meet across the dog-eared pages of the catechism book. He wets his lips. '*Shapen* in iniquity.' He clears his throat. 'How is the heinousness thereof discerned?'

'By three things. First – that it is the seed of all sin. Secondly, that it hath defiled the whole man. Thirdly, that it never ceaseth to provoke man to sin, as long as he liveth.' It has not yet been a day since I humoured Judith in her foolish game. I dreamed my lewd dream that very morning. And now I sit here and I speak of sin and defilement. Digging my nails into my palms, I feel suddenly that I ought to stand up, as though something execrable is leaking from my body and pooling beneath my skirts, around my seat. I do stand, as though compelled, and press a shaking hand to my brow. Master Edes looks up from the book.

'Rebecca – are you quite well?'

I do not know. Something has struck me with a purer terror than any phantom talon in a washbasin. My heart flutters and thuds. I realise in that moment that to be loved by him, or by any man worth loving, would be quite impossible. More than anything in the world I would have him see me, and know me. But if he saw me and knew me truly, he would despise me, despise what it is I hold inside me. I wonder if this is what all women eventually come to know – a choice each comes to make between obscuring her true self in exchange for the false regard of a good man, or allowing herself the freedom to be as she truly is and settling for a brute who couldn't care less if she is as broken, as coarse, as hopeless as he. Or is it only me? Am I, somehow, *wrong*? Perhaps other women glide unsoiled through their lives in magnificent simplicity, an inch above the claggy mud, unassailed by crude distraction or unholy impulse. All of this I think, and I am terrified, terrified both for and of myself. 'Oh,' I say. Just *oh*.

'You are pale as death,' Master Edes says. 'Here. Here, sit down.' He stands and gently takes hold of my shoulders, pressing me back down into my seat. Yes. I am desperate for him to tell me what to do, to instruct me. *Shaken by iniquity.*

I might be enjoying this, were I not so discomposed. 'Here. Have a little wine,' says Edes. He fetches a bottle of port and pours us both a cup, pushes one into my shaking hand. Unthinking, I take a gulp, and it is warm and fortifying in my mouth. I take another, and Master Edes smiles, resuming his seat. 'There now,' he says, cajoling. 'Drown the distemper down.'

I thank him for his kindness, but he waves his hand dismissively and snaps the catechism shut, taking a gulp of port. He pinches his sandy moustaches between thumb and forefinger, and his eyes settle at last upon my face. 'It may not be my place to ask,' he proceeds, nonetheless, to ask, 'or within my ability to render assistance, but—' He fumbles around with his words, '—does something trouble you, Rebecca?'

His face is open and earnest as he peers into mine. A high, freckled brow and tired, grey-blue eyes. His teeth are a little large, perhaps, objectively. But I like that. I like the liony flash of them when he throws back his head to laugh, which he does quite often, for a Godly man. It reminds me of the tale of Old King David dancing in the temple, lost in rapture.

I want to tell him. I want to speak to him. I grope about in my brain for something like a beginning. 'Many things trouble me, sir,' is the best I can manage.

He nods, slowly. 'Indeed. These are dark times, and readily we believe the Devil might walk abroad, sowing a corruption in our hearts that compounds our earthly miseries.'

I have never heard him speak like this before, of the Devil. 'Do you believe it?' I ask. 'That the Devil truly does his work among us?'

He smiles bitterly, his fingers clasping over the rim of his cup. 'Believe it? I know it to be true.'

'How?'

'Because I am a man, like any other. Even our Lord Jesus Christ was subject to the Devil's black coaxing. And by great fortitude alone did he resist.'

I see something new in him then, sitting across from me at the table. Something scathed. His head is bent over the closed book as though in supplication. His mouth and nose are a young person's, but there are deep lines on his brow, and his eyes are limned about with red. I remember that he has a day-life, an occupation, outside of our weekly audiences. A shipping clerk: long nights sat in front of dusty account books and pitiless columns of figures, the scratching of a lone quill by candlelight. Thinking of it makes me feel an unspeakable tenderness for him. I want to kiss the lids of his tired eyes, take his face in my hands and bring it to rest on my shoulder.

'I think I have seen him,' I say, quietly. Why do I say it? I regret it as soon as I have. Master Edes looks up at me, his expression darkening. Perhaps it is the wine, for I seldom drink. Either he will believe me, and find me forever tainted by the association – or he will disbelieve me, and think me nothing but a silly maid who entertains herself with flights of infernal fantasy. Or perhaps there isn't anything to believe in the first place, and all I am doing is thickening the tissue of deceit between our two hearts. What would I prefer? I grasp in the dark toward him.

'I know you would not say such things in idleness, Rebecca,' he replies at last, after a long, tremulous silence.

'Like a shadow, behind me. In the water,' I offer. An explanation that is not an explanation, and could not mean anything to him, but he seems to accept it. Accept it, or ignore it.

He rises. 'The days have grown so short,' he says. He begins to light the candles.

And I say that I should be getting back to Lawford before Mother misses me – but I make no move to leave, because he sits down all of a sudden, and as I am reaching for my shawl he takes my right hand in his, and presses at my fingers. His palms feel soft and cool. He says my name again, then, says *Rebecca*, but in a strained, contentious sort of way, as though I have tried to interrupt him. 'Rebecca,' he repeats, and I think how wonderful it is to hear one's name said aloud, to know that a much-beloved mouth shaped itself to the saying of it. 'I am saying that I know temptation, because I am a man.' His eyes, those damselfly-blues, are fixed intently on my face, where I feel the colour rising. I think I know what it is he is saying to me, but I dare not believe it, and much less dare return it in kind. I feel like an ear of corn is quivering dry in my throat, scratching at the sides of it. Master Edes' bed is at my back, in the corner of the room, with the clean white counterpane.

'Does the Bible not teach that women are worse afflicted by temptation, having weaker spirits than those of men?' I pipe, pointlessly, in the hope of filling the silence.

Master Edes seems encouraged by this, and tightens his grasp of my hand. His lip curls. 'Then perhaps we might *both* do well to remember,' he says, 'that the Devil, that Old Deluder, works hardest where he feels himself to be most despised.' He turns my wobbling girlhand upward in his lap, and traces his fingertips over the rough skin at the saddle of my thumb. Oh, *God*. My hands, rough-skinned, coarsened by lye and burning water and whisker-scars from hearth tending. Hands small and so, so crude against his long, eloquent fingers. I suppose the innkeeper does all of that for Master Edes, those daily chores. Or the innkeeper's wife. Or the innkeeper's girl. And then I feel a sudden and unjustified surge of proprietorship over Master Edes and his chamber both, and against whatever little slut of an innkeeper's girl there might be. I feel I should say something, and so I say his name, 'Master Edes,' and then I feel that bilious turn again. We are alone and he is touching me, and not in a manner to which I am used. Whether it is because it all feels so abrupt, or because my humours simmer still from the morning's orchard-dream, I could not say – but something causes me to withdraw my hand and glance toward the chamber door, which we leave always ajar for propriety's sake.

And Master Edes sees me look toward the door and withdraws his own hands, raising them, open in apology. 'Forgive me, Rebecca,' he sighs. 'You are troubled. I sought only to offer succour. But perhaps it is not my place.'

I know this to be a lie, but it sounds true enough to loosen the knot of nerves in my chest, and I am grateful for it. I watch him finish his port, then rise and refill his cup, and I do not know how to begin to explain what it is I want from him. It is strange, how you can want something terribly – like a man, or to die – and at the same time be frightened to the dipping point of the heart by it. Really, I think, as I watch him linger by the hearth with his head bowed, I know so little about him, and nothing he does not wish me to know. I would like to know a secret about him. Perhaps the best thing of all would be to *be* a secret about him. A precious torment. An unforgettable shame.

I stand, and the bells of St Mary's sound from somewhere between cloud and mud-clagged street outside, calling the devout to Evening Service, and quelling my voluptuary daring. Instead of moving to where he stands by the fire and pressing my tongue to the pulse of life on his soap-sweet throat, as I would like to, I stand stupidly by the table, and say, 'How fares Mister Hopkins at the Thorn?' with forced politeness and much too loudly.

Edes looks up at me, surprised. 'Mister Hopkins? Well. Business is ... slow, now, of course. Now that the weather has turned. Rebecca—' He looks away from the fire and up into my face, again, his tone quietly scrupulous, 'I think it would be best – that is, I think you have the good sense, to not speak of . . . of what we have spoken of here today to any other.'

The Devil and his temptations, or the business with the hand-holding? I think it best not to ask, and so I nod, obediently, and draw my shawl on around my shoulders. As I gather my things up to leave – my basket, cloak, ragged woollen gloves – a sense of desolation seems to creep on me. I take surreptitious looks at him standing over the fire, apparently deep in thought. We have somehow blundered about each other, the thread missing the needle's narrow eye. Thread and needle, *well*. But too late. 'Good night, Master Edes,' I say, standing at the doorway, and, 'God keep you. John.'

He nods, but makes no answer. I close the door behind.

Outside, Market Street is little more than a reservoir of churned black mud. A drizzle falls light, of the eyelash-clinging kind. There are scarce any abroad in the gloomy street, and the only sound beside the evening bells is the yapping laughter of the three Wright children, thin and poorly dressed. They berate and jostle at a fat black hog who has nosed his way through the neighbour's crumbling sty wall and into Goody Wright's shed, as hogs have a way of doing, because they are clever and frightened of nothing. Goody Wright herself, languid in despair, watches her broodlings' ineffectual assault from the stoop, the hog happily munching through her stacked winter provisions. How simple, the life of beasts, who were not made in the image of God. What they see and want, they move to take, happy as can be.

As I begin the long walk home, the closing parts of Gouge's catechism unspool in my mind: *In the end of the world the son of man shall send forth his Angels, and they shall gather out of his Kingdom all things that offend, and them that do iniquity, and they shall be cast into the furnace of fire: there shall be wailing and gnashing of teeth.*

8

Fire

In the winter I am sometimes glad to return home, though my mother be there. Glad of the fire and the bubbling stew, when they are there, glad of the sack of onions in their crackling yellow skins, the tonic fragrance of thyme drying at the doorposts. Small part of the world to loose myself in, where no one who matters will see. But tonight my mother is deep in one of her philosophical episodes, and limply melancholy, and prone to nip at my edges. She moons about the table wrapped in a greying shawl, her hair tangled, distemper writ in the deep lines of her face as she bends over the pot on the hearth. Up she peers when I come in and set to scraping the mud from my clogs. She asks me if I am hungry. Tells me she got a shoulder of mutton on credit.

I lie to her that I ate at the Moones'. I add that she shouldn't be getting anything on credit, either, given that winter will be lean and spring is likely to be more so, what with war being what it is (though far away for now, at least, a halter at the neck of the country).

She watches me, clutching a ladle in one thin hand, the other clasped at the edge of her dirty sleeve. 'And where is it you have come from so late, miss?'

'Master John Edes',' I say, shortly, in such a manner as I hope indicates I will brook no further enquiry at this time, as I thaw my tired feet by the fire.

'Did you see Margaret?' she asks.

'Mother Moone's hard to miss.' I am much pleased with the witticism, though all Mother does is click her tongue and return her attention to the simmering stew, muttering that I am being unkind. There is no conviction in her movements, her words, or even her chidings – she progresses about the kitchen like a wet ghost fated to re-enact the routines of a mortal life tragically curtailed, and by the Devil, it riles me. Sitting by the fire, I go through all the outrageous things I might now say to her that would scarce raise a grimace on her torpor-stricken face. It is like she is barely there. *I think I am in love with John Edes*, I could say, for instance, *and I would eat his beard trimmings if he asked it of me.* Or else *I think I saw the Devil last night in Judith Moone's washbasin.* But instead I say only, 'Where has my knitting got to?', and untie my sodden cap.

Mother passes me my knitting and says, lackadaisically, that she thinks we ought not to light the parlour fire for a while. It is only me that tends the parlour fire, and I have not lit it in weeks – but I haven't the energy to challenge her. 'One fire will be quite enough,' I sigh, unwinding my dark yellow wool. Vinegar Tom slides out from beneath the bench with a big, carnal yawn. He seats himself by the door, ears attuning twitchy to the sounds of the night just-born and squalling beyond the timbers. Of all my mother's moods, it is this, this sullen abdication of personality, that I hate most. It occasions greater loathing in me than having all the sack jugs in the Tendring Hundred hurled at my head. It feels like a betrayal.

Outside the clouds sweep their heavy skirts of wind along the Stour, and the chimney whines over the clicking of my needles. Mother sits opposite me, silent and frog-eyed, picking at the loose skin of her neck with idle fingertips. She chews her cheek. And then she begins to talk. She talks very quietly, as though for the benefit of no one but herself. 'It wasn't long after you were born,' she begins. 'Your father, God rest, was off and away – at Flushing, I think it was. And I was sat by the fire there, dandling you on my knee. Such a pretty babe you were. All that hair, soft as down. You won't believe . . .' Her voice folds up in a sad, faraway sort of smile. 'A night very like this, with a foul blast sucking in the chimney,' she adds, her smile fading as her eyes roll toward the wailing hearth, 'there came a man in black. The man in black came and stood there—' She raises a finger and points just before the hearth, to a spot at the edge of the knot-rug. 'A man in black with a high-crowned hat. I was alone one moment, and the next . . .'

I fall still and look up at her. I can tell she sees the man there now, her bloodshot eyes tracking the progress of some obscure visitant around the room, as a cat's might follow the flakes of dander dancing on a summer updraft. 'They do not tell you, before you whelp,' she says, quietly, her eyes still fixed on nothing, 'that one moment you are alone, and the next . . . you are still alone. You think, when you are young, that a child is like to a sailor's knot, or a hairpin – except you push it out rather than in.' She smiles ruefully. 'That the child will come and hold everything together, everything in place at last. But it don't. I mean,' she looks at me, at last, '—you didn't.'

What am I meant to say to that? I listen, needles poised still in my hands.

'And there the man in black stands,' she continues, 'in a long coat like a presbyter wears, and I sit still and quite dumbfounded. He says I would do well – *you would do well, Anne West*, I remember it, exactly that – *to throw thy babe in the fire*. Right then and there. So I kiss your plump little cheeks and I put you down there on the hearthstone, before I can think to know what it is that I am doing . . . and the man in black is gone. Gone as soon as it is done.'

I listen. I remember a tale of a young wife from Maine, New England, that was passed along the back pews of St Mary's a year or two hence. It sounded the way many stories that reach the parlours of Essex from the haunted pines of the New World do: our own domestic fancies dropping like a flock of grubby black pigeons on the barest scattering of truth. The girl, they said, was very young, and a simpleton, too. She found herself so transported and affrighted by the sermons of a local preacher that she resolved to throw her newborn babe down the well, and in broad daylight. Charged with killing the child, the Maine woman had said that as she was damned, and as she knew the babe was damned, too, there was little point in indulging either of them with such flummeries as earthly life. Had she not cleverly circumvented the cruelties inherent in God's plan, while bringing about a conclusion that would no doubt satisfy Him, and with great expediency? All that remained was for the Justices to complete the job, which the simple Maine girl begged they would with all haste. Duly they did. The girl was hung before the meeting-house, in a clearing amid the spruce, and her sad tale became a moral tract in a grubby pamphlet bought at the yard of St Paul's in London and read aloud to a thrill of Essex virgins by a travelling messenger. A lesson against presumption.

My mother continues. 'The embers were very hot, and soon enough you were squalling, and wriggling like a worm on a hook, there at the hearthstone. I watched, and I felt very heavy of a sudden, and knew there was nothing I could do even if I had wanted to. And your hair, all that black hair you had, was singeing. My legs were bound together tight. And then,' she smiles, 'there's a knock at the door. In comes Widow Leech – excepting she was no widow then – takes one look about the parlour and seizes you up and away from the fire, shrieking.'

Vinegar Tom interrupts with an unseemly mewl, galvanised by

all this talk of infanticide to resume his own tyranny over the local vermin, and therefore wishing to be let out into the yard. Mother rises from her seat at the kitchen table and opens up the door for him. Out Tom slips and in comes the wind. The candle flame gutters. I start up my knitting again. The violence of my mother's tale – the burning baby, the baby who is me – moves me not. Blistering skin on fat little arms. No. There is nothing in me for it. Still. I think of it, the man in black, the girl in Maine, the babies on the fire and plashing down the well. There is a pattern to it, like with knitting, a language of it, and it is women's, and held secret and grey-pink as guts.

'Leech gave me a sound slap, then grabbed up my hands,' Mother goes on, shutting the door tight and taking up her seat, 'and together we prayed.' She is silent for a while, and then adds, '—and I never saw the man in black again.'

'*A man in black*,' I repeat. It sounds like I am mocking her, I think. I hope it sounds like I am mocking her, and her man in black.

She looks at me askance. 'You think it was the Devil.'

I shrug. 'It was God that came to Abraham and bid him to slay his son.'

'God – the Devil. How is a silly woman who signs her name with a cross meant to tell the difference, their methods being so alike?' She sighs. 'Nothing more than my own fancy, maybe.'

I tell her to leave off, anyhow, or she'll never think of anything else, which would not do, seeing as we've mutton on the boil that needs paying for. And she says back that she bought it off Rivett, who is a drunk and will quite forget the extension of credit. And she calls me *Rabbit*, and tells me that if there is one thing that she, my old mother, can teach me, it's to only take credit off men with red-webbed noses. She musters a wink.

I say, 'The eleventh commandment,' and smile, so that she might think we have shared something between us.

The mutton is good, and lasts us the best part of a week, during which my mother and I find nothing very great to fall out over.

9

Maleficium

It is Saturday night. Thomas Briggs is stripped and deposited peremptorily in a tin bath filled with a half-inch of lukewarm water before the parlour fire. He gathers his skinny legs to his chest and sits there pouting at his knees. Priscilla Briggs, his mother, is secretly pleased by the incipient masculinity evinced by his intransigence in the face of ablution – but not so pleased she will allow him to attend church with rinds of estuary mud beneath his fingernails.

Mistress Briggs herself heads upstairs to lay out her best church gown of black stuff and collar of powdered lace for tomorrow's service. She instructs Helen, the housemaid, to air her coat. Then she warms a cup of milk with which to see young Thomas off wholesome to bed.

'And I hope you have remembered behind your ears, this time. Cleanliness is—' *But stop.* She pushes open the parlour door to the sight of the tin bath upended, and Thomas sprawled face-down on the flagstones, arms stiff and outspread like a corn dolly's, fitting and twitching.

Together, Helen and Priscilla carry the boy upstairs to his bedchamber while he hisses and kicks at them both, as wretched as a fox caught in a trap, his eyes rolling back into his head. *O God, my boy, my Thomas.* Priscilla gasps frantically over bed and boy, pushing his hair away from his damp face and trying to suppress his wild thrashing.

Helen watches mulish from the door. 'Thick as clot!' Priscilla shrills at her. 'Don't just stand there! Send Michael out for Doctor Croke.'

And off Helen dashes, tripping on her skirts.

'And the Minister!' Priscilla hollers down the stairs after her.

It is past midnight by the time Doctor Croke arrives, stately in his overcoat, with his long wisps of white hair and his hard little bag of pincers and pokers, urchin spines and saltpetre. Goody Briggs has left her son's bedside for just long enough to comb out her hair and throw on a straight gown. She feels mildly guilty for even this brief abandonment, but reasons it is ultimately done in Thomas's best interests, given that Doctor Croke is an eligible widower, and Priscilla herself expects soon to be a widow too, a circumstance she will aim to correct as soon as it is respectable to do so.

Thomas's thrashing has dwindled to a ceaseless tremble, but his eyes remain lucid and his skin hot with sweat. 'Poppets,' he gasps. 'In the scuttle. And they keep birdies as pets as well.'

The Doctor lifts the boy's nightshirt and presses a hand to his quaking belly. Thomas attempts to wriggle out from beneath the coverlet and to stand back on his feet. Priscilla gently protests, trying to press him back down to the pillows, but the Doctor silences her, and indicates that they should allow the boy to rise.

Thomas Briggs does rise. He stands shivering by the bedside for a moment, then begins to walk, to walk, dead-eyed and in ever-expanding circles, around the room. He drags his left foot crumpled behind him – a limp where before the boy had none – and releases a laboured, hacking breath at every footstep. Priscilla babbles quietly to herself, alarmed to see her son so compromised. It is as though the healthful lad she left grouching in the bath has been carried away by devils and replaced by a superannuated drunk – a discomposing, palsied thing hauling itself around the room in an aimless stagger.

Helen reappears at the doorway and says that the Minister has promised to come as soon as he is able. She fidgets with her apron and casts a nervous look at Thomas, dragging his left foot behind himself as though it is rotting off.

'Ha!' Thomas shouts, spinning on the spot and jabbing a finger at the housemaid. 'Ha! Sisters, and the fondling of sooty-ears! I saw her dugs once—' he declares, with an odd, lascivious smile. 'Lovely they were, though the left is bigger than the right. She feeds me on pins!' He releases a sudden screech and falls to the floor, as though something has lain its hands on his shoulders and pushed him.

Doctor Croke sweeps the lad up in his arms and returns him, at last, to the bed. Thomas is reduced once more to a collection of jittering limbs atop the blankets, and mutters in a sing-song voice, again and again, *The Captain brings a monkey for the King, though the red-skin died, the Captain brings a monkey for the King, though the red-skin died*, and whines and variously battologises. Helen backs away, a look of dumb horror on her face.

The God-fearing Priscilla is grave. She presses a hand to her mouth and mutters, 'Use not vain repetitions, as the heathens do,' through her fingers.

Doctor Croke renews his examination, tugging at Thomas's lower lids to inspect the veiny flesh beneath his rolling eyes, seizing the boy's jaw and holding his mouth open to peer at his tonsils. 'And never before has he had such convulsions?' the Doctor enquires.

Priscilla shakes her head. 'No, never.'

Doctor Croke makes a low, thoughtful noise, and sends for a wide dish and a wet cloth.

'Aye, and fetch me a Holy Book too, Helen,' Thomas interjects from the bed, in a high-pitched, needly voice that is not his own – and not like anyone else's, either – 'for I wish to make an evening snack from it.' He bursts out into guffawing and mashes his balled fists against his chest.

Goody Briggs snaps her fingers at Helen, who is very pleased to have this excuse to absent herself. By the time she returns, Thomas's affliction is modified once more, and Priscilla and Doctor Croke watch the boy with mute concern as he gallops and careens about the room as though he is riding an invisible hobby-horse, his hands tight around spectral reins. But where a child indulging in such play might usually click the tongue to denote hoof beats, Thomas instead barks like an angry terrier. His flagrant rejection of dramatic veracity is deeply unsettling to all. With great difficulty – and, for Helen's part, with reluctant compliance – the three of them eventually wrestle the boy off his ghostly steed and into a chair, then cover his head with a wet cloth so that the Doctor might administer fumes of hartshorn. The bedchamber is choked with a mealy, sour odour, like hot piss, and Priscilla gags and chokes as she helps Croke stall the boy above the steaming bowl. As soon as the wet cloth is removed from his head, Thomas begins a bout of vomiting miraculous in its longevity, and kicks the bowl over, and is returned to the bed once more, shuddering and slick with sweat and his own effluvium. It is a waking nightmare.

'A jaybird, plucked and disembowelled, is one remedy for the Falling Sickness—' Doctor Croke gamely interpolates, as he dabs a kerchief on his glistening brow, '—although I concede, a jaybird may be difficult to obtain at the present hour.' His black humour does not find an appreciative audience in the frantic Goody Briggs. But fortunately (though not for Thomas Briggs), all options are not exhausted. The boy is pinched and bled, heated and cooled, sprinkled with powders, spread with salves and a gritty mucilage of peony seeds and cat's cruor.

Minister Long arrives too late to corroborate the miraculous nature of the vomiting episode, and soon wishes he had stayed away entirely. He improvises a number of spiritual diagnostic techniques, and they reach a consensus that in his present condition, the usually devout Thomas is wholly unable to recite the Lord's Prayer without barking, which must be significant somehow. The Minister, however, sees which way this whole affair is going, and is chary of performing any procedure that might be thought by Doctor Croke and Goody Briggs too closely to resemble the Popish ceremony of exorcism. (Secretly, however, he wishes that the Pope were here, and thinks that he would have a better idea of what to do.)

By daybreak, it is concluded that the only explanation for Thomas Briggs' prodigious malady is bewitchment. Maleficium. By mid-morning, half the town has heard the same.

The Information of Grace, the wife of Richard Glascock of Manningtree,
taken upon oath before the said Justices, 1645

This informant saith, that there being some falling out between
Mary the wife of Edward Parsley of Manningtree, and one Helen
Clarke, the wife of Thomas Clarke (which said Helen is the daughter
of Anne Leech) this informant heard the said Helen to say, as the
said Helen passed by this informant's door in the street, that Mary
the daughter of the said Edward and Mary Parsley should rue for all,
whereupon, presently the said Mary the daughter, fell sick, and died
within six weeks after.

10

Sermon

The next day is one of winter pure and true, bitterly cold and overcast, and a powdered sleet falls over Mistley. Mother takes one look at the grit-bellied cloud from the kitchen stoop, and declares that she will not leave the house for all the silver in Seville, but I – being hard compelled by curiosity, which is, of course, the first sin of woman – decide that I will go in spite of it.

The pews are cold enough to blister your thighs through your skirts – but the congregation is nonetheless swollen to great number, despite the filthy weather, by the promise of gossip. Goody Briggs' unprecedented absence from her front seat only serves to confirm the outlandish rumours that have circled the slender hours, passed from door to door by errand-bound boys, and by the red-cheeked housekeepers emptying ash pails onto midden heaps (the Widow Leech among them). It is clear from the opening formalities of the sermon that Minister Long's auroral brush with Pandemonium has imbued him, in the eyes of his flock, with a certain glamour (Frances Hockett flutters a hand before her breast and declares she could just *eat him up in a pie*, which seems to me an excessively libertine pronouncement). Minister Long notices this newfound regard, and it seems to please him. He is a different man. He swaggers and swashbuckles at the pulpit, Essex's own Jeremiah, pushing his mop of brown hair from out of his eyes, his lace jabot at a rakish angle.

His sermon keeps even the restive back rows rapt. As we all know, he says, *as we all know* – God's work on earth is nearly done. Things draw, resolutely, to their close. As that celestial arrow of intent nears its target, the Devil redoubles his efforts to send it astray, and plunge the world into the thicket of anarchy. I think the metaphor somewhat torturous, but the congregants' eyes widen. The venerables in the front pew press their hands to their sallow throats.

'We grope,' Minister Long intones, 'even now, along a darkened path, beset by fiends. Hands reach out to us through the black. But how are we to know if they offer to guide us true, on our way through the shadows, or seek to lead us further from the way of redemption, and unto the very jaws of the Beast?' As the Prince of Hell is invoked a gust whips felicitously at the boarded windows. In the third row, I see Mary Parsley reach to clutch at her sister's arm.

Even here, he explains, in Manningtree, the Devil's servants abound, like rancorous toads at the bottom of the grain-sack, revelling in their own slime. And now their master galvanises them to mutiny against the town, against the neighbours who have long offered them protection and succour, against Parliament, and against England itself. 'The world will be made anew,' he says, eyes sweeping and reeling as though he traces the progress of some invisible bird over the front row of pews, 'do not doubt it, for it is written that the day of the Lord will come as a thief in the night; in which the heavens shall pass away with a great noise, and the elements shall melt with fervent heat . . .' He inhales. Blinks.

'A new world. But will it be a world for the righteous?' He moistens his lips and pauses, his eyes flickering closed in a subtle invitation for his congregants to envision the alternative: hedgerows bursting into flame, no doubt, and magpies picking at the faces of dead lambs, and pigs and dogs alike walking on their hind legs, wielding rusty cleavers of their very own.

'And he cried mightily with a strong voice, saying, Babylon the great is fallen, is *fallen*' – and some of our more tendentious neighbours, who know well their Revelation, bend their lips silently along to the familiar passage – 'and is become the habitation of devils, and the hold of every foul spirit, and a cage of every unclean and hateful bird.' Minister Long lifts his arms to the rafters. 'How much she hath glorified herself, and lived deliciously, so much torment and sorrow give her! For she saith in her heart, I sit a queen, and I am no widow, and I shall see no sorrow. Vigilance!' he shouts, smacking his hands down hard upon the lectern. A shiver passes through the congregants.

Of whom might Minister Long be speaking? There are many widows in Manningtree, and their number is growing. The general opinion concerning widows is that – once time has blunted the edge of their bereavement – they tend to fuss about and make unconscionable demands upon the commonweal. A knob of butter here, a loaf of bread there, *just until I am able to get back on my feet, Goodwife*. Some take to languishing abed while their homesteads fall to ruin and their children, unattended, make a nuisance of themselves in the streets. Some of them, having lost their own husbands, cast about for other people's, all heaving bosoms and wet doe eyes and *please just hold me George it's been so long since I felt the touch of a man*. Yes, the left side of St Mary's might be forced to concede, they can see how a woman like that, riven by emptiness, might find it consuming her. They can see how she might look for things to fill it with, set about stuffing the fissure with whatever ghostly shreds come to enwrap themselves about her shoulders at night. They say the Devil is a cunning trickster, a two-faced sweetheart. He dangles a patient ear as often as he does a pretty bauble. And women hate widows all the more because they are just a tumbling scaffold at the shipyard or a storm on the channel or a bullet from a hedgerow away from being one themselves.

'Vigilance,' Long repeats, intently. 'Vigilance and faith. He who overlooketh the sins of his neighbour sinneth himself. The Devil cometh amongst us in all manner of disguises, both astonishing and base: the wanton girl, the conjurer, the Cavalier with his feathered hat, bent on defilement and rapine: or else he appears as no more... no more than a rabbit by the door, the dog... the dog who walks in your shadow the whole road home. Ever His dominions increase, and encroach – from east and west, from north and south, and he hopes that he might truly be called King in this world! We must see to it' – he raises a trembling finger heavenward, here – 'that among the righteous, he findeth no recourse, no sanctuary. Be alert, saith Peter – for your enemy, the Devil, prowls around you as a roaring lion, looking for one to devour.'

He draws to a close, touching a hand to his pigeon chest. The church is silent, save for the rustle of collective in-drawn breath. I feel that I am being looked at – I am being looked at. Eyes round the white wing of a cap, a furtive hindward glance. I pinch hard at the skin of my wrist.

The churchyard is glutted with the last fallen leaves, shades of leathery brown and livid yellow, the earth turning up a leprous cheek. The women have made uncommon haste back to home and hearth, most half-expectant they will find cauldrons upset and laundry despoiled by spectral burglars in their absence, nasty fingerprints on their underthings. But the men remain behind and mill about, congratulating the Minister on his sermon, and discussing, with doom-laden expressions, the events of the preceding night.

'Bewitchment?' John Edes enquires of Minister Long, elevating his eyebrows. 'You are certain the boy makes not . . . well, mere sport? A jest by which he means to fright his mother? A fit of mulligrubs? Mistress Briggs is, after all, a woman of nervous disposition.'

The Minister shakes his head. 'If the boy play-acts, he suffers for it out of all proportion. No. In my opinion – and that of Doctor Croke – his affliction is very real. And its causes . . .'

'. . . are supernatural,' interjects Matthew Hopkins, his collar pulled high around his beard. He sets the word out with care, but also gratification, as if it were fine glassware.

Minister Long nods. His face, now he has left the pulpit and conceded the authority conferred by that elevated position, is soft, malleable and more than a little desperate-looking. In his pride, he has started something, he knows, with the talk of lions and defilement and nasty, filthy birds. He is like a child who, joyously up-ending a bag of marbles, ends up scrabbling to stop them rolling away into the dark. 'But. But I would urge against too precipitous judgement in the matter—'

'Was the boy's body inspected for marks?' Hopkins interrupts.

'Marks?' blinks Long.

'Witch-marks. The Devil stamps them about his children, to put them always in mind of the covenant they share. Or so I have read,' he adds, twitching his reddened nostrils.

Long peers up at Hopkins. They all do, gathered in their little knot by the church door. 'You mean to suggest that Master Briggs, himself, affects this ailment?'

Hopkins shrugs. 'Nay – but he is chosen as a recruit, perhaps. A lively, impressionable youth whose burgeoning vitality might be redirected toward maleficent ends.' He cocks his head, thoughtfully. 'Who else is of his household?' His manner is cool and authoritative, but the way he shapes his mouth to the cramp-words (*burgeoning*, *maleficent*) is almost titillated.

Richard Edwards, another neighbour, volunteers the information: 'Outside of the boy and his mother . . . they keep two servants, I believe. Michael Wright, bound over from Clacton, and a maid, Helen Clarke, who was recently wed.'

'I see,' says Hopkins. 'I trust you will be attending to the matter closely, Minister Long? Your sermon reassured me of your very great eagerness to protect our town from the scourge of witchcraft, even as it seared me with hot reminder of the depravity we face.'

Long tugs at his jabot and nods vociferously. 'Of course, Mister Hopkins. I shall render the Goodwife Briggs every assistance possible.'

'As will we all,' ventures Edwards, to a general murmur of assent.

They stand about there for a little while longer, narrowing their eyes against the saline wind, each absorbed in his own thoughts, each privately calculating the level of credence he is willing to venture on the paroxysms of an adolescent boy, the terrors of a lonely mother, and the professional guesses of a spineless cleric and dipsomaniac physician (the latter also widely believed to hold Popish sympathies). Then they leave, and the Steward extinguishes the dozen on dozen candles, one by one, taking care not to turn his back too long on the encroaching shadow.

Dark falls early over the little town, and the sleet rarefies into a silk mist, a devil's web spanning the dishevelled rooftops, smothering out the stars.

II

The Incubus

A week passes, and I hear nothing else spoken of in town but the bewitchment of Thomas Briggs: its symptoms, its nature, any possible cure – more pertinently, its cause. Precedents are found in literature by the learned men of town: Darrell's *True Narration of the strange and grievous vexation by the Devil, of 7 persons in Lancashire*; Denison's *Most wonderful and true storie of a certaine Witch named Alse Goodridge of Stapenhill*. These and suchlike pamphlets are passed about the inns and ordinaries, and much spoken over through mouthfuls of brawn. And meanwhile, Briggs' condition, like the weather, neither worsens nor improves. His teeth chatter in his head, his eyes roll back so that only the whites of them can be seen. The little Briggs body contorts and locks into dismaying postures the like of which all avow they thought the human body incapable of assuming. *He takes a thin gruel twice daily*, says Grace Glascock. *He vomits up dusty feathers and miniature teeth*, claims Mary Phillips, *like to an owl's leavings*. Doctor Croke arrives periodically to slather him in stuff. But no good seems to come of it.

The rumours begin sober and discriminating, traceable to those with immediate knowledge of the occult affair. Then more arrive at the Briggs' modest manor, which stands a way back from the road between Mistley and Manningtree in a sad little garden, dripping and denuded by winter.

I see visitors going in, gentlemen and goodwives. They carry cakes, pigeon pies and bowls of stewed pear, black pudding and sticky, exotic figs. This bounty surely does Mistress Briggs no good, as she is committed to fasting in penance for whatever transgression has caused God to forsake her household. But the relative extravagance or miserliness of each gift gives us something else to gossip over, at least. Grist for Manningtree's brute mill, *reputation*. I can picture it: the women sitting about Mistress Briggs in the parlour, praying most earnestly for the recovery of her Thomas, or else singing tuneless psalms ('Why standest thou so far off, Our Lord?' is a reported favourite). Most men will summon only enough courage to peer gravely around the door to the afflicted boy's room, I suspect – but perhaps the braver venture in to stand by the bedside, to speak merciful words of scripture over the bewitched, and shake their heads in despair at the ungodliness of it all – Thomas himself fixing a black, discomfiting gaze over the counterpane on whomsoever dares to visit him.

At first the visitors come one by one, but soon their visits overlap, and something of a moribund carnival atmosphere begins to take hold of the lower storey of the Briggs household: there stands the Yeoman Hobday and his wife, rigid and wholesome-looking, who have brought with them an entire blush-tummied trout, filleted and ready for poaching (respectable enough now, but we all know about the time Goody Hobday found out her husband had been at the girl who came to do the milking, and threw his treasured miniature of his mother into the pig slops as revenge while he was away at Ipswich). Here, Minister Long helps himself to his third of Mary Parsley's oatcakes and admires the scheme of pears on her collar, politely astonished to hear the wonderful broidery is her own work, though her hands be dropsical (they are not, in point of fact, her own work – they are mine). Mister Hopkins glowers over his book by the kitchen hearth. Richard Edwards shepherds young Prudence Hart out to the kitchen garden, his hand hovering disagreeably close to her bum roll. I hear people speak of visiting the Briggs' across the way much as they would if it were a May dance (though a visit to the bedside of a languishing child is a pastime far more agreeable to the Puritan sensibility than any such heathen spring frolic). Soon, those of us who have not visited become conspicuous by our prolonged absence.

An air of desperation clings. A sense that appearances must, now more than ever, be kept up. Small talk is made over the raucous crashing from the upper storeys. Priscilla Briggs appears to have aged so dramatically that it could almost count for a bewitchment in itself (or so I hear a cluster of women, thick-cloaked against the cold, muttering by the Market Cross). Her cheeks are said to be hollowed and colourless, her eyes, they say, boggle half out her pinched head. One afternoon, Goody Edwards sees her gold wedding band slip from her attenuated finger and roll right across the hearthrug, which all agree – once Priscilla has vacated the parlour to check on Thomas – can only be a portent exceedingly ill. 'She scarce seemed to notice,' reports Mary Parsley, who witnessed the event, to Robert Taylor, the victualler, who did not: '. . . just left it lying there on the floor. The Devil is in that house, and no mistake.'

If the Devil has made a bed up at the Briggs', his stratagems seem to me tediously shopworn, and his sallies into the open very arbitrary indeed. Gone to the garden to make water just after nightfall, Mister Stearne swears blind he saw a creature very like a winged monkey amusing himself in the undergrowth. A postman is thrown from his horse as he passes the gatepost. Michael Wright, the scullion lad, develops an unsightly rash, which he aims to hide by growing a spare (and even more unsightly) beard. Every morning, some say, Mistress Briggs finds a pin driven shallow into the soft flesh of Thomas's scalp, just behind the left ear. Some believe it. Most do not.

I suppose I want something like this to happen to me: I want to see an imp streaking red across the damp lawn. To find myself lamed. I want something to happen that might prove I am still counted on God's side. So this is why, on the first morning of December, I find myself at the Briggs' kitchen door with a basket of apples – which are yellow and past their best – and my heart in my mouth, thinking *Devil, hurt me. Devil, show me you hate me, for that I stand among the chosen.*

In the past weeks my thoughts have been much occupied by that uncanny sequence of events begun, I fear, by my own wantonness, and concluding – or so I must hope – here: with a sick child and a grieving mother. I shift foot to foot at the Briggs' front steps, feeling I am to blame for this. Not in the sense that I *did it* nor willed it done, but in the sense that I heaped my own sins upon the invisible agglomeration shedding its rot over all of us, manure for the Devil's dark flowers. Rabbit by the door, blindfold and cabbage, shadow on the water, dream of the orchard, baby in the fire, it cannot mean nothing. These are torrid threads in some ingenious design I lack the circumspection or wit to fully comprehend. Of course, I believe in the Devil. I know myself to be thoroughly beneath his notice. Had thought myself so. But then. *But then.* He can, after all, be in more than two places, even more than ten places. What is to stop him standing right behind me, there on that doorstep – or at Judith Moone's washstand – even as he whispers sweet fiendishnesses into the fragrant hair of the Duke of Cumberland, half the country away, as they say that he does?

But perhaps it pleases me, a little. There is a change in me that has been noticed, and found all at a loss to explain. My mother has commented, eyes narrowed suspiciously, that I look very well indeed. Perhaps it is my winter gown of russet wool setting off the colour in my cheeks. This dress is a hair too short, and last year its scantiness shamed me. But now I stride happily through town in it, threatening to disclose a flash of slender ankle with every foot-trot, and thinking baker or chandler or smith or whomsoever I happen to pass might be very lucky indeed to see a little slice of my white stocking. I touch my neck as I unwind my hair from my cap of an evening, and I feel it to be swan-like. I feel graceful as wingtips, as a woman loved by Sathan. But to be loved by God is better, because then your feelings do not matter. To be loved by God is to have your feelings blasted away by love. So ugly men – the kind who look as though they have been shaped to no other kind of love but God's – write in their books. These are my thoughts. I want everything, deserve nothing.

So I stand by the Briggs' back door, clutching tight at the handle of my basket, my breath rising in little puffs before my mouth. If it truly is bewitchment that has befallen Master Briggs, I am resolved to see it for myself. The neat face of the Briggs' manor – all good red brick and firm bleached beams – is cowing. They have an upstairs. Eight rooms at least, likely more. I count off the windows as I rap at the door, having reached ten by the time Helen Clarke arrives to admit me, in soiled apron and headwrap, black curls bouncing loose at her ears. The look she gives me as I stand there at the entryway is long, hard and reluctant – a look I do not understand, for the two of us are usually friendly enough (Helen is the Widow Leech's youngest, and our mutual ignominy thereby assured. But I am prettier than her, I suppose, even with my pox-scars, which is always bound to raise some enmity between two girls who can't spare a shilling for ribbon nor rouge to remedy their homely presentations).

'Helen,' I say, and smiling, dip my head. 'I thought I might come to see Mistress Briggs, give her my good wishes, and those of my mother.' I have practised these words in my head the whole journey over, and still it comes out wrong. She stands back with a grunt and motions me into the kitchen. A fire burns in the big grate. Copper pans and deep pewter dishes and stoups and porringers in huge number shimmer on the sideboard. A little money, so much beauty. I hear voices, three or four perhaps, in the parlour beyond.

'Better you had not,' says Helen, gruffly, taking my basket to inspect the apples. Helen Clarke is not *fair* in the way most girls might want to be, but she is soft and smooth-looking and pleasantly coarse, in that way that there seems to be a lot of her that wants a mouth putting on it. Aside from her dark hair, she is not much her mother's daughter – though she has inherited the Widow Leech's meddlesome tendencies, and a shadow of fine hair on her upper lip.

I stamp my feet to warm myself up. 'And why had I better not?'

She puts the basket down and fixes me with a challenging look. 'Who are we,' she hisses, jabbing a finger at her bosom, 'and who are they?' She points at the parlour door.

I laugh. It is a silly, mincing laugh. 'I haven't the pleasure of knowing yet.'

Helen's exacting gaze pares my false jocularity away. 'Lor',' she says, exhaling through her nose, 'never let it be said the West women want for audacity. There have been mutterings,' she herself mutters, 'of the kind that give rise to accusations. That Mister Hopkins has been round very often indeed.' She shudders. 'He is like a handful of snow down the back of your dress, do you not think? The way he looks at people—'

She pauses as the door to the parlour swings to. There stands John Edes, in a fetching narrow-waisted doublet of dark blue, fastening his cloak at his throat. I like these rare moments when I have seen him before he properly sees me – artless and natural as some baby animal he looks, frowning down at the fiddly clasp. He glances up, and does see me, rallying from his momentary surprise to bow. 'Miss West,' he says, gracious in confusion.

'Master Edes. A surprise to see—' *No. Don't say that, Rebecca. You are no London coquette. Start again.* 'Master Edes. I thought I would come to see Mistress Briggs, to give her my good wishes, and those of my mother. And – apples,' I repeat, feeling the colour rise in my cheeks as Helen peers between us with a slanting grin, and turns away to tend to the fire.

'Ah. And I am – I am certain she will welcome the kindness,' he smiles, weakly. 'I hope you will excuse me. I was just . . .' He gestures vaguely at the door by which I entered. I dip to curtsey, but he has already left the kitchen, without so much as a *God bless*. A person might think Master Edes wished to avoid my company. In fact, I know already that that is *all* I will think, for two hours at least, when I head to bed in the evening, and that my sleep shall doubtless suffer thereby. And I wonder if there is any kind of intimacy with another person that isn't also an indignity, and if some people enjoy this, or if everyone just pretends to.

Through the open door to the parlour I see a pair of folded legs in a seat before the hearth. Legs in high boots of black leather with spurs at the heel, spurs glinting where they catch the firelight. Mister Hopkins' boots. So. Edes came with Hopkins.

'Time to meet your maker, then, as they say,' Helen smirks by my elbow, following my gaze. She slaps a ball of dough down on the table and begins, truculently, to knead.

I take a deep breath and straighten my apron. I ask Helen how I look.

She glances up from her work with a sneer. 'What do you care? Your sweetheart has just departed.' And she is quite right. What *do*

I care? Nonetheless, I stand there smiling expectantly until she rolls her eyes, and says, 'Well enough, I suppose. Now, get thee.'

I enter the parlour with my eyes lowered in a deferential manner, and because that is how I spend most of my public life I can identify everyone in the room by what they are wearing from the waist down. On a low bench at the far wall, in thick black skirts, sit Prudence Hart (hands, as ever, curled protectively around her swollen belly), Priscilla Briggs and Mary Parsley, a mournful triptych. In a high-backed chair by the fire is Mister Hopkins, his gloved hands steepled in his lap. By the door stand Minister Long and Richard Edwards, who always carries a sword despite all knowing he has never done so much as wring a hen's neck for himself. And they all fall silent as I enter.

I dip, my hands folded at my back, and address myself to Goody Briggs' velvets. 'Good day and God bless you. I came to pay my respects, Mistress Briggs. My mother and I pray most fervently for Thomas's recovery. I – also I brought some apples. I – Helen sees to them.'

Before Mistress Briggs can answer, a querulous shout comes muffled from upstairs, and then a flurry of footsteps, appended by a bang. 'O ho!' cries the Minister, cheery as a child listening to a storm unfold over the bay. 'That was a big one!'

His excitement is not infectious. The women lift their heads to squint uneasily up at the beams, but Thomas's occult ambulation seems to draw to a temporary conclusion.

'Is he under watch, mistress?' Hopkins asks.

'Yes, sir,' Goody Briggs replies. 'Doctor Croke attends on him.'

When I raise my head I find that Priscilla Briggs' excitable eyes are fixed determinedly upon me. I try to smile, but produce what is probably more of a grimace. Mary Parsley reaches across her lap to take Priscilla's hand. Like any peculiar girl, I am well attuned to women's conspiratorial mischiefs: the double-edged laughs, the spider dropped in the ribboned slipper, the implacable nasties we drive into one another like pins into wax poppets. I know that women have a certain look about them when they have recently been speaking of you, just as men have a certain look to them when they have recently been thinking of you unclothed. And Priscilla, Mary and Prudence have been speaking of me. Prudence Hart leans over to whisper something in old Mary Parsley's ear.

'I thought,' I say, trying to stop my voice from shaking, 'I thought that I might see Master Briggs? I should like . . . I should like to convey my good wishes to him directly.' I bite my lip.

'I shall not have—' Priscilla blurts, and I know she intended for her next words to be *you going near him*, but a censorious squeeze of her hand from Mary Parsley reminds the Mistress Briggs of the requirements of propriety. Priscilla recomposes herself, straightening her back in her stays. 'I mean to say – Thomas is resting, at present. I think it would not be—'

'I will accompany Miss West to his chamber,' Hopkins interrupts, rising from his seat by the fire.

Mistress Briggs glances between Hopkins and myself, her mouth frozen in a tight O of surprise. I can tell that she would very much like to protest, but she will not – cannot – enter into open contention with a man. Besides, Hopkins is not just *a* man. He is *that* man, now, with his Cambridge education and his continental mores. They say he speaks French. His whole manner intimates a secret knowledge of the scheme of things. A sudden image comes into my mind of Mister Hopkins lifting his high-crowned hat to reveal an intricate mechanical replica of the world entire in miniature, like the inner workings of a clock, replete with a fur of cloud clinging to the midget oceans, as rot on a peach. Hopkins says it, and it is so.

Their five pairs of eyes are all fixed on Hopkins as he walks across the parlour toward me, his spurs scraping on the flagstones, and waves me toward the stairs. 'Please, Miss West,' he says, with a cold smile, 'follow me.'

Thomas Briggs' chamber is meagrely lit by reed, and wretched with a midden-stink. A sampler hangs above the bed: 'The fear of the LORD is a fountain of life'. Doctor Croke sits in a low chair by the fire, apparently asleep, but Thomas lifts his head from the pillow at the sound of our approach, his eyes shiny as a dor beetle's back. 'Oh,' he says, quietly. 'You have brought one.'

Hopkins places a firm hand on my shoulder, pressing me to the threshold. 'Know you this maid, Thomas?' he asks.

'Yes,' he replies. 'Her father died at sea.' His mouth twitches into something like a smile, as though his spirit is perhaps momentarily enlivened by the thought of nautical jeopardy. So there is still a little boy somewhere in there.

'And after that?' Hopkins continues, his fingers tightening on my upper arm.

I begin to tell Thomas that I have come to wish him swift recovery from his present indisposition, but the boy seems discomposed. He begins to whine, and slam his sticky head back into the pillows most violently as I speak. His thin arms rise up, shaking, and wave about in the air, as though he is attempting to wrestle some invisible aggressor away from his heaving chest. 'Make her stop!' he croaks. 'It hurts me!'

I try to step back, but Hopkins' gloved hand twists at my shoulder and holds me firm. 'Tell me what you see, Thomas. What is it that assails you?'

Whatever it is seems to vex Thomas so wonderfully that he can barely form words, his arms spasming back and forth through the air, his face bloodless. 'It – it sits on me,' he wheezes. 'Like a shadow. A dark thing!'

'Good God!' Doctor Croke is finally woken by the boy's wailing, and leaps to the bedside. Before I can know what is happening, Hopkins has wrenched me back from the threshold by my arm and into the next room, slamming the door closed behind us. I am frightened. As soon as he releases me, I back as far away from him as I am able, and peer about – a bench, a broken spinning wheel, an empty bookcase. Hopkins stands with his shoulder pressed to the door, a dark, gloating look on his face. My shoulder burns where he held it. I touch the place where there will be a bruise.

'How did you do it?' he asks. He is smiling.

'Do what, sir?'

'The Incubus,' he replies, simply.

I tell him I cannot begin to know what an *Incubus* is, sir, much less summon one. There is a tarnished candlestick on the bookcase, by the window – if I could just get to it – *then you would what, Rebecca? Beat him about the head with it?*

'An incubus is a demon, Miss West,' Hopkins breathes, moistening his lips. 'A demon conjured from Hell, to serve a witch, by the power of her compact with the Devil.' Hopkins is excited. Excited in the way men get when they read about wars or Turkish dancing girls. His pupils have grown wide and a single black ringlet clings to the corner of his wet mouth. A little sunlight must break through the cloud and fall through the window at my back, because my shadow slides across the dusty boards, touches his boots.

'I *saw* nothing, sir,' I insist. 'Much less *conjured*.'

Hopkins takes a step toward me. 'Is not your mother the Beldam West? She spoke a malediction upon Master Briggs as the child played by the quay. Her own companions told me so.'

I make a noise indicating something between fear and mirth. He knows nothing of *my* spiritual infractions. It is my mother who is the focus of his interest. My mother, the Beldam Anne West, at the crux of all things, the middle of the creaking wheel, as ever. The larger body I grow upon, canker-like. 'Mister Hopkins,' I say, finding my voice clear and firm. 'Sir – if cross words on my mother's part had any weight, then I would be riding an invisible horse of my own to Maldon and back.' I keep my arm across my breast.

'Mother and daughter,' he says, hoarsely, still advancing, still narrowing the space between us, 'all alone, in a house on the hillside.' His smile. 'When women think alone, they think evil, it is said.'

'If you think I have both the mind and the means to do harm, sir,' I say, 'then perhaps you ought to be more careful of me. I wish to leave now.' As I say it I find that I am doing it. Before Hopkins can move to detain me again, I have pushed by him and out through the door. There is much commotion in the corridor, where the women, roused by Thomas's mewling, stand pensively about – I streak past, hustling Goody Hart aside as I make for the staircase, the blood beating in my ears. I snatch up my shawl from the kitchen and hurtle through the door, leaving behind a stunned Helen Clarke and a basket of yellowing apples.

The Examination of Helen Clarke
taken before the said Justices, 1645

This examinant confesseth, that about six weeks since, the Devil
appeared to her in her house, in the likeness of a white Dog, and that
she calleth that Familiar Elimanzer; and that this examinant hath
often fed him with milk-pottage; and that the said Familiar spoke to
this examinant audibly, and bade her deny Christ, and she should
never want, which she did then assent unto, but doth altogether
deny the killing of the daughter of the said Edward Parsley.

12

Mass

He removes the apples from the basket carefully, one by one, inspecting each. There are six in total. Their stems are brittle, their flesh cool and very slightly yielding beneath the puckered, porous, icteric skins. He throws one experimentally on the fire and crouches low by the hearth to watch it burn. There is an odour, though barely detectable – sweet and acrid at once, like horse dung. The dermis slowly blisters then cracks, the juices sizzling out, and within minutes all that remains is a charred core with two scorched frills of leather, like the brow bones of a death's head.

The second he punctures with a long iron nail. There is a pleasing suck as he draws the nail out again, and then he holds the glistening metal up to the flame of a candle. He smells the juices on it. He touches it to his tongue, but the ferrous quality overpowers the apple's sweetness, reminding him of the taste of blood. The third apple he slices in exact halves. Black pips settled in white meats, like little comical, owlish faces (he's always seen faces in things – on grey river water, in flowers, in shadows). The fourth he leaves on the windowsill in his study, for observation. The fifth he buries in a shallow hole in the yard.

The sixth he has pressed to his lips as he lounges on the settle before the fire that evening, when John Stearne asks, idly flipping the tacky pages of John Milton's *Animadversions* back and forth: 'And what news from the Briggs', Matthew?'

Matthew Hopkins sighs. 'There was little change in the boy.'

'Ah, well. At least the consistency of his symptoms ought to disprove suspicion he counterfeits.' Stearne scratches the side of his nose as he leafs through the pamphlet. John Stearne is a pale, watery-looking man in his middle thirties, hopeful and blundersome, seemingly a walking confutation of that age as the *prime* of anything. Swelling and leaking to fill the space his money bought him. Matthew finds that something in Stearne's admittedly notextraordinary appearance triggers an immediate repugnance. He is a bit like a bladder filled with milk, membranous and near whitely blond, quivering this way and that. But one cannot argue with his connections, of which he has made liberal use in helping Hopkins establish himself at Mistley. The Thorn Inn is set on the edge of a narrow bend in the road to Harwich, where the estuary deepens and widens. Freshly whitewashed, it is the cleanest-looking thing in miles, save for the swans that circle the Gamekeeper's Pond. It stands empty tonight, there being few willing to leave their own home fires for the biting chill without. The gentlemen make use of the parlour at the back of the lower floor.

'It is little matter if he does. One cannot counterfeit what does not exist,' Hopkins reasons. Stearne sets the pamphlet down for a moment and frowns, trying to trace the contours of Hopkins' argument, which he knows must be sound, even if he does not fully understand it. Hopkins sighs, and expands: 'Even if the boy merely apes bewitchment, it suggests two things: firstly, that something has instilled a great terror in him, to drive him to such extremity of behaviour. Secondly, that he has from somewhere gained knowledge of the forms by which bewitchment is made manifest. Corruption flourishes in this town, unseen and unchallenged. The innocent are always the first to see it. *Out of the mouths of babes and sucklings...*'

'Psalms, eight-four,' Stearne shoots back, with schoolboy superciliousness.

'Eight-two.'

Stearne flushes. 'It is true,' he concedes, clearing his throat. 'I can think of no obvious way a boy such as Briggs might come to learn of such things. Bewitchment, possessions... We have had no witches in these parts for, oh, a generation or more. Not since old Mary Clarke... There was the St Osyth affair, I suppose...'

Hopkins looks at Stearne, piqued. 'Clarke, you say? Any relation to the Briggs' girl? Helen, I think it is?' In actuality, Hopkins is certain her name is Helen, because Hopkins doesn't forget things. But there is no cause, yet, to put too fine a point on his suspicions. A frightened witch is apt to flee, or worse – provided she has the resources to.

Stearne rubs his cheek and takes a gulp of wine. 'No, no. She was Elizabeth Clarke's mother, if you can believe a hoary old crone like that ever had one,' he chuckles. 'I was just a boy at the time. We swam her in Mistley Pond, just over the way.' He gazes toward the rafters, nostalgically, before adding, 'Helen is the Widow Leech's eldest.'

Hopkins nods, slowly, pressing the apple to his bearded cheek. 'Leech. It is commonly thought that a tendency to the heresy of witchcraft is passed from mother to daughter, you see. There is near unanimity among all authorities on the matter. Whether because mother tempts daughter to join her in her Devilish compact, or by some shared debility of the soul more severe than is usual in the weaker sex, that renders both vulnerable to his seducings...'

'Well,' mutters Stearne, rising from his seat and pulling his cloak onto his back, because he has only so much patience for Hopkins' arcane invectives, 'twould be easy enough to believe it of a queer old hag like Mother Clarke.' He reaches for his wide-brimmed hat. 'It is late, Matthew. I had best be making my way back to the farm before Agnes begins to worry I have myself fallen into Sathan's clutches.' He throws back his head with a chuckle and drains the last dregs of his wine, eyebrows elevated. 'Mm. Thanks for the claret.'

Hopkins waves a hand in distracted farewell and listens to Stearne's staggering footsteps through the front of the inn, and away. After a short while, certain he is alone, he rises and goes to the armoire in the corner of the room. The top panel clicks open upon his private library: King James' *Daemonologie* and the *Malleus Maleficarum* sit alongside the cracked spines of Del Rio's *Disquisitionum*, Bodin and Rémy, the *Tractatus de Hereticis*. And, of course, an admirable selection of the neoterics: Perkins' indispensable *Discourse of the Damned Art of Witchcraft*, Streete's *Astronomia Carolina*, the *Ephemerides*. Beside these, countless well-thumbed booklets and tracts recounting the trials of the Devil's handmaidens in Warboys, Berwick, Pendle and St Osyth, Jutland, Copenhagen, Carrickfergus and beyond. He knows the women who writhe within those pages. Knows their names, their bodies that moulder in unmarked graves, or float as ash. Knows their methods, too. It is his own journal he eventually withdraws.

The first snow of winter is falling outside the window. Big, lovely flakes that collapse under their own weight even as they splash against the panes, undersides illuminated by candlelight. It is a moonless night, and nothing else is visible, no beyond. Instinctively, he switches the apple in his hand for the one rested on the sill – a hemisphere stiff and cold from proximity to the glass.

He returns to the settle with the apple and the bottle of claret. He undoes the top buttons of his doublet. The sixth apple, he eats.

*

He wakes to find a huge tree has grown in the corner of the chamber, and the far wall crumbles around its gnarled roots, allowing the violet light of moon and stars to flood the Turkey rug. All is silent but for the drip of melting snow from the smashed rafters. The fire has long since burnt out. Hopkins rises from the settle, numb-foot and dishevelled. The tree is huge, with thick, scored bark, and wreathed about with ivy, like painted-on smoke. He looks up into the darkness of the canopy. Fitting his fingers to a knot in the bark, he begins to climb, up through the broken thatch and into a night sky replete with a sepulchritude of stars. From his seat high in the crown of the tree, he looks down on the black fens and pasture-lands of Essex stretching off to the horizon like a damask lain over England's bent back.

Then the witches come. They land one by one and throw off their cloaks, their naked bodies silvered by moonlight. Some are young, some old, some fair, some dark, some fat, some thin, all beautiful, all horrible. Some fly, some ride in across the fields on peculiar, lumbering beasts, which he sees, when he looks more closely, are *men* – men bent double on their hands and knees with their faces stuffed into bridles.

A great feast has been prepared, with a five-bird roast and a twelve-bird roast, steaming red breads and silverware overburdened with sweetmeats and cherries and blue grapes. There are pineapples, dishes of fine sugar-like powders and bonbons iced with dark insignia, and three fat suckling pigs with shrunken human heads in their mouths where the apples ought to be. The centrepiece of this sulphurous spread is the whole, vexed head of a black hog, crowned with candied grasshoppers that have been cleverly positioned into attitudes of flight. Tiny human ears are strewn about the table like rose-petals.

Old Elizabeth Clarke is the first to take her seat, at the head of the table, so frail she appears almost iridescent, supporting herself with a staff of polished bone. Invoking the Prince of Air, she raises with both hands a huge goblet of dark liquor. She drinks, and it is blood that spills from the corners of her mouth and runs in red rivulets down her pendulous breasts. Her sisters join her in the unholy sacrament, white arms raised to the night.

But where is their host? Soon all manner of vermin creep from the hollows and hedgerows and slither through the wet grass to join them, impudent in their nastiness. An adder cools his belly in a shallow dish of rose-water. Four little rabbits gather in the soft lap of Rebecca West, and she fondles them sweetly as she dines. A fat brown centipede wraps its armoured body about the wrinkled throat of Elizabeth Clarke, as a seed-pearl choker might sit on the neck of a lady. The horror rises in him, but he cannot look away. Must not look away. Now they pass around a book, each pricking her finger and writing her name. Old Mother Clarke raises her voice to the sky, and says that any there who breaks their Compact, sealed in blood, and reveals what has passed there that night will be torn apart with pincers and scattered in a great furnace. She asks each who has gathered there what the Devil has promised them. The answers are cried out in response, one after the other: a scarlet gown, a songbird, a husband, years of peace and plenty, for misfortune to befall all those who have wronged me.

He moves among them, then, and they flock to him, and fall down on their knees, the ground alive with a mass of insects and small beasts, spiders, weevils, roaches, earthworms, moths, so that it looks like bubbling tar where he parts the folds of his black cassock and plants his cloven hoof, and they bend to kiss his cloven hoof and fawn over him. He reaches out his dark hand and each long finger bulges with jewelled rings, and he touches each woman upon the crown of the head, as though delivering a blessing, or else fondles their breasts. But then he straightens, something catching his notice, and turns his face to peer up into the branches where Hopkins hides, his eyes like two black pips in white meat. Hopkins feels his grasp loosen, then he falls—

His mouth is very dry when he wakes, and a drubbing pain gathers at his temples. The sunbeams bouncing in through the parlour window feel like hot spindles to his eyes, and slice right through the soft, compromised meat of his head. Groaning, he looks about himself. By the edge of the settle, the empty bottle of claret (he thinks it was actually the third) and an apple, the flesh browning around his bite-mark.

Shakily, he rises and goes to the window. The fields are covered over with immaculate, unbroken whiteness, and the sky is utterly empty above the thin line of trees. Without stopping to find his coat, he runs out to the field. But he can see no evidence of the unholy ceremony. Nothing more than the slender tracks of a fox leading up over the hill. There he is, shivering and bareheaded, his breath a vapour before his uncombed beard. The snow outspreads all comprehension, annihilates all thought, so bright it makes a purblind of him. He prostrates himself in the caustic whiteness, and there, most ardently, he prays.

A man in his shirtsleeves lying face down in the snow was a very queer thing for William Calfhill to see as he walked his lurcher in the next-door field, and it is no wonder he tattled to half the town regarding his new neighbour's quite unaccountable behaviour.

Winter lays down hard frosts, vitrifying the roads and the rooftops, enforcing seclusion and imposing fasts. Pigs freeze to death in their pens. News slows to a trickle. Letters go astray and are intercepted, the heart's-blood missives of young lovers and the sober bulletins of generals alike. The rumour is that both armies are quartered away for Christmastide, but no definitive word on this subject arrives. An army is a very large thing to lose; losing two begins to look like carelessness. While marching orders and tactical directives deliquesce on the brumal winds, the pyrotechnics of imminent apocalypse shimmer just as rosily on the ice-bound horizon as they ever did. In Ipswich, a sorceress is seen shrieking down the Orwell on a pole, wielding lightning bolts. In Brentford the *divided pieces of a woman abused to death* are found.

In Manningtree itself there have been most strange and inexplicable happenings that could be accounted for only by infernal malice. William Rawbood, the brewer, tells of a most perplexing incident – his wife, the new Mistress Rawbood, was sat in the kitchen one cold Sunday morning, just before they were to leave for church. All of a sudden, she found her skirts all full of lice – 'so many you could have swept them from her clothes with a stick'. This is stranger still, for Mistress Rawbood is a most cleanly woman, and broadly agreed to be of sound mind. Catching one of these horrid creatures under a glass, Rawbood found it was unlike any louse with which he had heretofore had the displeasure to find himself acquainted, long and lean as a lady's little finger.

Filial relations, too, are strained. Confined to the home by inclement weather, sister turns against sister, brother against brother, maid against mistress and husband against wife. Thighs are pinched raw beneath dining tables, dumplings pilfered from plates, noses thumbed during the grace, account books defaced by cack-handed toddlers. The same grey dress laid out on the bed, the same grey fog rolling in off the Stour, the same wooden crucifix on whitewashed plaster. Eventually you want to prise a nail out and turn it upside down, just to have something a little different to look at. You know what they say about the Devil and idle hands.

The day itself passes without gaiety – the word 'Christmas' being shod as it is with that most Popish of lexemes, 'Mass', most of the town's Godly populace think it best to pretend it had escaped their notice. St Mary's stands closed, and the shops are opened (though there is little left for them to sell). A week or so later, on a frostbitten Twelfth Night, news comes in the form of a local agitator ridden up from Weeley, who stands at the Market Cross brandishing a sodden copy of the *Mercurius Civicus* and yelling something about Cheshire to a crowd of bemused onlookers. At Barthomley in Cheshire, he says, the King's Men, under the command of Lord John Byron, had found a party of Parliamentarians – twelve, or closer to twenty, or closer to one-hundred-and-twenty, depending on whom you ask, and good Puritans all – holed up in a church. The Cavaliers set a fire to draw them out. The men stumbled, choked and singed, into the frosty brightness of Christmas Eve, whereat they found themselves viciously set upon by Lord Byron's men. They were stripped naked, beaten, each punctured one thousand times and in one thousand parts of his body by the King's bright swords.

To men and boys who are hungry and cloyed by boredom, the news is welcomed, after a fashion, as cause to renew the looting that had broken out in fits and starts across the Stour Valley all that preceding year. There being very few confirmed recusants left within convenient riding distance, a mere suspicion of Popish sympathies becomes sufficient prerequisite for their attention: even the benign Doctor Croke wakes to a brick through the window of his study and three jars of pickled cabbage missing from his storehouse.

Grand houses are ransacked and cobwebbed oil portraits piled in the manicured gardens for burning, painted faces bearing gracious witness to their persecution from above antique ruffs of starched lace. The boys return home with their breeches sodden and sticky to the knee with good port from flooded wine cellars, looking for all the world as though they've been wading through blood. One lad rides his mare at a gallop down South Street, a tattered dress of yellow silk tied to his saddle, shouting, 'Death to Queen Mary and Hell for the Bishops!' And some applaud them, and some say they are little better than Levellers, to do such things. And those that still have fine jewellery or good plate go out into their gardens at night and bury it in the hard ground as best they can. There is the off chance, after all, that the cataclysm might be a few years in coming yet.

They couldn't bury Thomas Briggs, who was eaten up of a seeming fever in the second week of January. He was a small boy to begin with, and worn down by the end to little more than a switch – but nonetheless, there will be no grave deep enough until the earth is thawed. His body lies, slowly putrefying, in an outbuilding. On hearing this, the ragged Wright children break into the shed one night and dare one another, breathlessly, to touch it, to touch the boy the Devil and his handmaids carried off to Hell.

1644

'And yet there are some of opinion, There lives in the world some, and of those some, a small party in *England*, that know more than they utter, and, either by Vision, or verbal Colloquie, have the knowledge of future events, yea, even from the blessed Angels.'

William Lilly, *The Starry Messenger*, 1647

13

Vagrancy

Picture a crooked old woman dressed in rags, who labours through deep snow, alone. Now fray the hem of her gown and soak it in meltwater, cover her balding head with a thin shawl of worsted. She smells – you can smell her from an arm's length away – of grease and chicken shit and mildew and embarrassment. The hair she has left, leave to matt and tangle into yellowing snarls and charm-knots. Choke the lucid blue of her eyes with a scum of cataract. Now hunch her over a walking stick, and set her to trudging. Slow. No – slower still than that. Perhaps a few crows rail at one another in the glassy hedgerows as she passes, but otherwise, all is silence. She is alone on the rolling fields of deep, unpromising white. Now empty out her belly. Now decide. Will you offer to help her? Do you even want to touch her?

Old Mother Clarke is known, in part, for her chickens. She sings to them, old songs, sailors' songs. At the start of winter she fetched them into the house, and it brought her joy to watch them picking diffidently around the novel bulk of the bed and the cauldron, oily and reptile-eyed. She paid no mind to the white streaks of excrement on the table legs, nor the stink of their moult. When the chickens began to die she could not bring herself to eat them, so she carried them out to the midden heap, so light in her hands, and the foxes received them gratefully. No one came to Old Mother Clarke's for a week or more. Not one bright-eyed baby-filled miss up from the town, nor any absent-minded granddam soliciting the help of Saint Peter and Saint Paul to find a missing keepsake ring or buried bracelet through the twist of sieve and shears. No Beldam West, no Margaret Moone, no Widow Leech. Not me, either. She supposes the roads up from town have become impassable. Or that she has been forgot. Or that she is perhaps already dead, and these fields of uncanny, unbroken white are the silent demesne of Limbo.

I cannot imagine what might have occupied her, alone and hungry in her little hovel, those icebound weeks of deep winter. But now she is picking her way across Wormwood Hill. Perhaps she fancies she is the only one left alive across the whole sorry countryside. That she slept through the sounding of the trumpets, and that the angels, pulling everyone crumb-eyed from their beds and hauling them up to Heaven, happened to overlook her. Perhaps she daydreams that when she reaches the Millers' farm she will find it standing empty, and in she will go, and there will be a steaming pork chop sitting unattended on the kitchen table.

Take an old woman. Cut off her leg and empty her belly. Leave her to her neighbours' mercy. Put in her mind the picture of a pork chop, good and juicy, with apple sauce and a mug of good beer. Feel her mouth moisten at the prospect.

Rounding the top of the hill, Mother Clarke sees a thin ribbon of smoke unspooling from the Millers' chimney. James Hockett, the farm boy, is trimming wood in the yard at the time of her arrival. Shading those eyes against the mid-morning sun, grievous bright, Hockett straightens his back to look at the crumpled shape advancing through the snow toward his master's homestead. He sees the old woman carefully pick her way down the slope, open the gate, and proceed, hobbling, down the garden path that he cleared of snow that very morning. Before Mother Clarke can reach the door, Leah Miller – his mistress, a handsome woman of twenty-five, with a child a-dozing in her arms and another apparent in her puffing belly – opens it. Goody Miller regards Mother Clarke charily. So does the child, sucking her thumb against her mother's breast. A lovely child with curly blonde hair – the kind one imagines when told a fabulous tale of the colonies, about the Red Men plucking a little girl from her bed in the night and stealing her away for their feathered king to eat.

'What ho, Goody Miller.' Mother Clarke raises a palsied hand to shade her good eye.

Goody Miller keeps most of the door between herself and her visitor. 'Good morrow, Mother,' she says, without enthusiasm.

'She's getting to be a big one now, isn't she?' Mother Clarke ventures, indicating the Lovely Child, who watches wide-eyed from her mother's grasp, little able to distinguish this ancient caller from the lachrymose ghost of a bedtime story.

Leah Miller allows herself a gracious smile. 'Aye. She will turn four come spring. God willing.' God willing, because all sorts of horrible things are known to happen to Lovely Children.

'May the Lord bless you and keep you both.' Silence. Mother Clarke stamps her peg leg as though to dislodge a stone. Hockett sees how she wobbles over her stick. 'Might I ask—' She lowers her head, more from fatigue than in supplication, '—see, I came to ask if I might trouble you for a little bread, and perhaps some butter.'

Goody Miller's mouth flattens. She peers over her shoulder into the house. 'I do not know as we truly have any to spare, Bess. The children,' she adds, weakly, hoping this invocation will serve as explanation enough for her miserliness. And perhaps it is true. All over Essex, stores are running low. Nobody knows when they might next see sugar, or good bread. A strawberry would be coveted like a garnet-stone.

Mother Clarke trembles and sniffs. She struggles just to remain upright – that much is obvious. 'Anything – any bare thing you might find it within yourself to give, Mistress Miller. I have not a crust left, and no hope of getting into town. God bless thee. God bless thee,' she repeats, and repeats a third time, barely above the level of a whisper.

Leah Miller touches her lips with another guilty, backward look. Slowly, she shakes her head. 'I am sorry, Bess. I cannot.'

And that is it, poverty. A life slowly narrowing around you like the trick walls of a tomb. You have things and then the things fall to pieces, and then it begins to empty your body out as well, and your mind. No dreams, just hunger. A hole whose edges begin to fray, become undone. Elizabeth's voice is hoarse. 'Then . . . then might I at least warm myself by the fire, for a short while? I do not wish to cause thee any difficulty, Leah . . . I would be most grateful.'

'Wait here.' Leah sighs, and closes the door.

Love thy neighbour, God commands. But also, *thou shalt not suffer a witch to live.* Is Old Mother Clarke a witch? She is cunning, and the distinction between the two is imprecise at best. Poor Thomas Briggs, God rest his soul, doubtless bucks and reels through Leah Miller's mind. A witch? So some say. Her mother was, most assuredly. And she certainly has the foul looks of one. For all her debility, there is a presence, a canniness, behind the tarnished eyes. She drags around a motley, elaborate odour, as though she had recently raised herself, Lazarus-like, half-rotted from the grave. At base, it just doesn't seem wholesome, that a person should be that old and that poor, and yet persist in living. What could give her cause to cleave to so miserable a mortal situation, save the promise of eternal suffering thereafter?

It is not Leah Miller who returns to the door, but her husband, Richard. His jowls wobble with indignation as he mounts the stoop. 'Mother Clarke,' he declares at the shivering bundle of woman, 'we have no victuals to spare for you, nor any other – and I will not stand to have my wife so importuned, in her delicate condition.' He plants a fist on his hip, impressed with himself. 'I ask that you take your leave, or else I shall inform a Constable of these vagrant carriages.'

As with many women of a certain age, Mother Clarke knows no more effective tonic than indignation. She draws herself up on her stick. She explains her predicament slowly, as though to a child, and edges the stump of her peg leg out from beneath the hem of her skirts for pictorial emphasis: 'Would you have me starve, master? I have no food, and no other hope of coming by any. Show a little kindness to a lame old woman.'

'That,' Richard Miller replies, 'is what the church dole-cupboard is for, mistress. Perhaps you would know that if you attended service.'

On what was said after this, all agree. 'A pox on you, Richard Miller,' is the first thing, by Old Mother Clarke. 'A pox and piles on you.' She holds her head askance like a dirty bird, training her good right eye on him as though it were the sense of some cruel instrument. 'And I wasn't asking *you*, at any rate – I was asking your *third* wife,' she continues. 'And she is very comely indeed – but dost thou not feel some ways cuckolded, sir? Married her too soon after she was widowed last for that lump under her laces to be thy own work, after all.'

James Hockett stands by the woodpile with his splitting-axe in hand, and gulps down a laugh. Leah jostles out from behind her husband, a hand splayed over her swollen belly and her freckled cheeks turning deeply scarlet. 'Why, you filthy mare!' she sneers. And there is a little of the Leah Miller of old back in her then – Leah

Wright, of legendarily intransigent spirit and loose gold hair, who was said to trade kisses with river men for sweetened rum.

'Oh, lay off, *Goody Miller*,' spits Mother Clarke. 'I have no qualm with you. We all have mouths need feeding, after all. Mayhap if I had known the price of a morsel, I would have worn my Sunday gown.' She lifts the hem of her tattered dress and minces in a pantomime of seduction, her movements jerking and puppet-like. She grabs at her withered left breast, with a sneer.

Hockett and the Millers watch her menacing little jig with increasing revulsion. There is indeed something devilish about it, something uncanny, in the way she twists her body into a parody of allure, like a goat with a girl's slender ankles dancing in the margins of a grimoire. Now Leah lets out a sob and draws back into the house, disturbed. Yeoman Miller remains firm at the threshold, and slowly shakes his head. 'I see,' he says. 'You would come into my home to warm yourself by my fire, and to what accursed end? Secrete away a lock of my wife's hair for use in a poppet? Send one of your imps behind the skirting board to nip at us in the night, feast upon our blood? I am not ignorant of witches' methods. God above,' he sighs, placing a meaty hand over his heart, 'I wish I was. But no man has the luxury of innocence, in these dark times.'

'My imps,' laughs Old Mother Clarke, 'my imps need no doors, sir. They go where I tell them. Through any crack, be it narrow as a nun's or wide as your wife's.'

Miller swallows an incensed breath of winter air. Before Hockett can decide if he ought to help or hinder his master in driving away this vulgar interloper – and how he might best effect either – Miller grabs up his cane and stamps down from the threshold toward the reeling Mother Clarke. He draws the club up over his head. The old woman moves backward with a catlike yowl and falls, a crumpled heap in the snow.

This is how Master Hockett told it to my mother, when he appeared breathless at our doorstep and bid us come out to the Millers as fast as we could, for there had been an *accident*. The trip is an hour-round, and a moonless night is closing in fast behind us by the time it is completed, half-carrying half-hauling Mother Clarke and her wooden leg. The Millers had left her there, lying in the snow, like an animal. Then there is the wrangling over whose cot she is to be put in, which, in the end, is mine, of course. I express my displeasure at this arrangement, given that the old woman smells worse than a brace of polecats, but Mother says simply that it's the lice I ought to be worrying about, and bids me get the fire up to warm her.

We strip off the invalid's sodden, filthy clothes, and I take them out to the yard for burning. Vinegar Tom strides imperiously between parlour and bedchamber, overseeing the whole affair as though it is most vexatious to him. Very like a man, only lovable. Soon the fire is up. Mother takes Liz Clarke's limp, dirty hands between her own, and rubs them vigorously, left then right. She tries to spoon a little watery pottage into her slack, unresponsive mouth. And I watch all this from the doorway and wonder at my mother, and how tenderly she cares for our neighbour, that flake, that practical nothing, a near-friendless outcast. It will seem absurd, but I think of Mary Magdalene, then – Mary Magdalene drying our Lord Jesus Christ's feet in her beautiful hair. And for a moment it feels very clear to me. It all makes sense. God does, I mean. Not so much as the self-satisfied brute that Minister Long is wont to expound upon, but as what they call the Spirit; the warmth rubbed into the rigid hands of an invalid, the kissing away of tears, the alms, and all of that. Mother Clarke's rasping breaths smooth and swell. A flush soon enlivens her furrowed cheeks. She returns from that point of crisis, the moribund crossroads, and simply sleeps, warm and fitful.

My mother sits back in her chair by the bedside, rubbing at her tired eyes. I draw up a stool and join her there. Something must be said, though I have no idea as to how to go about saying it sensibly. 'They think she is a witch,' I say, in the end. 'And that you are a witch, and that I am one too, I suppose. Hopkins and the other Godly folk.'

Mother smiles tiredly and draws the cap off her greying hair. '*Witch*,' she mutters. 'You pay too much mind to gossip, Rabbit. *Witch* is just their nasty word for anyone who makes things happen, who moves the story along. A man like Hopkins, or like that dolt Richard Miller, will pray every day that God might strike his rivals down, or that a pretty young thing might look his way. And should it happen, he counts it a miracle, a marvel – proof of his standing among the righteous. All a supposed *witch* does, it seems to me, is everyone the courtesy of saying those prayers out loud, and in company.'

'The witch says her prayers, and it is the Devil as answers them.'

'And if the Devil is truly so affable to a poor old wretch like old Bess Clarke then perhaps he is worthy of worship indeed.'

I know I need to make her understand. But she is testy, unpredictable. If I told her of the incident with Hopkins, what would she do? No doubt it would further imperil us. Because it is *us*. We are bound by name and fortune and blood, and there is nothing else. I reach across to grasp at her wrist. I remind her it is a crime. A hanging crime. *Maleficium*. Already there is one dead body, and it is never very difficult to find more.

'Peace, Becky,' she huffs. 'It isn't like it used to be, back in the Queen's day. They cannot bind thumbs and toes to swim you in the Mistley Pond. Cannot hang you wrongways up by the ankles, any of that. If they start knocking off every poor sod who's ever chafed a Puritan, half of Essex'll be treading wind by midsummer. Believe me. I have been through all of this before.' She nods inwardly, once, twice. Rubs her calloused thumbs together in her lap. 'No. Jurymen want proofs. Proofs, or a confession. And in our case, they shall find neither. Will they, Becky?' She looks at me.

I am silent by the bedside.

'*Will* they, Becky?' she asks, again, her brows knitting.

Tears of frustration suddenly burst up out my eyes like the waters of a flood-swoll brook, and I lower my head to my apron so she cannot see, and say that I simply do not understand why it is that we must be the kind of people that folk rumour to be witches. Pressing my face down into my skirts, thick with darkness and damp smells from our labour through the snow, feels good and protective, like burrowing must to a beast. The tears are hot on my cheeks. And then, I feel a hesitant hand on the small of my back. Mother pats me, haltingly. 'And you would rather we were what kind of people, hey?' she tuts, with gentle reproof. 'Rather I was the kind of mother that would marry you off to a yeoman Miller as soon as you had learned to wipe you own arse?'

'No,' I protest, meekly, 'but Master Edes . . .' And saying his name, I feel unworthy of it, and I am choked up by tears again.

'There now. Quit your squalling,' sighs Mother, drawing me into a wary sort of embrace. 'Poor girl. You're just a little cunt-struck, is all. Or whatever a maid be that is like to cunt-struck.'

I laugh a little at that, despite myself, and then I say, 'I don't want to die, Mother.' And upon saying it realise that it is what I am afraid of – dying. And so the weeping.

Mother rolls her tired eyes. 'Well tough,' she blusters. 'Because everyone does, sooner or later. And your time will come – far from here, and many years hence. Believe me, I know these things.'

And I think of my mother then, and her own peculiarities. Her reckless taste for surviving, that makes her like an animal, wild and unknowable. Her pride, of which she has so much, and which she wants to pass on to me, as other women give their daughters fine linen and pearl earrings. She wants to give me pride but I will not take it, because I have seen how desperately she has had to fight to keep it. But a knack for surviving – that is a more promising inheritance. And if we are to survive, we will only survive together. So I breathe in slowly, and then say all at once, 'I told Master Edes I saw the Devil.'

I feel her arms stiffen around me. She says nothing for a short while, and I listen to Bess Clarke's slow, wheezing breaths. One, two of them. 'Where?'

'In the water. In Judith Moone's bedchamber, the washbasin.'

'The Devil in water . . .' she mutters, her chin pressed to the crown of my head. 'The Devil in water stands for evil deep in the heart.'

I begin to whimper again, but Mother gives my shoulders another awkward squeeze. 'Peace, Rabbit,' she tuts. 'Not *your* heart, child. The Devil doth govern our world by God's consent, it is true, but his mere image holds no special power. Who knows what 'king' means, these days? Let alone 'devil'. Strange times. Much that seemed it would always be melts away under us from the fire of men's hearts. Aye,' she sighs, 'and women's hearts too. Your life will not be like mine. It will not be like the life of anyone who went before. I know that rightly enough. You will live to see I'm right. Tooth and nail, Beck. That's all we need.'

We embrace for quite some time there at the bedside, listening to the shudder of the fire. I think she is wrong, but I love her for it.

14

Warrant, Testimony

The next morning Stearne has his boy saddle up his best horse – a fine bay mare named Cassandra – for the ride over to Bradfield Hall. I have never seen Bradfield Hall, but I have heard that the Baronet keeps white peacocks and that the house itself has no fewer than six chimneys.

A fine vapoury sleet falls, melting the snow, and Stearne is soaked to the bone by the hour of his arrival. Cassandra trots down a wide drive of oak, through to the Baronet's extensive stables. The horse is unsaddled and a liveried footman leads the rider through to the office of Sir Harbottle Grimston, 2nd Baronet, deputy lieutenant of Essex. Stearne must wait. His boots squeak wet on the polished marble. He sits, then stands again, then removes his hat. The second-richest man in Manningtree he may be, but he remains a simple rustic in the eyes of so lofty a personage as the Baronet, with his six chimneys and innumerable peacocks.

While he waits, he inspects a dusty tapestry hanging by the door: a fox weaves his way through silver grasses pursued by a clutch of huntsmen in antique hose and doublets, and a flock of agitated ducks with gold-tipped wings bursts across the blue velvet sky. I like to imagine that Mister Stearne realises – just as the door to the Baronet's office swings open, and he is ushered in – that he quite desperately needs to piss, and that he sits there rocking uncomfortably to and fro in a damascene armchair before the Baronet's vast mahogany desk for the duration of their audience. But none witness Stearne's meeting with the Baronet to tell of it. He leaves with a warrant for the arrest of Elizabeth Clarke, orders to search whatever property the vagrant woman has, and instructions to elicit, if possible, a confession of *maleficium* (before no fewer than two respectable witnesses, as Deuteronomy exhorts).

I spent the day on my knees scraping rotten chicken shit off the flagstones of Mother Clarke's cottage, in preparation for her return. I am alone. There are things I do not want to touch: a shrivelled, sour-smelling item like a prune studded with nails beneath her pillow, oily little vials of cloudy liquid. By mid-afternoon the sleet has stopped, and low grey clouds transude instead a filmy sunshine. On his way home, Mister Stearne must have ridden across the top of the village green, and from there looked out over the damp thatched roofs of Manningtree, and the mudflats beyond shimmering ever so prettily. In the distance, ships' masts cluster round the smoky harbour of Felixstowe and the perpetual fires of the wrights' yards. Melting snow drips from the gutters and sills all down South Street. Already, it seems, spring is sweeping winter briskly away, the sap is rising in the meadows.

Allow me to conjecture. He is pleased with himself, pleased with the way his audience with the Baronet has transpired. He knows he has a busy week ahead, that there is much work to be done. Testimony to be collected and formalised, witnesses to be rallied. As Cassandra trots past the Red Lion, Stearne is seen to smile magnanimously at the simple folk gathered beneath the eaves with their tobacco pipes and mugs of beer, at the butcher's boy scraping pink-tinted slush from the stoop of his master's shop, at sweet little Prudence Hart tripping down the hill with her basket of cakes and a bellyful of baby. Their innocence is touching to him. They cannot hear the furry imps nibbling at their claws behind the plaster, cannot see the hexes blasting through the ether above their heads. But Mister Stearne of Manningtree can.

John and Matthew. I suppose they think themselves like the Apostles, putting on all of God's armour, raising high their swords of flame.

The men walk about town together in a little company, and with a sense of purpose – a purpose everyone knows. They are inquisitors. Hopkins leads, tall and Bible-black, his spurs click clicking on the rain-chilled cobbles. Next the portly Mister Stearne, wearing his fine-furred riding cloak and his wide grin of money. A few paces behind them walks my sweet John Edes, his hat pulled low over his eyes, a battered leather portfolio of loose-leaf papers held tight under his arm. There are some addresses at which they know to call. Certain individuals they summon through the Wright lad, who would labour up and down Sinai itself for a glittering penny. Still more, hearing of the gentlemen's righteous undertaking, volunteer themselves for interview, cautious or defiant, pious or vengeful – it makes very little difference to Hopkins. All can agree – things haven't been right for a while. Our conjoint misfortune has been too rigorous, runs the tattle. Our newborns are sickly, our pies raw in the middle, cats scream in the alleys all night long and the butter will not turn. The world froze over, and now rots from within.

They begin to call Hopkins 'Witchfinder'. The ragged little children chase after him in the street as a dare, or prance over the mud in the wake of his determination, singing of Old Mother Goose and her fine gander. Some say he carries a book about his person in which are written the names of all Sathan's servants the world over, and that either the book must be very large or the writing in it very small and cramped. This is, of course, untrue. He holds all our names in his head, and has no need of such banal memoranda.

Master Edes – a true professional – is, they say, methodical in his record-keeping. At the Thorn, or at a meagre kitchen table, or even on the carpenter's workbench, he spreads open the portfolio, lights a candle stub, slices a fresh quill, and arranges pounce pot and ink well. I wonder if the ritual of it soothes his unease? I wonder if he feels any? In crisp hand, he dates and titles a fresh leaf for each separate visit: March 1. 1644, March 2. 1644, March 3. 1644. The Testimony of _____. Whereas Hopkins' method is apparently inconsistent, and consistently mystifying. Of course, sometimes he need not employ *method* at all; some know what it is they must say, what names they ought to mention, and what compelling detail they might provide. Others must be prompted or cajoled like children before the grace – have their mouths opened for them, the black ribbon carefully unspooled from their tongues. Be told, in so many words, what it is that has happened to them. Some require assurances that they will be protected from further harm befalling them. Others seem to desire it, because anything is better than being overlooked, even by the Devil himself. I hear of two who wept. I can guess the ones who raged and blustered and banged their fists against the table, causing Master Edes to besmirch his perfect shorthand with a jump in his seat. Some, I imagine, were embarrassed by the oddity of what they had to tell. Some, I suppose, made it up word for word as they went along. I think of the maids. The maids, like me. The maids who perhaps knew me. The maids with their white sickness and dainty lace collars. How might I have behaved, confronted with the diligent attentions of three men, two of them young and unmarried? Blush and giggle, or else fall into embarrassed silence? We never want to say what has happened to our bodies, to describe what thing it was that sat on our breasts, or what we felt stroke at our bellies. I imagine it was hard to bring answers forth from the girls. I imagine that they did not want the men to notice they had bodies at all. Or else they wanted it too much, tugging on their stays and smearing chicken blood on their cheeks to serve as rouge. You would not think it to look at us, so alike in outward semblance, but there are many different sorts of girl, many different thoughts beneath our little starched caps of perfect white.

Minister Long is one of the first volunteers. I picture him trembling on the parsonage settle, beneath a sampler stitched by his predecessor's rheumy-eyed wife. The Minister tells of how, a little over a year ago, he was riding back from Colchester. He had a copy of Sandys' new *Metamorphoses* in his left breast pocket (this detail embarrasses him, for the frontispiece depicts two bare-breasted goddesses, but Hopkins assures the jittery young Minister that he is likewise an admirer of the pagan poet, though he would not ordinarily boast of it).

The Minister tells how he passed a dog on the other side of the road, at the turning overhung by the old oak. A big dog like a deerhound, with dark fur. The dog trotted on by, seeming to pay no mind to the Minister and his horse. 'As if the beast had pressing business of his own up in Colchester,' Long chuckles, nervously wetting his lips. He relates how a peculiar feeling came over him then. The skin prickled at the back of his neck. Seeing that no master followed after the hound, the Minister drew his reins and went to call to it, whereupon he saw that the great dog had paused at the turning and was regarding him over a matted shoulder. He saw also that its eyes were not like a dog's eyes, nor like the eyes of any other animal. He says how those eyes seemed to flame red and drip black all at once, set in a long face like a frayed rag. His horse – a very sweet and placid mare – started from the spot. The Minister was thrown to a verge not half a mile from that inauspicious turning. He must have fainted, for a time, and surely that hellhound would have come to rip his gut hot from his belly, was the power of God not greater than that of the Devil. His horse, however, pined and wasted to death within the month.

Robert Taylor, the victualler. Above his shop on Market Street, where the good sourness of onions masks the smell of muck running in the rutted road outside, he tells them his story. Taylor is a stout, weather-bitten man, and I picture him relating it with a certain degree of scepticism, one beetle brow upraised throughout. His tale concerns Liz Godwin – a new name, but not an entirely unexpected one. Taylor tells of how Godwin came to his shop a few weeks ago, asking if she might be trusted for a half pound of butter. Not in the habit of extending credit to the meaner sort of Manningtree folk, Taylor denied her. 'So off she goes,' he says, chewing his lip, 'muttering and mumbling all peculiar.' A short while later she returned with money, and so he cut her the butter after all and thought no more of it. That night as he knelt down at his bedside to pray, he was disturbed by a noise from the shop below. 'A tumult – a strange . . .' Frowning, he slaps the palm of his calloused hand against the table, demonstratively, rattling Master Edes' ink well. 'A shaking, in the walls.'

Out he went in his nightshirt, lantern in hand, and followed the noise round to the stables, where he found his old mule in a most excitable state. In a seeming frenzy, she bucked and threw herself against the walls of her box, again and again, so hard her fur was stippled over with blood. She could not be calmed, and Taylor knew not what could have affrighted her. So he called a farrier, and then a second farrier, and both said there was nothing else that could be done but restrain her and hope the distemper would pass. So that is what they did. But all night long she whined at the halter and rolled her desperate eyes, as though assailed by some invisible swarm, as though white-hot sparks burned holes in her greying hide. Taylor says he had never seen the like of it, leastwise not in a mule, 'except,' he gulps, his eyes moistening—

'Except you have,' Hopkins interpolates, delicately. 'Master Briggs. God rest him.'

Taylor nods, slowly. The seams of his eyes glisten with moisture. 'I have heard much sermonising in my years, gentlemen,' he sighs. 'Many presbyters with their talk of sinners afire forever in Hell. But I never did – I never could *see*. . .' He wipes his running nose on his shirtsleeve, clears his throat. 'She was a good old thing.'

The Minister has lost a horse and the victualler a mule – but the Yeoman Richard Edwards, not to be outdone in anything, lays claim to a virtual shambles. Stroking at his fine whiskers, he tells of driving his herd through to pasture on Wormwood Hill one bright Sunday afternoon, hard by the hovel of Old Mother Clarke. All of a sudden, a white heifer keeled as though lame and promptly expired, her eyes rolling back into her blunt skull. On the following Wednesday, at that very same spot and that very same hour, a black also met her end. And another, and another, each as if struck by invisible lightning. He had them opened up, these cows – set the farmhands to comb every inch of steaming viscera – but no pustule nor poison could be discovered that might have caused their abrupt demise. He could find no explanation for this mysterious – and costly – plague, at least not until now. He is a Godly man, and a righteous one, the father of four healthy sons. The Lord has seen fit to shower him with all manner of blessing. Why would he turn heel and look to curse him now? He feels himself to be interfered with, and it is embarrassing for a man of his quality to feel interfered with.

Master Edes perhaps feels a twinge of dubiety as regards Richard Edwards. 'The way he tells it,' he leans across to mutter at Stearne, 'you might think Old Mother Clarke was crouched at her kitchen window with a musket.'

For most in Manningtree the loss of a healthy steer or a good milker ranks among the greater calamities. The loss of a child, especially a girl child, is a more minor misfortune. Of course there is weeping, and fasting too. But people do not speak of it openly, because it happens all the time, and because God wills it. There can be scarce a house the whole town over that lacks the little unsanctified spot nestled beneath the bramble-patch, a name or three struck over on the inside cover of the family prayerbook. But this time is notable for there being so few healthy babes born in Manningtree, and still fewer living to be weaned from the breast. I suppose Hopkins, Stearne and Edes visit with midwives and wet-nurses, hearing stories of mysterious fevers and limbs contorted in cradles. As though the Angel of Death had passed over unbidden in the night, as happened long ago in Egypt. The thing that came out of the mother with three lolling, dead legs sprouting from each hip. The big-eyed boy found cold in his cot. The toddler who lost her footing at the creek. Doubtless they saw much women's weeping. I wonder if they found it unseemly? I wonder if Hopkins, ever composed and gracious, offered to pray with them – if he took their hands in his and knelt, and said, 'Let the little children come to me and do not hinder them, for to such belongs the Kingdom of Heaven,' or else, 'In my father's house are many rooms. If it were not so, would I have told you that I go to prepare a place for you?'

And if, once their prayer was done, he would ask the downcast woman where her babe died, and who she knows liveth close by, and who hath taken the babe to nurse, and had laid a hand on it and called it a pretty child, touched the cheek? And which answer he received – West, Moone, Godwin, Clarke, Leech?

15

Fornication

I am alone in the house when I hear a knock at the door. This can only mean trouble, as it is near to midnight, and if it were my mother returning from the inn she would bray at me through the window to open the door sooner than do anything so genteel as knock on it. So I take up the iron poker from the hearth and open the door up the barest crack. There, panting at the threshold, stands Master John Edes, his collar drawn up high over his face and the brim of his hat glittery with raindrops. His eyes move from my head – which, blushingly, I remember is bare – to the poker in my hand. 'I came alone,' he blurts. 'Fear not, Miss West.'

Aye, I think, *but why did you come?* I have not seen Master Edes in nearly two weeks. In truth, I have kept well away, for where Edes is, is Hopkins too. I open the door a little wider and peer out. There is a rare clarity to the damp air – the moon peers from behind a shoulder of cloud. In one direction, an evening rain velvets the estuary and the distant rooftops of the silent town. In the other, the open country and wide, wet unsown fields where the pipistrelles make their nightly sport. He came alone, all right. I settle my eyes back on his face. Now, I am circumspect enough to have wondered, before, if my attachment to Master Edes – my overwhelming faith in his personal beauty – is genuine, or the result of a severely curtailed experience; my idle fancy stretching her aery hand for the lowest-hanging fruit, and buffing it up to shine. But there he stands with his hand hooked into his belt, chest heaving as he catches his breath, blue eyes tilted upward into my face, and I feel thoroughly vindicated in my adherence to the credo of Edes. I also feel a soft twisting sensation between my thighs. I have said nothing yet. What to do? What am I doing? Hurriedly I grab my cap and shawl up from the bench and arrange myself beneath them as best as I can. 'The Beldam's out at the Red Lion,' I explain, and prop the poker down by the lintel.

'I came to see *you*,' Edes replies, wholly missing my meaning, God bless him. But as I step out into the drizzle I see that his face is grave, and pale. And I realise – something has happened. Not a usual thing. This is the look of a man who has broken faith.

'You have come from the Thorn?' I ask. 'Hopkins?'

He nods, significantly.

So, well. Our time is limited. I bid him wait and snap the door shut, finding a cloak and a candle stub, then move back out again, shielding the dim light with a shaking hand. 'Does he know you have come?' I ask, shoving my stockinged feet into my pattens. I take another look down to the distant glitter of the Stour, the huddle of rooftops and chimneys stacked at the estuary's hip.

'No,' he says. 'But I shall soon be missed. He sent me to fetch the Minister . . .'

'Come.' I take hold of his arm and lead him around the back of the house and up the narrow hill path, the thump of my clogs muffled as the trampled dirt of the yard melts to the mulch of the wood. I do not know what it is that I am doing – almost. It feels automatic, instinctual, like a cat crawling under the bed on its belly when a stranger calls. In the house I feel bad, exposed, I need to go somewhere I am able to think. I need to go somewhere something can happen, if I feel I need it to. There are trees. They close in over our heads, releasing a silver music of drips when our passage disturbs the lower branches. Eventually we reach a clearing, and I stop, and Master Edes stops a yard or so behind me. He is finally recovered from his sprint, wan in the candle's tiny light.

Where, possibly, might we begin? It is Master Edes who speaks first, fast and grim: 'Mister Stearne has secured an arrest warrant for Mother Clarke,' he says. 'And he gathers evidence against your mother, and Margaret Moone, and—'

'Judith?'

'Judith Moone is at the Thorn. Seemingly she is bewitched.'

I stare blankly at him, feeling the cold rain slide down under my collar. He begins his story. He explains how earlier that evening Hopkins, Stearne and himself were gathered by the fire in the Thorn Inn to collate that day's testimony, when there comes an unexpected and timorous knock on the door. It is Judith Moone – or, as Stearne called her, 'that little redhead with the scabby mouth'. At the door, she declares to an astonished Hopkins, 'I have come to tell thee of the sins of Margaret Moone, my mother, which are many, and very grave.'

Judith is shown into the parlour, where Edes sits massaging his blemished hand. Hopkins bids her take a seat by the hearth, and Edes notices that she is clutching at her sleeve most anxiously (because she had not thought so far ahead, and realised then she would have to extemporise, I think, bitterly). The three men cluster opposite her, at the other end of Hopkins' study. Hopkins motions for Edes to turn a fresh leaf, and for Judith to begin her story.

Judith tells them how some months ago her mother bid her to go and fetch wood from the yard, but as it was the time of her bleeding, and as she was racked with great pain (Master Edes flushes as he relates her testimony), she said that she would not. 'My mother threatened me then,' Judith claims. 'She said I had as best go fetch the wood or . . . or something very terrible would befall me.'

Hopkins asks, did Margaret Moone speak *more precisely to the nature of* this terrible evil? And Judith says, she did not. But the next night as she lay in bed she felt something clambering about on her legs. Groping for the candle, she searched through the bed covers – but could find nothing there. Hopkins blinks. Master Edes could tell that he was disappointed (expecting the crimson burst of infernal flowers, he has received only a damp squib).

But there is more, Judith insists. Margaret Moone utters profanities, and often speaks of matters so lascivious that Judith dare not, for modesty's sake, repeat her words. Margaret asks for the *Devil to take* so-and-so, or the *Devil to dog the steps* of him or her. She keeps an imp! Hopkins leaps to attention at this. Edes underlines the word twice – IMP. Can Judith describe this imp?

It is small and grey and 'very like a mouse', she says. But it is not a mouse? The girl shrugs.

'Does the imp have a name?' he next enquires.

Judith scratches at the corner of her mouth. 'Jack,' she answers.

And what of her coven? Hopkins proceeds to ask all manner of questions concerning the Widow Moone's presumed confederacy with Mother Clarke and the Beldam West. To Judith's knowing, have the three women ever met at strange hours, perhaps in a meadow, or the wood? Judith says, unhelpfully, that she cannot rightly remember any such meetings being spoken of.

At this point in the relation of the evening's strange events, Master Edes lowers his voice and gazes stolidly down at his feet, as though embarrassed. I take a small step closer to hear him explain that Hopkins then asks Judith if her mother bears any witch-marks, or teats, perhaps about her secret parts. Judith pulls a face, and says – Edes' cheeks are crimson as he tells me this – 'I have not seen her *secret parts*, sirrah, since I came from them. But if you would care to look for yourselves . . .' And then she laughs, and they all see a strange and wicked brightness come into her eyes. Throwing her head back and slipping her narrow hips forward, she begins to hitch her skirts up over her thighs, baring her naked calves, and laughing ceaselessly. Master Edes averts his eyes from that strange, sordid spectacle. Hopkins, however, moves to admonish her, and reaches out an arm to take hold of the girl's quivering shoulder – at which point she throws her chair out behind her with a terrible bawl and falls across the hearthrug onto her back, tearing at her bodice and cap.

Mister Hopkins cries that the girl is possessed, and presses down upon her shoulders while Stearne endeavours to take control of her flailing legs. 'As we draw near the truth, the Devil stops her tongue!' Hopkins cries. Edes is ordered to fetch the Minister at once.

Edes springs to his feet and asks if he ought to bring Doctor Croke with him as well, but Hopkins insists a physick will not be necessary – he does, however, bid him to make haste and fetch a Godly woman, too, perhaps Mistress Briggs or Mary Parsley, for to search the girl for witch-marks. And while he instructs Master Edes in all this, Judith twists and howls on the floor between them, her face glistening and contorted. 'God! Deliver me!' she screeches. 'Deliver me from evil! He fills my mouth with his – all up with his . . .' And she begins to choke and gurgle obscenely. The Devil is there in the room with them, and Hopkins could not look more pleased at finally having drawn the man himself down from the gossamer barricades.

Master Edes describes how he watched Hopkins bear down upon the trembling maid, beads of sweat prickling on his brow, and was filled with an unaccountable horror. Hopkins was correct. There was a presence in that room, unnameable and undeniable and full of wickedness, a shadow crouched somewhere above, with forked tongue unfurled. Hopkins stood, then, and peered about the study still and poised, like a scent hound readying himself to flush a rabbit out. 'I know you are come,' he said, appearing to address thin air. 'I know you are come,' he repeated, louder, to compete with Judith's pitiful whimpering, 'and I shall cast you back into the abyss. For yea, he would raise his throne above the stars of God, and make himself like the Most High!' Then he fell to his knees beside Judith, and took hold of her shoulders and thrust her back hard against the floor, shaking her. 'But you are brought down to the realm of the dead, to the depths of the pit! Begone, false prophet! Begone!' he shouted, and Judith quivered and retched in his arms, as though a charge passed through her body. And Master Edes fled, then, with Judith's infernal wailing ringing in his ears, and the brightness of the fire burnt violet in his eyes. He ran – not southward toward the parsonage as Hopkins had bid him, but toward Manningtree. He passed the Briggs' now-empty house, the garden snarled with weeds, and the Parsleys' cottage by the water, and the Wormwood Hill path. He ran here. He ran to me.

All this he relates with the look of a man haunted, starting at every benign forest sound, and struggling to meet my gaze across the wretched flame. When he is done he takes a deep, rattling breath, and appears to brace himself, as though preparing to meet a blow. But I laugh. I cannot help it. I laugh, loud and full, and stamp my patten into the muddy ground. *Of course.* That is what I should have done. That is how I might have protected myself. Clever Judith felt what way the wind was blowing. I wonder – would it be too late for me to do the same? Turn up at Hopkins' door and throw myself upon his mercy, the Devil's wounded dupe? Master Edes peers at me, confused. 'Do not worry,' he reassures, uselessly, 'Judith is . . . is quite well.'

'Oh, I'll bet she is.'

His lower lip quivers. I see that he had a notion of how this would all go. He presumed that I would think him heroic, for shucking the bonds of his complicity with Hopkins. He presumed that I would be grateful to him, for bringing me this warning. And now I am none of these things and he is left standing alone on the arid spire of his expectation. 'Rebecca . . .' he mutters, helplessly.

'She feigns, you realise? She feigns it to save herself and damn her mother.'

'I—' Master Edes narrows his eyes and tweaks at the corner of his wet moustache. 'The thought had entered my mind. I did not wish to impugn your friend—'

I let out another hollow laugh. 'Oh, I know very well she is a liar. And an actress. I just feel a fool for not thinking of it first.' I begin to pace back and forth across the clearing, pressing my hand to my brow. The candle fizzes close to my bowed face.

'Perhaps—' Edes ventures, 'perhaps it would be best if you leave. For the time being, at least. Until their fervour cools. There will be tradesmen bound for Colchester – you could—'

'Colchester?' I interrupt. 'I think it might take more than ten miles to deter Mister Hopkins. He has the wind of angels' wings at his back, after all. When will they come?'

The deputy lieutenant's warrant for Mother Clarke will b[e] filled on the morrow, he explains. They will go to search h[er] house on Wormwood Hill, and there apprehend her.

I steel myself. I stop in my tracks. 'Why is it you[ ] ask him. Though I think by now I know very well [ ] I decide I will no longer allow him the privilege [ ] matter. He must speak it.

He wets his lips. 'Because whatever dark[ ] at work – I know you are innocent of the[ ] them unwittingly, or against your will, perhaps, by your mother,' he says, his voice fervent. And then he moves toward me and takes hold of my arm, and our faces can be no more than a palm's-length apart when the candle gutters out, extinguished by the rain, and I lose his eyes to the moonshadow cast by the brim of his hat. 'I am a Godly man, Rebecca,' he says, his voice hoarse, his grasp of me tight.

Innocent, he thinks me, of *whatever dark connivances may be at work.* I laugh again, I cannot help it. I know it is a nettling, delirious laugh. He takes hold of my waist, and I feel my legs weaken beneath me. And I am angry then, quite suddenly, like a cornered thing, thinking *how dare he, how dare he.* 'Am I?' I find myself asking. 'Innocent, indeed? Because I do not feel it, sir. I say my catechism and sing the psalms and I feel nothing, no grace. Cold and dry as stone inside. And perhaps that is what the Devil is, really. Not your lion, not your Frenchman in a tall hat – a nothing. So what do you feel, John? *Godly man* that you are?'

I am shaking in his arms and near to weeping, and it is at that moment he chooses to kiss me, his beard cold and wet and all the blood rushing to pullulate at the surface of my skin, and when we part we are both shaking. I cannot see him but feel him, his heart beating against the worsted of his doublet, and then against the thin stuff of my nightgown, and through the smooth cold glass of rain. The candle stub slips from my hand as that hand finds a way to the sliver of skin at his throat, where I feel his pulse, warm and quivering, *soap-sweet.* How strange it feels to be so close to another's real animal of a body, the hum of their blood. I gulp. I tell him I want someone to tell me how it feels, that I need to feel how it might feel to be loved, to be loved by God.

And of course we fall, then, to the forest floor. I feel my patten from my foot as he moves on top of me, fumbling with his belt, his knuckles grinding against my hip, and there – there it is inside, a curious feeling, a sting at first, but pleasant enough after a fashion; a kind of precious agony. I close my eyes so that I might better commit the feeling of it to memory. A heat at the bottom of the belly, an all-you-are gathered together and tied together with a crimson bow. He thrusts back and forth, breathing onto my neck. *I am being deflowered*, I think, to make it real. *I am no longer a maid. I am sinning. I am sinning, quite decisively. I am fornicating with Master John Edes, the Clerk.* I find myself admiring the dainty filigree of the interlocking treetops. The mud is cold and gritty between my toes. Thrust, thrust. I wonder if he has done this before. I want to ask him if he has done this before, in some other forest on some other wet, climactic night? Would a *yes* wound me? Probably. Are these irregular thrusting motions practised? Do they show evidence of experience? I cannot tell. How and where is it that men learn these things, anyway? Or is it an inborn knowledge? I try very hard to remain present in the moment, to savour his vigour and weight as it nudges at the edges of my terror, as it fills me up. I wish freely to embrace the deliciousness of sin. To sin with abandon is, after all, the only prerogative of the damned. An image comes into my mind of a baby, falling to the bottom of a well, where it melts away to nothing like a cube of sugar, and of a slender body swinging at a gallows amid the lush New England spruce. I am not right. You see for yourselves how I am not right. Devil leer over me. I was born to be this way, it is inheritance, take your pleasure sir and grind me down to nothing. Stop.

I try to occupy my mind with thoughts of Master John Edes, of Master Edes only: John Edes laughing, a wave of his hair caught in the brisk estuary wind, John Edes happy and neighbourly, kneeling down to work in Goody Wright's garden. The back of John Edes' neck pink with sunburn. John Edes in his settle, bathed in the mellow light of noon, turning a page of *The Plain Man's Pathway to Heaven*. But it is no good. He moans and moves in that jerking way once, twice more, and then is spent, I suppose, and shifts, and is still. I notice my breasts are bared, and his cheek rests rough and wet between them. I feel it for the first time, the cling of the slick dirt on the backs of my thighs, the tangle of my nightdress wet beneath us. I try to clear my mind of everything but the sensation of his immediacy, but feel instead the chill progress of a raindrop along the curve of my neck to the hollow of my throat. It will not do. Lowering my hand, I touch at the tippet of his ear through his sodden hair. 'John,' I say, though I have no notion of why, 'I love you.'

He jerks away from my touch, like a man waking from a nightmare. I cannot see his face in the dark – just his still shape in outline, his breath rising as a vapour. My eyes on the nothing of him and his on the nothing that is me. Something rattles in the treetops, then, and he climbs hurriedly to his feet, his hand on his belt again. Without a word, he pulls his cloak tight around his shoulders and stumbles off in the direction of town, in such haste that he forgets his hat. I turn my head to look at it, moonshine tracing the swell of the crown. I turn it over in my hands. I hold it over my face and breathe the smell of his hair mingled with the warm must of bruised leather. For a little while I hold it experimentally over my heart – then I think, *no*, and toss it away into the dark. And there I lie in the mud alone, prone and splayed and of a mood unaccountably tranquil, until the cloud thins and I see the moon above, resting like a silver dish against the canopy. All is peaceful, and all is gently spangled – as I might have wished for it to be. I think I would quite like to sink down into the mud and feel it close over my face, tender-black and suffocating. It is done. It has passed, and I lack the energy to give it signification. I stand up, and peel the despoiled stockings from the gooseflesh of my calves, and am surprised to realise that I weep – a hot tear splashes down on my bare knee. *Stop.* I brace my shoulders against the bole of a tree. 'Do you hear me?' I ask aloud of the darkness, the grave trees – and none make reply. 'They say when the Devil is called, he comes. Well, a fine mess you have got me in, sir. I hope it amuses you. A pauper, a witch, and now a whore.'

A breeze urges the boughs to a petty, answering laughter.

Mister Hopkins finds himself unable to sleep, after the thrill of his encounter with the Prince of Hell. He tosses and turns in his big feather bed, the heavy hangings seeming to billow and pitch with spirit-gusts. The whereabouts of Master Edes is likewise of some concern. The clerk never returned to the Thorn, and it seems peril is attendant on a Godly man's every footstep, these days. After a few fitful hours of semi-consciousness, Hopkins finds himself wired and taut on South Street, bathed in the first gelid light of the day. The incipient sunshine shucks the mist off the bay as he makes his way into Manningtree, with little notion of where it is he is going, or why.

Providence and intuition lead him up the hill to Lawford. He knows the Wests' cottage on sight, having had it described to him: a meagre, low little building of sun-washed red stone, with a sloping roof and wild gorse breaking up through the foundation, a rose-hip bush shading the kitchen window. He hangs back across the road, half-hidden behind a neighbour's abandoned sty. He supposes this is where the pig lived – the pig John Edes told him of all those months ago. The pig the Beldam West sliced across the wattles. He watches the cottage, and imagines Rebecca West sleeping within. At first in the ordinary manner, tucked beneath a counterpane, her breathing slow and soft. Then, suspended mysteriously from the rafters in the manner of the bat. Finally, he imagines her sleeping tucked in the dark crook of the Devil's own armpit, her pretty pocked face buried tick-like in his coarse black fur, her arms wrapped about his neck. Hopkins waits, but no smoke curls from the chimney. The little windows remain shuttered. Confident he goes unobserved, Hopkins picks his way across the dirt road and through the Wests' yard, round to the back of the house.

A cock's crow splices through the silence of the morning, and he presses his back against the outside wall – but all remains still, save for the shimmering of the bluebottles that rise from a daub of chicken shit as his long shadow passes over their backs. There, he notices footprints – two sets of footprints, leading into the wooded patch at the yard's end. Naturally, he follows them. Inevitably, they lead him to the clearing.

The first thing he finds is a burnt-down candle stub, sticking up out of the churned mud like a loose tooth. This he picks up, inspects, and puts into his pocket. Next, he notices a lumpy, brown shape that he takes at first to be the body of an animal. Moving closer, he sees it is not an animal, but a hat. He lifts it and wipes it down with the corner of his cloak. The square brass buckle on the band identifies this hat at once as belonging to Master John Edes. He has a feeling, a feeling as of someone gathering his entrails up in a clenched fist. He turns it over. It is the hat that Master Edes wore the preceding night, there can be no doubt. Hopkins surveys the mulchy forest floor, breathes deep the petrichor smell, and finds his eye caught by a point at the base of a nearby sycamore, where the misty sunshine catches on a pale thing wound shimmering about the thick tree roots. Not thing – *things*. A pair of wet stockings. He unwinds one in his hands, translucent and crisp with dried mud like the filmy discard of an adder. They could be anyone's – but they are not anyone's. They are Rebecca West's. He tucks the hat and stockings away beneath his cloak. He leaves. Stockings. He can conjecture what occurred there, in the wood, quite well. Its full hideousness hatches slow and chimera-like – a wriggling beast half-Edes, half-West – in his mind, as he tramps back through the waking town, ignoring every friendly *good morrow* that is called to him. He goes back to the Thorn, where the bewitched Judith Moone languishes in an upstairs guest room.

Returning to his chamber, he climbs into bed once more, and draws the gaudy drapes tight. He dreams of slender ankles and white necks. Of a girl peeling her skin off like a snake. It makes him hard. It makes him feel sick. These, his delicate firebrand-darlings—

16

Arrest

This is what would come to be outwardly recognised as *the beginning*: Wormwood Hill, a late-March evening, and the sky over the estuary is full to bursting with annealed, blood-red cloud. The cows tumesce in the fields, waiting on a storm. A small party walks the hillside path. John Stearne is first, with his warrant and a set of manacles beneath his cloak. Matthew Hopkins, his assistant, follows, upright in his scholar's black. Then the Constable, then Priscilla Briggs and her sister-in-law Abigail, slender bookends in high-necked gown and starched cap. Master Edes is still nowhere to be found, but the clerk's absence is of no consequence – the events of the night to come will prove indelible in the memories of all who are to witness them.

Stearne knocks at the door, and Mother Clarke answers, hesitantly. She has been returned to her cottage for mere days, and it hasn't gone back to feeling like home yet. Rebecca made it too clean, too sparse of odour. Stearne raises his voice above the stertorous wind to deliver the news that by the authority of Parliament and the deputy lieutenant of the county of Essex, she is apprehended on suspicion of *maleficium*, and her person and property will be searched for evidence pertaining to such wrongdoing. Their torches, redundant against the sanguine wash of the sky, sputter and flare quite dramatically.

'How many of you?' she is reported to have asked, narrowing her poorly eyes.

Stearne tells her there are five, but more may follow.

'And so it is,' comes her reply, and she hobbles back to allow them entry.

And more do follow. In they come, and see a little old woman sitting in her smock and bound at the wrists, before the hearth. She watches as the men overturn her cot, her stewpot. They rifle through her linens and flour sacks. They sniff at bunched herbs and rusted hairpins. A greasy old candle end, bloated to anthropoid semblance, causes particular consternation. The midden heap is full of gnawed-up bones. The old woman is tired and the ropes chafe at the loose skin of her wrists. She is heard to repeatedly invoke the name William Bedingfield – a name none recognise. She offers to help the searchers, if only they might tell her what it is they seek. She asks if she might have her tobacco pipe, and is denied.

Having overturned the miserable abode, the men leave. It is time now for Goody Briggs and Goody Hobbs, who know they must be brave, who know that they must put on the whole armour of God. They have been instructed well. They have been taught that they must neither look into the witch's face, nor heed her remonstrances. The Devil, they know, is adept at beguiling; he can make his black eyes round and wet as those of a kitten caught out in the rain.

This is how a witch is discovered. The suspect is laid out on her back. Her skirts are unlaced and her smock drawn up to cover her head. In Mother Clarke's case, they are presented with a body pale, puckered and tiny beyond expectation – but the task at hand is nonetheless onerous: moles, blemishes, spots, styes, pimples, wrinkles, boils, corns, scabs, bruises, bites, sores, suppurations, cankers, ulcers, lesions. Each must be thoroughly inspected. There are always more, on every body, than you would expect. Each must be pricked with a needle. It is best to work methodically, starting at the top and moving slowly down. Mother Clarke's blood is slow to run, but bleed she does, eventually, little constellations beading across sagging breasts and belly, Serpens and Ursa Minor of warm ruby. They handle her limbs with the impassive efficiency of midwives. They peer into her armpits and the shrivelled blue folds of her sex, unblushing. It must be considered a privilege, an act of trust. They are looking upon a woman's body in a way that can properly be sanctioned only by God. They join hands and pray over her body as the scarlet buds on the wool of her smock. *Because you did not serve the Lord your God with joyfulness and gladness of heart, because of the abundance of all things, therefore you shall serve your enemies whom the Lord will send against you, in hunger and thirst, in nakedness, and lacking everything. And he will put a yoke of iron on your neck until he has destroyed you.* Awl meet flesh. Let nothing be hidden, and knowing flow. They say Mother Clarke had a mark at the crease of her thigh from which no blood could be drawn, red and swollen as though sucked upon. They say she was compliant, which means she felt nothing, because witches are made of wood, and that is why they float, and that is why it doesn't matter if you strip them and stick them with pins. The crueller rumour is, she wept.

It is dark by the time the men re-enter. There is Elizabeth Clarke, now clothed again in her soiled things, sat at the end of her cot; rocking back and forth. Hopkins draws up a stool and sits opposite her. He asks, *do you keep imps, Mother Clarke?* – moderate, matter of fact. Of any shape, bee butterfly polecat red cock cat white dog like unto a man in a suit of black. Do you keep imps? Have you ever kept imps? Do you know what an imp is?

She rocks back and forth. She says she has a rabbit visit her, sometimes.

And does this beast feed upon her? Feed upon her blood?

She laughs at that and does not answer. She is confronted, of course, with the facts: she spoke a malediction upon one Mister Miller, and she threatened too that she would set her imps upon him. Marks have been found upon her body – teats by which the Devil has been given suck. Does she deny it? The tiny cottage is full of men dressed head to toe in black. She could not count them, and does not know all their names. Tall hats reaching practically to the rafters, candlelight dashing their shadows up the scrubbed plaster. She is hungry and tired. *I do deny*, she says, tongue thick and dry as the tread of a boot in her mouth, *that ever I had traffic with the Devil or his demons in any form*. And she asks, please sir, for a little water to drink, and they say that if it be water she wants there is a jug there, on the kitchen table, and Stearne and the Constable laugh as she moves to fetch it but cannot see to grasp the stem with her bound, bungling hands, and over goes the jug and over goes Old Mother Clarke, the water plashing out over the flagstones.

Hopkins' mouth twitches. 'Mother Clarke. Why would you threaten to set your imps upon Mister Miller, if no such imps exist? Where are they? Where are your familiars?'

She laughs again – a desiccated sound – and begins to chew at her lips.

Hopkins fans his hands in a gesture of apparent capitulation. *If you will not answer, I will wait.* And unlike Old Mother Clarke's, Matthew Hopkins' threats are not idle. He waits. They wait hours. They wait through a long, warm night. Whenever Mother Clarke comes to the edge of sleep, when her head lolls forward and her eyes flicker closed, then Hopkins will say, 'Come now, Mother Clarke – when your imps arrive you must be ready to welcome them.' And then she is rudely hauled up from the bedstead by her elbows, and made to walk, to walk around the kitchen table, in circles, ever more delirious. Dawn comes, spreading dirty roses over the floor. Stearne dozes in the corner, by the chimney breast. Hopkins sits opposite Mother Clarke, his scrutiny unrelenting.

She moistens her cracked lips. She asks him, does he not tire in his watching?

Hopkins smiles. Hopkins quotes Psalms: 'I will allow no sleep to my eyes or slumber to my eyelids, until I find a place for the Lord, a dwelling for the Mighty One of Jacob.'

The pale light of morning crawls over the disarray wrought by the searchers, the smashed crockery and scattered cornhusks. Then it ripens to a mellow gold, and climbs the walls. The world is narrowed to that one bare chamber, and neither Mother Clarke nor Hopkins sleeps. There sits Hopkins, so eminently hateable, knitting his fingers over his chest and leaning back in his seat, with something of the air of an apprentice bricklayer idling in the sun after a long day's labour. For his next trick: he begins to scrape his spur against the flagstones. The metal rasps and squeals. It seems to Mother Clarke to squeal on the very inside of her skull. *Please, sire,* and with much puling and groaning, she presses her bound hands to her brow, shoulders hunched in abjection. He asks again for the names of her imps. *You will tell me, Mother.*

She swears she has none, and has laid no curse upon the Millers.

Has the Devil come to thee in the form of a man, then? And she laughs weakly, and she is hopeless, and she titters an 'Aye, the Devil came as proper a Gentleman as any in England, and with a laced band.'

Good, Hopkins says, softly. *Good,* intently. And will she name her imps for him now? Will she hell. With a dry sob the little old woman bends in on herself, scratching at her scalp and tugging at her scant white hair. The sight is pitiful. Hopkins begins to scrape the spur again.

The Briggs sisters bring a light repast for God's intrepid inquisitors (bread, cheese, beer). Mother Clarke is dragged, debilitated, between Stearne and the Constable in a last circuit of the kitchen table, her horny foot blistered raw now, swollen and bleeding where it trails over the mucky stones. Oh, her swimming head, floating like a puff of thistledown between thrown shadows and half-seen visitations, the gloss of *mira* crowding at the dead edges of her vision. If someone would just touch her, lovingly (she once had sons). She feels a deep pinch at the back of her neck, and thinks she sits on the cot again. Words ripple into her mind arbitrary and uninvited, like 'eel' or 'gunpowder'. She remembers her mother, too – they tied her thumbs and toes and wound a rope around and under, waded her out to the pale green rushes, *goodbye*. She looks down at her own hands, shrivelled and thin, which rest on her belly, and her belly under a smock all spotted with blood, which shocks her. She cannot remember how it was she became so bloodied. 'Where,' she asks, quiet and startled, 'did all this muck come from?'

Hopkins leans eagerly forward in his seat. By now he has been two days without sleep, and it must have begun to show in his appearance – eyes blotched with shadow, hair greasy and tousled. But powerfully attentive to the task at hand. 'Tell me, Elizabeth Clarke,' he asks, 'what are the names of thy imps?' Oh, he enjoys asking it. He *loves* to ask it. He could ask it every hour on the hour 'til Shrovetide or longer. So says the oblique smile, the finger hooked nonchalant in his pistol-strap.

Mother Clarke is looking down at her bound hands. Her head is held aloft at a cramp-angle, as though she is about to vomit. 'William was my husband's name,' she says, at last, opening and closing her hands in her lap. 'Forgive me. I am as poor as Job.'

She has been doing this for a while now. Speaking nonsense, her consciousness worn threadbare, flickering between the present and an apparently preferable past. The Constable, just outside, says to Stearne that surely, if Sathan counted the old hag his menial, he would have interceded by now?

'Your imps, madam?' Hopkins asks again.

Stearne sighs. 'Matthew,' he mutters, moving forward, 'this is fruitless—'

At that moment Old Mother Clarke, rocking on the spot, was said to let out a long, keening whistle. There were ten witnesses. What can be said? First a dog, or a thing like one, which was plump and white with sandy spots was said to come, and this called Jarmara. Then a second just-about-hound-shaped thing, thin with long legs, and called Pyewackett. All are doubtless a-shudder at the infernal hideousness of these strange appellations, these names which are surely beyond mortal invention. She says a black imp will come next, and come for Mister Stearne, who grabs up a pistol from his belt and wheels on the spot to confront this invisible assailant. Nothing more comes, and all that came before is gone, yet Priscilla Briggs seizes up her skirts and leaps onto a stool, while her sister Abigail clutches shrieking at her waist. There are several as would confirm every particular of this story, and of the imps that were called Pyewackett and Jarmara. And they said also that Mother Clarke did tell them that herself and my mother kept many more imps besides these two, so one can only think that the innumerable horrible things must verily have fought for a suck on her witch-mark like piglets round the belly of a sow. And in the midst of all this tumult comes a confession from Mother Clarke, though it is no longer needed, so many having seen her execrable pets.

Matthew Hopkins calls for peace, and seizes the old woman up by her bound wrists, and demands to know if she conspired with the Beldam Anne West, and if she knows said Anne West to be likewise a servant of the Devil?

'Anne West,' she repeats, as though it is a name she knew in a different life. 'She said she pitied me my poverty, my deformity. She said she knew ways and means by which I might live better.' This is all she says of the Beldam, but it will suffice. All argument is moot, irons clapped on. First witch, fire-seed. They take her out into a gusty night. The clouds are once more flush in the setting sun, bruisy and doomfull of rain. She crosses the threshold for the last time in chains.

Hopkins takes Mother Clarke gently by the elbow, then, and she looks up at him with her empty grey eyes, and says, 'James, it is too cold to go down to the river tonight. We can see the boats tomorrow morning, after church, if you are a good and Godly boy and listen well.'

Then passes a moment of strange and miraculous tenderness that is spoken of for weeks, and makes a place for Hopkins in the heart of every Puritan mawk. Hopkins lowers his head to meet Mother Clarke's gaze and takes a gentle hold of her shoulders. He says, they say, this: 'I pray God will forgive you, Elizabeth Clarke. Your body has known much suffering in this life, and I pray that you will recant, and cast your sins away, so that your soul might be spared the torments of the next.' He takes her wrinkled cheeks in his gloved hands, all gentleness. Stearne and the Constable watch in silent bafflement. 'Even now,' Hopkins whispers, 'God reaches out to you, full of mercy, and full of love. John saith, if we confess our sins, the Lord is faithful and just to forgive us our sins and cleanse us from all unrighteousness.' And then he presses a decorous kiss to the old woman's brow. *Quo modo deum.*

Mother Clarke looks uncomprehendingly up into his face. There can be no malice left glinting behind the lacteal scum of her eyes.

Is there even life? She asks, rocking on the spot where she stands, if she will now be permitted to sleep.

Hopkins smiles. He tells her she is to ride into town with Mister Stearne, and then she may sleep for as long as she might wish.

17

Coven

Of course, fleeing seems the wisest thing to do, once you no longer can. But then again, where would I go? I hear them coming up the hill. They are a small rumbling troop now. Their number has swollen since Mister John Stearne rode triumphant into town, erect in the saddle, with Old Mother Clarke trembling at the pillion seat behind him, her hands tied. A witch divested of her power. The men have come out from their houses to follow Matthew Hopkins, the Witchfinder, who rides ahead of the crowd like some adumbral ensign, his torch held high over his head. Some of the men wield pikes or swords, or else lathes and axes seized up from woodpiles. They do not know what it is they might do with them – they just felt the need to be suitably accessorised. They have come to watch, to see. Come to see what? A woman clatter up to the sunset on leathery wings? A black dog twisting at the end of a rope?

The noise of them grows louder, and I think I would see them, too – a speckle of fire-lights wending ant-like up the shoulder of Lawford hill – if I would, if I could, move to the window. But I cannot. I am too frightened. I stand in the dark with my back pressed tightly against the cool plaster of the parlour wall. I can feel every organ in my body. Then a red flush fills the window and I hear the hum of maybe a dozen voices, the yelp of an excitable hound. They have reached the garden fence. I imagine the Constable and his militiamen pressing the throng back from Mister Hopkins at the gate. Reverently they comply, falling into a hush of anticipation – as if what lies beyond the little garden gate is not our muddy walkway, our chicken coop, our unplanted flowerbeds choked with charlock, but Nebuchadnezzar's Furnace itself, a conflagration none but the Witchfinder might emerge from unscathed. There is a collective gasp as he clicks the gate open. A deep bray of admiration as he walks, alone and fearless with his black cloak billowing behind him, up the Devil's garden path.

And then reality comes face to face with my frightened fancy at the point his gloved fist knocks once, twice at the kitchen door, and I must decide what it is I am to do. Not later, when I have had time to think about it, but now. Each possibility and its possible consequences spread many-branching out before me. Might I wriggle out a back window and make for the wood? But they will have – they do have, I can hear them – hounds. Just answer the door? The door. There is a thin thread of flame quivering beneath the door. Just answer it. Fine. Or stay here leg-locked like an oaf until they batter it down. A shadow moves across the window. Someone is peering in. Slow, slow and shaking, I find it in myself to move. It feels good to move. I want the outside air, suddenly. In fact I thirst for it. I have not left the house since Mother Clarke's arrest.

I open the door. The air is cool and good, then hot on my right cheek, for Mister Hopkins stands at the threshold, just as Master Edes did four days ago, holding a torch. 'By the authority of Parliament,' he declares, 'and the deputy lieutenant of the county of Essex—'

'She is gone,' I state, fast as you please, meaning my mother. 'I mean. She is not – she is not here, sir.'

Hopkins pauses. An ember drips from the torch and dies on the wet stoop slab. When did it rain? I wonder. How long was I pressed waiting against the parlour wall? I look past Hopkins' shoulder at the men's weather-blasted faces, shining like dirty pennies in the firelight. I see Joshua Norman, who was fined once and put in the stocks for turning up drunk to church. I see, with a twist of disappointment, Yeoman Hobday, leaning on his hayfork. I see young Master Hockett, who we all laughed at when he said that God could not send a dead man to Hell if he were buried in a scapular, no matter how he sinned in life. And of course, Mister Hopkins. His lip curls as he looks up into my face. I want to tear that smile right off him and hold it up to show the men who crowd around the gate. *Look*, I would say. *Look – he is enjoying this.* His smile would hang red in my tight fist like a gypsy's silk and I would shout at the top of my voice, *Woe to those who call evil good and good evil, who put darkness for light and light for darkness*, because I also know my scripture, and lo, how the men would tremble then, and scatter off down the sides of the hill. Mister Hopkins, Witchfinder. His eyes are hidden in the shadow cast by the brim of his hat. He is just that smile, private and peculiar. I am shaking. As he moves to answer, I slap him hard across the face.

A gasp rises from the crowd and the militiamen jostle to hold them back. Hopkins lowers his head and rubs at his smarting cheek, a nerve jumping in his jaw. He takes a deep breath, then straightens up again. He is no longer smiling. 'May I enter?' he asks, by which he means, *I will enter now*, and he pushes past me and into the parlour, followed by the Constable – who I realise is binding my hands before I have thought to protest – and two of the militia, who make to search the house. One begins by causing a great din when he pulls at the tablecloth, precipitating a massive clatter of pewter to the floor – I think he does it for no other reason than to play on my nerves, for I shudder most violently at the noise. It is strange seeing the house, my home, with a man in it. With men in it, bringing all their smashing and their shouts. They are everywhere. I have seen no man cross that threshold since my father – and now four come all at once. I stagger backward and Hopkins guides me to the bench.

'Where is the Beldam West?' he asks.

'The Red Lion,' I answer, unthinkingly. 'Or else, that was where she meant to go.' I ask him if I am to be bound over. Hopkins does not answer. A ghastly howl chivs the general commotion of the search, and then a shout, then a nasty, bloody thud. I make to rise, but Hopkins pushes me back. The Constable cries triumphantly from the bedchamber that he has *killed it quite dead*, and re-enters the parlour panting, cudgel drawn, carrying a limp sack of bone and bloodied red fur in his free hand. 'Beat the brains out, sir,' he says, swaggering at Hopkins, 'most wonderful.'

He has Vinegar Tom hanging beat limpen in his fist. Or what was Vinegar Tom, and now is a mess of fur with holes and meat and blood, and blood coming out the holes. And I think how there is so little keeping anything alive, keeping the warmth inside and the force out. I put my hand over my mouth to deny the interlopers the satisfaction of my sob. The Constable passes the shaggy mess of fur over to Hopkins, who inspects it with a scowl. 'Are there more?' he asks.

'None that I can see, sir,' the Constable answers, wiping his big hand on his trouser leg. 'Some chickens out back, though,' he adds, hopefully.

'It is naught but a cat!' I find I have said – sobbed – at the Constable. 'A cat, sirrah.'

Hopkins sighs. 'Yes, a cat,' he repeats to the crestfallen Constable, handing him back his trophy by the gory scruff. 'Throw it on the midden.'

Tom's front leg twitches. Three drips of blood on the bare boards of the table. I cannot look at the caved-in head – I fight myself not to look at the caved-in head. I taste the bile rising in my throat like a cold finger, a branks, pressing on the root of my tongue, and my head is lightening. The next thing I feel is rain on the back of my neck, and the sway of a trotting horse beneath me. I lie draped across a stranger's knees, my vision swims, and I feel I am being taken down, down the hill. *Useless useless.* I gulp bile again, upturned. Doers of damage, bodies of sin, I can see our cottage growing smaller, fizzing. It fades to a blurred, black shape in the distance, retreating, wreathed all about with torchlight, with dancing specks of fire.

The men who did not join the Witchfinder's grim processional up the Lawford hill have gone out drinking in town to discuss it, instead. They crowd into the market ordinary, with its floor of trampled dirt and hay. They press three-deep along the narrow stretch of paving by the White Hart, where the sign swinging above their heads bears the image of a deer beguiled all about with gold chains. They wonder which of us can fly. They wonder which of us is Sathan's favourite fuck. A good night for a barnyard cockfight – a better one for Manningtree's two whores.

The Red Lion, crouched low at the corner of the village green, is packed to the smoky rafters. A shifty little man in a grey biggin cap moves from table to table plying a solid trade in palm-sized fragments of painted glass in emerald and scarlet; painted glass he claims that Parliament's men knocked from the windows of the grand cathedral down at Winchester, though he cannot explain how he came by it after. The men of Manningtree divide themselves to social degree by drinking hole as reliably as they do by church pew, and the Red Lion is home to the worst sort: a squalid, very illiterate mass with fewer teeth than fingers, for the most part. And so when a boy comes in to tell them the Witchfinder and his Godly men have taken me – 'the West girl' – away, this news is welcomed with no great show of righteous triumph, but with a murmur of general bemusement. The sailors, smugglers, sowgelders, pedlars and ploughmen crowded at the bar have no special stake in this intrigue, but observe it with a mild, lateral interest, like Mennonites caught in a fist fight. Misfortune and suffering are, to them, too commonplace to warrant attribution either to a higher power or to an infernal one, the hunting of witches, like the hunting of anything else, a gentry diversion. 'Come again when the girl's hanging,' calls some cut-up from a corner stall, 'that'll be something we can all enjoy.'

I like to think that perhaps my mother's blood, in that moment, thickened. She knew it was coming, doubtless – but perhaps she did not know how fast. There she stands, alone by the door to the wagon yard with a half-empty beer mug and her only child in the hands of the law, her resources suddenly reduced to whatever she thought to carry on her person when she bid me farewell and left the house earlier that evening, in the happy expectation of a few languid hours spent drinking. An Egyptian day. She finds, perhaps, having taken a fumbling inventory of her apron pockets, that these resources consist of no more than thimble, needle, cracked clay pipe and a few pennies. Doubtless, she wonders why I did not run. Likely she contemplates, for a moment, doing so herself. But she does not. Instead, she calls out, 'Where did they take her, boy?', and pushes her way to the front of the inn, where the messenger stands panting in his ragged trousers, cheeks bright after the long sprint from Lawford. The room falls silent as the redoubtable Beldam West stares it, defiantly, down.

'Well,' says Moses Stepkin, the pedlar, 'if it ain't the Queen of Hell herself!'

'The Prince of Air a mettlesome bedfellow, Nan?' leers another, thrusting his loins against the back of a chair.

'Fie, gentlemen,' my mother barks, setting her feet apart and her hands on her hips. 'You know well this Puritan folly is like to turn lawless. But what do you care? Shakerags and rascals, nothing left for the taking but your very lives, and even they would hardly be worth the bother.' Her invective is met with a dissolute cheer and the slop of rotgut on tabletops as mugs are raised and clinked together. 'Now—' Anne shouts over the tumult, 'will it please a man to tell me where this so-called Witchfinder has taken my daughter?'

'To bed, if he has any sense,' haws John Banks, to renewed corporate hilarity – God save us all from men when they are drunk together. My mother stamps her foot in frustration.

'Why not ask the man yourself?' calls a wily-eyed newcomer from the entryway, plucking off his hat and smoothing a hand through his hair. 'Passed him on my way up the market street seeming bound for the green – Mister Hopkins, and the Constable's men with him.'

This mention of the Constabulary swiftly curbs the communal merriment. The smugglers and card sharps in their dark cloaks edge grumbling toward the back door, the glass-seller tips his wares out an open window into the hedgerow outside. Mother dips her chin to this information. 'I thank you, sir,' she says, and, 'I think I will do just that.' She draws back her shoulders and walks out into the street, prompting a flurry of activity as the Lion's remaining patrons gather up hats and cloaks, in a state of high excitability, and file out to follow the Beldam down South Street. Toward her doom or Hopkins', none can quite say what he expects or would prefer; but certainly it will be a thing worth seeing.

They do not have far to go. The rain is falling heavier now – big plashing sheets of the stuff. My mother stands at the throat of South Street, atop the hill, as Hopkins and his Godly assemblage round the corner at the bottom and begin their climb toward the Red Lion, torches seething against the downpour. At their head rides the Witchfinder.

'Matthew Hopkins!' My mother shouts the name down the street. The Witchfinder's party halts in its tracks at the bottom of the hill. There is murmuring, until Hopkins raises a hand for silence.

'I will speak with thee, Matthew Hopkins!'

Some bare twenty yards of waterlogged road separate the formidable Beldam from the Witchfinder. At the top of South Street a motley collection of the Red Lion's rustics and delinquents elbow into position behind her, fidgety and watchful. At the bottom, on Hopkins' side, the chary Puritans stand firm, muttering prayers and brandishing their hayforks. With a sidelong look at Stearne, Hopkins chucks to his horse and trots out – God's righteous General – to meet his quarry. He draws up before her with an ironical tip of his sodden hat. He addresses her, *Mistress Anne West*, and speaks then the solemn words of binding over. *By the authority of Parliament and the deputy lieutenant of the county of Essex, I apprehend thee*, etc.

She snorts, undaunted. 'Hopkins. Where hast thou brought my daughter to?'

'To the Thorn, madam,' he answers. 'Pending further investigation of Mistress Elizabeth Clarke and yourself – known to be notorious wantons, and termagants, and feared to be servants of the Devil himself.' A hoot rises from the crowd gathered outside the inn.

'Matthew Hopkins, I will have my daughter back.'

'Madam, she is the daughter of God,' he laughs, the rain dripping from the brim of his hat. 'Matthew saith, call none on earth your father; for One is your father, He who is in heaven.'

'Aye,' Mother spits, 'and she hath done no wrong in his eyes, and was raised up Godly enough. You have no power to keep her.'

Hopkins arches a brow and glances pointedly over his shoulder at the ranked Puritan men in their heavy black cloaks, the militia propped nervous at their pikes. He needs make no answer more than this look, because he knows already what most women come to learn: the men will not save you.

The Beldam's canny eyes dart about. She softens her voice. 'We are but poor women, Mister Hopkins, yea—' she begins, 'but in our poverty God has bestowed on us a spiritual lucre—'

'Then perhaps these sad events might teach thee *ways and means to live better*, madam,' Hopkins interjects, watching her face closely.

They are words my mother recognises, surely. 'Bess Clarke.'

Hopkins enjoys watching this understanding move over her face, the knowing close in around her. 'Mistress Clarke has confessed, madam,' he continues, 'to the most hateful crime of *maleficium* – and named thee her confederate.'

'She lies,' my mother answers, not missing a beat. The men who crowd behind her have fallen silent now, sensing that higher stakes ride on the outcome of this confrontation than they had thought. We all like to have a lark or three, but no one *actually* wishes to see a woman hung, her skirts soaking with piss and throat's blood froth on sackcloth. It is a horrible thing. Not amusing any more. Or do they? It is a curious thing in human nature – even in such weighty matters as death and life, most seem to find themselves concurring with whomever spoke last. The Witchfinder and his bright armoury of smiles, my mother wet to the bone and visibly shaking, for all her fierceness – some of the observers on each side begin, reluctantly, to peel away from the crowd and head homeward over the green, thinking it begins to look a bad business. Others mutter among themselves, angrily. To think, perhaps, that the women, the termagants, may have been hard done by. The likes of Clarke, West and Moone have, after all, been clung to the ragged verge of Manningtree for many years now – who is this upstart Suffolk Puritan to trouble the town's hard-won peace, tenuous as it may be? The big war is bad enough. We need concoct no little-brother-war of our own.

'Aye, the Old Mother lies,' one of the men is heard to mumble.

Hopkins lifts his head and passes a gaze over the assembled, their faces blurry and indistinct in the pummelling rain. 'If you are innocent of any wrongdoing, as you say, madam, then you have nothing to fear in accompanying us. It is only our reverence for thy—' He churns his slender, gloved hand in the air here, as if searching for the correct word, '—thy most *tender* femininity—' It is the Puritans' turn to laugh, now, '—that has given us cause to demur from seizing thee by force.' There is a flint edge to his voice.

I picture my mother's face, fierce and carved out in the flickering torchlight. She trembles. Her chin lowers, and she tells him *God will judge us all, Hopkins.* Numb-boned and broken in the rain, she offers out her wrists, at last, for binding. *God will judge us all –* 'and you,' she says, looking up into the Witchfinder's shaded face, 'will taste blood.'

'Amen,' he answers, with a smile, and turns his horse about, leaving the Beldam West to be hauled behind by the militiamen.

18

Iconoclasm

I wake fully clothed in a strange, hard bed. I know this is the Thorn. That whitewashed, unjolly bone wedged in the throat of the estuary. I am held somewhere on the upper storeys. The door to the chamber has been locked without; this much I established the preceding night, in a state of high panic. It is morning now. Carefully, I listen to the croon of the floorboards below, the deep of men's voices, the wheeze of a staircase. There is an art to understanding the language of a house, and ordinarily I am an adept – but the Thorn is wholly unknown to me. Who is to say if this scrape or that snarling noise be a woman held in the adjoining room, or merely a rat nesting in the wall? What is to be done with me?

Somewhere outside a cock's crow overtures the watery dawn. I rise and go to the window, where I can see the sun casting a pristine glitter on a slice of the bay. It looks to have rained all night, and the empty cobbled street shines with a latticework of reflected sky. A rider in black trots from the wagon yard below, due west, his face turned away from me. I look around the room. A candlestick, an empty dresser, a washstand, thin curtains of starched yellow net. The door opens. John Stearne's pale face appears there at the crack. He clears his throat. There is a riding cloak folded over his arm. 'Miss West?'

I make no answer.

'An – a – a rider has been dispatched to Colchester,' he continues. 'We are to take you to the White Hart, and there await the militia.' The Hart – Master Edes. I feel my belly jolt, but not in the agreeable way of old.

I look down at my stockinged feet. 'I have no shoes, sir,' I say.

'We are to ride,' he says, roundly dismissing shoes in concept. He is cheered, I think, by my seeming docility – probably he thought I would fly hissing for his watery eyes like a cat. In Stearne comes and begins to bind my hands again, humming to himself a sprightly Roundhead ballad. I hear a peal of laughter – rueful, a woman's – from a nearby room. So there are others held here too. He brusquely fastens the cloak at my throat. It is too big and stale with tobacco smoke. He pushes me out the door and into another black-cloaked figure. I raise my eyes to find myself face to face with my mother. Her own eyes are weary and bloodshot, her head and shoulders uncovered and bent, and she whispers *Becky*, with a dubious sort of relief, because here I am, and alive. But also – *here* I am. I think we move to clasp each other, then, but with our hands bound we are able to affect only a mere fleeting sort of collision before Mister Stearne and the Constable pull us apart again.

'Well, isn't this nice,' says Helen Clarke, from the stairwell. She looks to have been seized from her own bed while still in rumpled smock. Her hands are bound, a dark scowl fixed on her face, and the hand of a militiaman on the back of her neck.

I am about to ask her when she was brought here, but Stearne gives me a little shove toward the stairs, and our sad party is pressed down toward the common room, where yet more men sit folded at the bar and smoking clay pipes in the high-backed chairs, pistols and swords in their laps – Hobday, Hockett, Edwards, Norman, Wright, even the Minister. A whole swarm of Puritan, come to see the thing through, tired and pleased with themselves. No Master Edes here. Curiously, no Matthew Hopkins neither.

'They have Bess Clarke as well,' Helen calls back over her shoulder as they hustle her toward the door. 'I saw. This is all her doing, you know. Her mouthing off,' she laughs, bitter and derisive. 'Just watch. I shall choke that old 'agtail with my bare hands.'

'Why not let these kindly gentlemen do it for you?' my mother mutters, leering sidelong at the assemblage. A few of the more courageous return her gaze with solemn curiosity, fingering the pistols arranged across their knees; but most keep their eyes averted from the Devil's 'eft-hand brides, from either guilt or superstition. A witch can, after all, curse by looks alone.

It is bright and chill outside. A salt wind hits me full in the face, like the world wants me to know it has missed making me uncomfortable during the time the men took over. There are horses, saddled up and stomping, and Stearne lifts me into the pillion seat with an undignified wheeze, before climbing up behind. It is all too much to feel real – here I sit on top a horse and assailed by the wind, when any other morning I would be yet to squeeze the sleep from my eyes. On the estuary, white birds rise through the haze of dawn. I watch them over Stearne's shoulder, watch them wheel and flock as he chucks the horse on to Manningtree at the head of our spare procession. There is a rosiness like a crust of sugar on the wet chimney stacks and the distant spire of St Mary's. I remember April is nearly come – wide and wet April, the season of hare coursing. And my twentieth birthday, a bare week from now.

We are soon at the town proper. The crowds of the preceding night are not dispersed, but prowl the roads wakeful and raggy from the immanence of Sathan, as though he might come tripping round the corner at any given moment, and could be scooped in a net like a butterfly (with a prize for the first man to do it). A whole desultory mess of townsfolk line the High Street and throng about the Market Cross, and the sun still barely risen. There are shouts and some tipsy whooping when we are spied approaching.

A dockhand with a livid bruise on his right cheek breaks away from a group gathered at the bottom of South Street and falls into step alongside Stearne's horse. 'My brother,' he says, 'my brother Joshua Turner, who was cast away at sea,' he calls, reaching out to pluck at the hem of my skirts. 'Had the Devil a hand in his drowning? In God's name, tell me!' He splashes sour wobble at his mouth from a jug in his hand.

'Away, man,' shouts Stearne, and spurs the horse to a brisk trot, but Turner holds step, grabbing up a fistful of my petticoats. I kick at his wrist, but his grasp holds. 'Joshua Turner,' he demands, 'my brother! He was to be wed at midsummer!'

'Turner, you say?' my mother hollers from the Constable's horse behind. 'That was my work!' She lets out a good barking laugh, and as she no doubt intended, the dockhand lets go of my skirts and reels on the spot. 'My master bid me fetch his soul. It was I who raised the storm and called the sea to gulp his hoy, good lad. Pray a minister could hear to shrive him over the clapping of the thunder, else he burns in Hell!' This raises gasps from the massed crowd and a howl from George Turner, who calls her the Devil's whore and runs toward her, beer plashing over the stones. The Constable draws his pistol, and I see pale faces clustering at the windows, brought from their beds by the ruckus in the street, by George Turner's anguished wailing.

'Peace,' cries Stearne, pointlessly, 'peace!' But his money and authority is forgot now.

A window squeaks wide. 'Murderess!' screeches the baker's wife from her ledge, and who knows which of us she means – and the cries of *witch*, and *she confesses*, and suchlike grow, and of Exodus 22,

so commendable in its clarity: *thou shalt not suffer a witch to live.*
More flock down from South Street, jeering and pointing at us,
drawing their fingers slowly across their necks in cut-throat fashion,
and my mother laughs and waves, blithe and near-queenly, until
little Edward Wright scoops a handful of sodden muck from the
gutter and dashes it at the Constable's horse, and a cheer goes up
as her cheek is spattered with slime. The horse rears and then the
narrow street rings with a deafening crack, the Constable having
hollered and discharged his pistol into the thinning mist. A cloud of
smoke and the white stone of the Market Cross in the slant light of
morning, then I am grabbed up from behind and bundled, uncere-
moniously, inside.

We are lined on a bench in the upstairs parlour of the White Hart,
shivering in our various states of underdress: Old Mother Clarke,
who was brought here first, then Helen Clarke, Liz Godwin, myself,
and last the Beldam West, proud and prickling. Our hands are
bound in our laps. The crowd is gathering in the street outside,
lively, baying. Hopkins and Stearne remonstrate with the Constable.
The Constable insists that the rabble can be held off until the law
arrives from Colchester.

Hopkins is grim-faced. 'Half the town quarrels in the street – and
two more yet to be brought.'

A glance is passed down our bench. 'Two more,' Mother sighs.
'Snatched Queen Mary herself away from a black mass, have they?'
I try to shush her. Hopkins' cold eyes flick toward us.

'The Baronet,' Stearne interjects, patting at his glistening upper
lip, 'the Baronet will not brook this. They are riding in even from
the villages . . . Misrule. Utter . . .' He trails off and peers out of the
window, with a whimper of desperation. If the tendentious Baronet
himself were to describe Stearne's situation, he might say the man

was caught between Scylla and Charybdis: to keep the Baronet's favour, John Stearne pretends to greater influence over the townsfolk than he actually possesses, and thereby puts himself in danger of losing that favour when the townsfolk do something the Baronet does not like, that Stearne could not have stopped them doing even if he had tried. What does the loss of favour mean to him, with his big house, his fine apparel, one of Manningtree's two looking glasses? The loss of favour does not mean death. No, nothing even close to it. And still he sweats like a pig.

The clamour grows as a band of militia approach – Widows Leech and Moone in tow. The women are squeezed through the morass under a slop of shouted curses and rotting produce before they are brought, shaking, to join us. A curl of lettuce quivers in Margaret Moone's expansive bosom. Their faces are puckered and pale beneath their shawls.

'Hello, Mother,' Helen sighs.

The Widow Leech sighs and shakes her head, with some *Oh Jesus wept, oh Helen,* and so on, and we all slide down the bench to make room.

'I cannot speak as to the others, but I am no more a witch than thou art, sir,' Liz Godwin blurts suddenly at Hopkins' back.

'God in Heaven,' mutters Leech, 'save your breath, Liz – and the rest of us aches in the head.'

In come Mary Parsley, Priscilla Briggs and Abigail Hobbs – now seasoned witch-prickers all – their hands primly knitted before red-speckled aprons. Anne Leech and Margaret Moone both bear marks, Mary soberly informs Hopkins – the Widow Leech as many as three teats about her secret parts – 'and they are not piles, sir,' Goody Parsley adds, earnestly, 'for I know well what those look like, having been troubled by them myself.' Hopkins clears his throat and thanks the good women for their service, extending God's own gratitude, too, as garnish. Then they leave, to lay their bodies down at last in their hard, spotless beds. Helen manages a laugh. My head aches and there is a gnawing in my belly, as I have not eaten a scrap nor taken any water since the night before, and it must now be nearing noon.

Margaret Moone settles and peers down across the bench. 'What is this happening?' she hisses. 'Where's my Judith?'

I tell her in a whisper that Judith is bewitched, supposedly.

'Oh, is she now?' Margaret sits back with a whistling sigh. 'That little slut.' Then she starts and sits up again, rounding on me. 'I wish very much you had not told me,' she says, panicky-voiced.

I tell the saucy creature that I only told as she asked me, and Margaret begins, frantically, to explain that now she is the one who will be supposed to have done it, the bewitching, 'because how else would I know of it unless I had done it? Unless I am to feign surprise when they tell me,' she continues, twitching her bound hands in her lap, 'but I cannot dissemble – oh, mercy . . .' and so on. Her face trembles most pitiably.

My mother rolls her eyes and says it matters little what any of us did or did not, and says we ought to keep our heads and hold our tongues. And I, being sick to my stomach of my mother and her great act of knowing best, tell her to shut up, and tell her that all she has done so far is to make everything worse for all of us, with her talk of the clapping of the Devil's thunder, and that, indeed, the crowd would have strung us up then and there, were it not—

And just as I am hitting my stride we are all scared out of our skins by Hopkins slamming his pistol down hard on the table, and shouting that he will have silence. I oblige. Never before have I seen Hopkins forfeit his composure. His slender body twitches with threat, like a whip in the hand of God. Stearne squints dubiously at his companion. We may have fallen silent, but the crowd without have not. Singular cries and complaints stick sharp out from the generalised din: *cozenage, Pope, prodigies*. Even the racket of a summer fair or barn fire might not rise to rival it.

Mister Hopkins takes a fortifying breath, and adjusts his hat and doublet. 'I will go and speak to them, Stearne,' he says, a strange light coming into his eyes. 'As the Lord calmed the storm on the Sea of Galilee – and the disciples were filled with great awe, and said to one another, *who is this, that even the wind and the sea obey him?* Keep them—' And here he waves a hand toward us, '—keep them silent.'

Stearne moves to grasp Hopkins' arm, saying, 'Matthew, are you sure it is wise to—' but Hopkins is already gone.

We hear the crowd fall hush as the dark figure of the Witchfinder emerges from the inn. An attentive silence, a soliciting silence. Those at the back of the ten-deep crowd, those from the neighbouring towns and villages, crane to get a better look at this champion of God. Is he as they expect? I wonder. Younger, probably, at twenty-five. Brittle and drawn as a scholar, his hair hanging black and uncombed around his shoulders. His long, rigid figure, held with cultivated grace, suggests a near-arachnoid watchfulness. He looks as though his heart has been many times broken. As if, beneath his black velvets, it quietly breaks at that very moment. Here is Matthew Hopkins, Witchfinder General, with the hard soul of a warrior and the famished cheeks of a saint.

A nervy woman standing at the front of the crowd reaches over the linked arms of the militiamen who stand guard at the doorway to pluck at the lace of Hopkins' sleeve. 'They say,' she gulps, voice shaking, 'that the witches held a mass in the wood...'

Slowly he turns to look at her, and reaches out to take her hand in his, *imitatio Christi*. 'Fear not, Goodwife,' he says, 'their cozenage has ended.'

As he speaks the dam breaks to an inundation of remonstrance, gossip, query and simple terror. One woman crows that there are no soldiers, and Essex is left unprotected.

'Aye,' her neighbour pipes, 'and if London falls to the King—'

'You don't want the soldiers here, love – believe me,' haws a pungent shipwright, in response.

Another agitator insists that the Papists are landing ships at Harwich every night, sent over by Queen Mary. He has witnessed it, in fact. 'My dear neighbours—' Hopkins begins, but his words are lost in the general fulmination. The crowd teeth and bicker and press up against one another, a brindling mass of rags and pox and fear, their grain blue with mould, their cattle keeling in the fields, their worlds wrung out of shape by the red hands of war and hunger. 'My good people—' he tries again, but finds himself now beset by a coughing fit. The taste of blood. He presses a kerchief to his lips, and the linen comes away scarlet-flecked. He sees the scarlet flecks. Swiftly he presses the rag into his palm, and closes his fist around it, hides it. But not swiftly enough. How many see? Enough that I later come to learn of it. Those nearest to him, at the front – the woman who touched at his sleeve – fall silent, aghast. *By the blood of the lamb. Brown apples.* Swallowing down a mouthful of imbrued spittle, he wipes his lips on the cuff of his sleeve. At last he speaks, hoarse and wet-eyed. 'My good neighbours,' he hails them, again, 'for surer than e'er before, I know ye to be righteous. They say where God has his proper church, there the Devil will build his chapel. My name is Matthew Hopkins.' A thrill runs through the crowd, a murmur, a swell specked with the dismal -itch of that new and baleful appellation – *Witchfinder, Witchfinder. Matthew Hopkins, Witchfinder.*

'Aye,' he continues, finding his strength again, his mouth curling into that unassuming smile, his words driving up through the brank of red phlegm in his throat, 'Witchfinder, some call me. But I know naught but God's word, see naught but that which He chooses to reveal unto me. Seven women we apprehended this night,' he continues, gesturing expansively toward the inn behind him – expansively, and unwisely, for the crowd become riled again and his voice is drowned. Now comes a cry of *Hang the witches*, and a stone that clatters against the inn's whitewashed fascia – *The Devil will be driven from here!* – and another. The crowd surges again, the militia straining to push them back with their pole arms, swearing and spitting; Christ is arisen in them indeed, like a boiling milk that threatens to spill from the pail.

'My good men!' cries Hopkins, desperate now. 'Be not afraid, for the Lord giveth strength to his people, the Lord blesseth his people, his elect, with peace! These women are to be tried in accordance with the laws of our land. For do they not disdain us as lusty rebels, Godly folk that we are? And lovers of anarchy? They say we are but a company of cobblers and butchers and shop-men who frolic in and make sport in misrule! It is not so! Our new and hallowed nation will be a—' Hopkins' efforts to quiet the crowd are vain, and he retreats, wide-eyed, toward the inn.

'It is no wonder the Prince of Hell hath come to work his darkness here, where no saints nor roods remain to fright him away!' shrieks some poor wretch at the rear of the throng, and these Laudian sentiments prompt a ruction of howls and execrations. *Death to the bishops* and *thou shalt not make unto thee any graven images*. Word elaborates to blow, then kick, then brawl, and the goodwives scatter in all directions, shrieking like geese, or else tear up fistfuls of their sisters' hair and beat their little hands against the cloaked backs of whichever bystander they can reach. Black and red and rumbling, riled halfway to rebellion, and if the Devil himself did walk abroad among them none would be any the wiser, so preoccupied are they. One of the Bergholt men – a huge brute bursting from his ragged doublet – has carried a sledgehammer over. He raises it to the forget-me-not sky and brings it down on the mossy stone of the old Market Cross (which had stood there, some said, since the Confessor's day).

We sit and listen to the riot unfolding in the street below, there being nothing else we can do. We watch Stearne watching at the window. We try to read the twitching movements of his face as a sailor reads the infinitesimal shudders of a compass point, and thereby assess the likelihood of our being torn limb from limb in the burnished sunshine of this late-March afternoon, while the baby birds trill brightly from the thatch. All is unmade, just like that. His kingdom come.

19

Suspects

The day wears on. The crowd thins and its rage becomes diffuse. Some begin to limp ale-drunk back across the fenland to their own villages. Some retire to the Red Lion to fill themselves with meat pie. Others go with the rooters to the churchyard of St Mary's, to watch as the faces of angels are scratched from the headstones. By the time the wagon arrives at sundown to take us on to Colchester, shame, exhaustion and a fleeting spring downpour have conspired to clear the streets, and Mister Stearne leads us unassailed, hobbling barefoot, out into the dusk. Where the Market Cross stood there is now nothing more than a blunt horse-tooth stub, the mud strewn all about with whitish chips of rock. Our hands remain bound, our clothes dirty, and our faces sour beneath our caps. All of us are hungry, but only Liz Godwin is foolish enough to say so, whining to the waiting Hopkins that we have had nothing to eat all day as a militiaman hands her up onto the wagon. *You are hungry. So what,* I think, ungenerously. *All England is hungry.*

Hopkins ignores Liz Godwin. Hopkins seems to ignore everything. He stares off into the nullness of the blue-grey sky, upright in the saddle, and there is no exultance in his face as we are led away. I think perhaps he feels guilty, for we must make a sorry sight, Moone, Leech, Clarke and Mother and me, in our varying states of undress and incapacity and unwholesomeness. But no, it is not that. It is because, I think, this is not an end but a beginning. Binding our hands will not close the matter, and neither will shutting us away in a cell. No. The cat is out the bag, as they say. The cat, in fact, bounds hysterically off between the clouds and out across the county, where the warm unplanted fields wait for thunder. I wonder if he feels foolish, having made such a work for himself. Probably he feels foolish because he is dying. Is there any endeavour that does not seem exceeding trivial to a man faced with evidence of his mortality so vivid as red blood from his own body in a white kerchief? We all saw it, hanging from his pocket as he remonstrated with Stearne and the Constable. We all heard the coughing, the gasp, beneath the open casement. Blood. Your own blood is meant to stay inside you. This is something every Christian agrees upon, Papist or Puritan. As far as I know.

I am the last to mount the wagon. Hopkins looks toward me as I haul myself up onto the bed. 'You have much work ahead of you, sir,' I say.

'God grant me fortitude,' he replies, quietly, and turns his horse about.

The wain draws out of Manningtree, and Helen and I rest our chins side by side on the endboard and peer out from between the flaps to watch the town diminish in the last largess of the evening sun, until the rooftops are little more than brassy flecks at the hip of the Stour. 'What a kelterheap,' Helen sighs, scratching her chin. I feel her black eyes shifting sidewards to my face, and I stare resolutely out over the horizon, feeling in no mood for tattle. But my feelings count for naught. 'Pining for your dear love already, are you?' she says.

'What? No.' But I am. I am thinking of how he did not come. How John Edes was nowhere to be seen. How we lay together, and

I told him that I loved him, and then he left. Left me at the mercy of Hopkins and Stearne. Left me to die, for aught he must know. I turn to peer at Helen. She is some years my senior, a worldly girl. Or as worldly as they come in Manningtree. I could ask her what it means that he did that, and if she thinks he will come back. But I do not, of course. Instead, I ask Helen if she has had word from her husband, Thomas, who fights for Parliament. Within the question is another: *and will you send word now? And will he come back, and put reason between us and death?*

'Not since before Christmastide,' she yawns. 'He was garrisoned at Taunton, then.'

'Where's Taunton?'

'How the Devil should I know? Out down west somewhere.'

I ask if she did not think to follow him into the army, as some women do their husbands. She wrinkles her face in a sneer. 'What? Join the baggage train with the whores and the bone-grubblers? I think not. Besides, have you heard how the King's men are wont to treat with the wives?' Her eyes brighten: 'Slit your nostrils and slash your cheeks with their dirks, then say, as I heard it, "A favour I do thy Godly husband – hereby freed from the bondage of lust."' She laughs, briefly happy and cruel, and I think it a shame she was born a girl, and is therefore unable to ride to war and indulge her happy cruelty as fully as a boy might. She is perversely unruffled, with a few stray wisps of black hair peeking from the corner of her frayed cap. Plump, pretty Helen.

'I would take a gash or three to my face sooner than be hung,' I reply, and look pointed into the wagon, where the older women sit slumped about on the thin carpet of straw. They have been lulled to sleep by the cart's gentle rocking – all but my mother, it seems, who sits upright in the furthest corner, behind the driver's box, her lips twitching.

'No one's going to hang,' Helen mutters, lifting her eyes to the deep blue evening. 'No one's going to hang *me*.'

'They hang the Irish women,' the Beldam remarks, darkly. 'The Gaels.'

We turn our heads to look at her, Helen and I.

'The Irish women in the baggage trains, who follow behind their husbands that fight on the King's side. The Roundheads string them up quick enough.'

'They're Papists,' Helen shrugs.

'And you, madam, are a witch,' my mother smiles. 'Which is much the same.'

We fall silent, and listen to the rain sputtering out soft against the bonnet. As the sky clears and the wagon turns northward over the rise to the Colchester road, the setting sun paints Hopkins' shadow stark against the canvas as he rides alongside – every detail, down to the gadflies troubling about his horse's muzzle. Old Mother Clarke murmurs to herself through a fitful sleep.

At dusk our short convoy stops just outside Dedham. We are given water to drink and bread to eat – the first sustenance I have had in the greater part of a day and night together. It is a sultry duskfall of the kind that often comes with the in-between days of spring: the grass a hard enamelled green in the low rays of sunshine, already a crust of young moon visible over the treetops. But it is hot in the wagon, and we all quite quickly become vindictive toward each other, so confined, sweating into our soiled gowns. It begins with Liz Godwin ruminating over her last bit of bread that she might escape our current predicament by claiming she needs to piss, then running down across the fields and into the wood, where she might slice off her bindings on 'a sharp rock'. The Widow Leech scoffs that Godwin has read one too many pamphlets, whereat the Widow Moone expresses doubt that Godwin can read. Godwin insists, resentfully, that she can. My mother suggests that she would like to see Godwin attempt to enact her escape plan, and that she ought to try, given that we could all use a laugh. Godwin says we are become cruel, and Helen gasps in frustration that 'sirrah, so has the world entire'. Liz Godwin then attempts to close the exchange by saying that perhaps we all ought to finish running our mouths for the evening, given that the reason we find ourselves in this situation in the first place is because some of us enjoy to speak – and be spoken of – more than is proper for Christian women. 'Fie,' my mother snaps at that, 'no need to peck around the point, Liz. Speak thy mind,' bristling all ironically in her stays. 'Liz Godwin, with her husband and her airs, and the husband an air himself for all the good he's done her. Where's thy dear Thomas now, eh, Liz? Riding over from Manningtree to save us all, is he, a regular Bevis of Hampton?' Liz Godwin begins to cry then, and the rest of us glance around at one another, wall-eyed, none able to summon the energy that comforting her might require.

A few minutes pass, and peace seems at last re-established, when Helen gets it in her head to poke the bear again. 'At any rate,' she says, settling her shoulders back against the endboards and grinning, mighty pleased-seeming with herself, 'it is Mother Clarke who has brought us here. If we *are* to be setting out blame.'

And Old Mother Clarke, far away on the faded meadow of her wits, smiles a vacant smile to hear her own name spoken. 'I told him,' she says, 'that we could go down to see the ships.'

And Helen, riled, throws her bound hands up with a 'Lor! And cracked now too, is she?' Then my mother calls Helen a cross-grain slut and tells her to hold her tongue, and Liz Godwin continues to wail over the top of all of this, and Margaret Moone hisses for peace and asks what good quarrelling will do us now.

'Mistress Moone is quite correct,' says Mister Hopkins, who has ridden unnoticed to the rear of the wagon and parted the canvas with a gloved hand to watch this skirmish unfold within its rancid confines. A kerchief covers his mouth. We all promptly fall silent as you please, and he gazes down at us with an obscure curiosity as though we were specimens of something pinned to a baize. He lowers his kerchief, and there is his infuriating smile. 'Why not turn your evidently restless energies to prayer?' he suggests, and the suggestion is somehow a taunt. 'Entreat God for the deliverance of your souls, rather than—' Here his eyes flick to Liz Godwin, '—plotting to effect bodily deliverance by your own . . . misguided enterprise.' His horse huffs and swings her tail and we all stare down into our laps, like children caught in a lie.

'I did not mean it, sir,' Liz says, quietly, drawing her knees up to her chin. 'It was idle talk.'

'Good,' Hopkins replies, and assures us that for all our earthly suffering might bring us closer to God, it would bring him no pleasure to have any of us whipped. He drops the curtain and trots his horse away again, his shadow heavy on the lambent canvas, to summon back the militiamen and driver. We sit in silence as the horses are hitched, and soon the processional moves on, away from the setting sun. 'They will be dismayed,' Mother Clarke mutters, quietly, rubbing a gnarled finger down her nose, 'pangs and agony will seize them, and they will be anguished like a woman in labour. They will look aghast at one another; their faces will be aflame.'

And Liz Godwin primly declares that as she recognises the aforesaid as a passage from Isaiah, she hopes all question of her being a simple and illiterate person might be put to bed.

20

Colchester

Colchester is smelled before it is seen. Sewage and smoke and the bitter underworld odours of gunpowder and churned black dirt on the humid evening air. I have never before seen a city. I draw back the canvas and peer out into the twilight. The wagon moves along a road in the midst of a wide scrubland, scored around with deep trenches and earthworks, big fences of sharp stakes jutting half-visible into the dark sky like the teeth of a thin-mouthed piscivor. I feel Helen jostle in beside me at the endboard. She seems, thank God, at last lost for words. These are what are called fortifications, which I have read of before but not seen, and I think that Jonah himself cannot have had a more terrible view than this, even as he slid down the gullet of the whale.

We must reach the gates, for behind us comes the demand for papers, the requisite underfed cry from the wayward watch-boy of Parliament, or King? We twitch, we draw our ragged shawls about ourselves as best we can, as the gatekeeper tugs up the canvases to inspect the wagon's human freight. His face is mottled like a collop in the light of his upraised storm lantern. 'Well,' the guard laughs, peering through the gloom at the white shapes of us, 'they don't look like much, but they certainly smells like a lot.' And though half of us have in the last day been spread down naked and had near-strangers press pins into our bodies, this feels like the greater humiliation: that this stranger, this Colchester man, should be given licence to look on us, to count us off, to say how he finds us all smelling.

'Their malice may be concealed by deception, but their wickedness will be exposed in the assembly of the righteous,' Hopkins says, Proverbing mirthlessly from atop his horse, and I hate him very deeply for it.

'Aye, I suppose it will,' the watchman says, jovial.

Then Hopkins says some other, brief, official things.

'Seven for the castle!' the watchman calls. I hear the gate creak open. Here, too, rumour has preceded the Witchfinder. The militiamen must ride ahead to clear a path for the wagon through a high street thick with the refugees of the Essex countryside, burned or starved or in other ways driven from their homes, gaunt faces and hands upraised to the Godly gentleman in his velvets of immaculate black. I keep my eye to the crack in the canvas, because I must know what a city looks like. It looks like cripples shuffling along the streets with begging-bowls and signs hanging round their necks that read PLEASE I AM HUNGRY GOD BLESS, while other men hardly less poor preach outside the inns and meeting-houses to knots of solemn onlookers, against walls peeling with postings for bear-baiting and piss-prophet empirics. It is a vagrant who keeps a lousy, half-bald little monkey upon a leash, dancing to the keening noise of a reed flute. It is a lot to look at, but very much more to smell: the vinegar of sweating horses, woodsmoke and hammers, the piss and beer and malady, feast of herring and open sores. Seeing the wagon with its escort of soldiers, a streetside divine shouts out, 'The wages of sin is death!', and the contents of a ripe privy pail are plashed against the canvas. A woman bent in the stocks, grey hair hardening around a deep red bloodied gash. A city, it appears, is like a famine, and also a pleasure. And there are other women, women I think may be whores, their gowns of dirty bright taffeta cut halfway down their breasts, their hair arranged in sticky piles of ringlet and trim. Some of them look so beautiful, leaning from upper-storey windows with their rouged cheeks and men's arms around their waists, and I wonder that their lives can be so full of sin and yet they do not seem to suffer for it, as I do. Then I wish to be them, though that is a sin in itself.

And then it is gone, all gone. A heavy iron grille drops between myself and the world and sin that will continue, I suppose, to happen, and was happening before, though I did not know of it.

The wagon squeezes across a bridge over a fetid waterway and into a second deeper maw, this belonging to the castle. I lean right out through the canvas and over the endboard to see the full height of these towering walls. It is doubtless the biggest thing that I have ever seen, the battlements seeming lost as high as the pitchy cloud, and crows flapping speck-like round the higher gullies. We are unloaded in some kind of gatehouse, and Mister Hopkins stands attendant as the gaoler exchanges the ropes that bind our wrists for heavy iron manacles. At first it is a relief, to be able to roll my shoulders and move my hands again. But before very long, the iron chain grows heavy, a whole fat baby's-weight on the arms, and we are sent single file down twisting corridors, a staggering retinue in rags, and there is that aimless manhood smell again – top notes of gunpowder and steaming leather – for the upper levels of the castle house a garrison of parliament soldiers.

We come to a long passage lined with cells. The prisoners know the gaoler's heavy tread as wicked children know their mother's. He moves down the narrow corridor like dawn, and they stir, they make their suffering known. These are the sounds: shouts, banging, weeping, belly-laughter, all blent into one long animal whine, an opulence of pain and want. And the smell is worse, too, of leavings and slime, bread left to go bad. It makes me think of the Bible, and what the Bible says of Hell, and I think that this cannot be what God intended when he decreed it all – that men would take the most memorable parts, the juiciest bits, and use them as a playbook, by which to make their earthly world be full of tiny hells under roofs of thatch and slate, over which they claim they have dominion, in which they shut each other up. But of course, he is God – he must have known exactly what men would do, and not cared, or else figured it into his arrangements.

The man in the last cell is notable for his silence. I look between the bars as I pass, last of our miserable line, and see a gaunt man propped on a narrow cot. At sight I know this man to be what they call a Cavalier, one of the King's men, and wonder how it was he was captured here, in a parliament city. It cannot have been long ago, since he still has his clothes – a high-crowned hat, and a coat of deep blue velvet with a rip at the shoulder and a silver of lace at the cuffs, and this draped across his legs like a blanket. His dirty hair is worn long. He catches my gaze through the bars, cocks his head and grins. 'Oh,' he says, in a voice like a purr, 'I hear you have been very wicked girls.'

21

Gaol

We are locked all together in two dank, windowless chambers in the bowels of the castle. Windowless, in this instance, does not mean possessing a narrow skylight through which a shaft of early-morning sun or a peal of birdsong might trip, sweet and aliment, though faraway; it does not mean having a mere barred cavity that admits the gales and spitting April showers; it does not mean furnished with a rough aperture overlooking a bare, featureless courtyard in which the daisies, rolling their pale yellow eyes up from between the broken flagstones, might become allegory for fragile hope in adversity; it means windowless. Two windowless chambers, about twenty yards by twenty yards, floors of rough board covered over with straw, two pails for our muck. We must burn candles all day to have any light at all, and these at a cost of two pence for each stump of tallow – a debt that is dutifully recorded in the gaoler's log book to be paid upon release. Or by our reluctant relatives, if these exist, upon our death.

There is nothing to indicate what time of day or night it is, in these chambers, except for the muffled rhythms of the castle above. Our bodies lose their unique character in the perpetual gloaming, and in my eyes a Rebecca becomes a Helen becomes an Anne becomes an Elizabeth becomes a Margaret, greying rags and tattered cap, the specificity of a shape of a leg, or the sharpness of a collarbone jutting from the disordered neckline of a nightgown, lost. We sleep heaped atop one another. Our bodies twitch in our sleep as though already strung from the gallows. Mother is quiet. Mother is, cruelly, sober. The gaoler comes once in what must be the morning, to empty the stinking slop bucket, and once again at an indeterminate later hour to bring stale bean bread and water. It is by his visits that we tally the length, in days, of our captivity. In the first weeks the miserable prison victuals give us gripe in the guts, and our cells are choked with the hot stench of run-off and worms. Animals know greater dignity. Animals have scraps of meat, bones to chew. Three days and my teeth want so badly a thing worth biting at.

The gaoler himself is a man with a shining bald pate and long, fantastic whiskers. He is named Edmund Ferriter. He has a reputation for extorting most of his charges with a rare and almost endearing brio, but he is frightened of us, the Manningtree Witches. At least at first. Down the rickety staircase from the upper storeys and into our cells he shuffles, quickly quickly as he can on those bandy legs (the legacy, I think, of childhood rickets) to haul away our slop bucket or deliver lights, with the Lord's Prayer trembling constant on his lips as talisman against our underworld power. Like an animal, however – let us say, a magpie that slowly becomes accustomed to the presence of a sleeping dog – his confidence soon grows, and he begins to hang back at the threshold of the cell, and pick curious circles about us, asking if we might show him some of the Devil's proper cunning, show magicks (or else Helen a little more of her lovely ankles). Helen obliges, a wanton smile and a flash of dirty calf. Her manacles are duly removed. Her mother's, too, in exchange for a few kindly looks, a little fondling of his long black moustaches.

A week passes, then ten days, then another few days, and it has been two weeks, and then our system fails us because Master

Ferriter the Turnkey is visiting more often to make eyes at Helen, and because, having nothing else to quarrel over, we naturally settle upon the day of the year as a point ripe for contention. My mother will insist it is Mayday, at most – the Widow Moone thinks it closer to Midsummer. This is what passes us for sport.

We have other games, as well. We pick the lice off one another and feed them carefully into our precious candle-tongues, watch them pop and shrivel. We make a competition of our tender reminiscences of the sky, lying prone in our bed of straw with our itchy heads pressed close together, staring up at the dripping roof of the cell. Old Mother Clarke begins, saying how she remembers one high gold summer morning all mottled with tiny clouds, like the angels had bickered through the night and torn off handfuls of one another's wings, and these came to settle in the sky as though against a glass (Mother Clarke is too helpless now to hate, though Helen tries very hard to, and will not play the sky-game). I remember how I saw the seabirds rising massed through fog on the pale green water, so perfect it looked painted. Widow Leech remembers a night when the fumes beneath the moon appeared to arrange themselves into a perfect fleur-de-lis, and this she took to be a very ill portent of Popish supremacy.

Once a fortnight has passed, I begin to see these dungeons are not rightly like Hell at all. Suffering here is not like a burning lake of sulphur – nothing so absolute. It is a slow and vexatious accretion of a matter at the nostrils and behind the ears and in the tear ducts. It is itching and smelling like a vagrant's mutt. There are a whole host of creatures, mice and lice and rats and the rats' fleas, all gathering at the thin boundaries of the flesh. I wonder what I look like to the intrepid harvest mite, with his six red hungry legs, nosing through the crusted dirt of the Via Solis to find a soft pouch of blood at the base of my forefinger? I watch him, almost fondly, like he is a pet.

Little Red. It is ours no longer – our skin, our blood. There is no keeping it clean, there is no keeping it with modesty, there is no using of the body in a proper way.

Upstairs, the gaoler tells us, a summer fever has set in. A cutpurse and a cattle rustler have died in the night with their eyes wide open – a bad omen – the meat of their bodies cooked over with weals. 'It seems the Devil followed you here,' he tells us. There is a wailing in what must be the night. I suppose there are ghosts in very old places like this, trailing green ermine through the twisting corridors, their pennants rippling in the odourless winds of Limbo. It does not frighten me. Here we live together, under-ghost. And under the Old Devil too. Mother Clarke speaks to him in her sleep – or at least I hear her talking to someone. 'I have brought them,' she will say, in her wafer of a voice, 'I have brought them for you—' and sometimes she adds, 'Banbury cakes, as you like them so well, my dear,' and I know she is dreaming of nothing more untoward than puddings, but sometimes – sometimes she does not.

I keep one eye open, always, in the dark. He could be here, right beside me, and I would scarcely notice. We could light a candle to find him reclined in the corner, dandling a red velvet slipper off his slender foot, smiling proudly at his work. I did not know what I believed before, but now I know even less. An arm – it could be anyone's – is thrown across my breast. Cold fingers brush against my cheek. In the dark I see my mother curl in on herself, pressing her hand into her side as though digging out elfshot – the cramp-pains attendant on an emptied belly.

I dream. Taste a mouthful of forest and roll over, opening my eyes to find Master John Edes staring back at me, his eyes simmering with reproachful tears. Or else Master John Edes but dead now, maggots and luminous crawlers in the sockets where his eyes ought to be. Sometimes I dream of the Devil, who rolls me up in the waxy petals of some great flower and tells me to be very still or else they will catch me. But I can never remember what his face is like, upon waking, or who it was he meant to hide me from.

Helen draws a skein of cotton from the fraying cuff of her night-dress, with which we play at Cat's Cradle. The others watch in rapt silence as we count the figures off over our crossed knees: cradle, diamonds, fish, saw-horse, the two crowns. Our other entertainments are not so wholly frivolous. We discuss at length who we think it is that put us here, where we are always hungry, where we are going quite mad. Names are thrown out, repeated like a chant, our daily commination: Goody Miller, Goody Hart, Briggs, Hobday, Taylor, Croke. 'The Devil take them,' sneers my mother. 'The Devil take them all. For I will it, now – though it cost me my soul.' None of us argue.

'Do you think they shall cut off our heads?' gulps Margaret, massaging her pouchy dewlaps.

'*Madam* Moone,' smarms Helen, mouth downturned and marked near the centre with a sore. 'Airs even as she trembles by the side of her grave. They won't cut off your head, dear – they'll string you up like a thrice-damned whelp.' She makes a *chh-* noise, pops and rolls her bright black eyes. *Airs* are some of the worst things a woman can have.

'God help us,' Margaret whimpers.

'He won't,' answer three others, all at once, but I do not know which three, the candle being extinguished, their voices joining in the dark.

The Widow Leech tells us of a woman in Ipswich, when she was just a girl, who was burned at the stake for witchcraft. 'Murdered her husband with a Black Fast, so they said.'

'Women are only burned for treason,' explains my mother, our expert recidivist. 'So killing the King, or killing a husband. Or asking the Devil to do you for either, I suppose.'

'But half the country wishes the King dead,' says Liz Godwin, frowning.

'I'll do it for them, if they'll let me out,' Mother coughs.

We eat, sleep, stare, think, stink – though each but the last, only barely. The unending nature of our confinement begins to make in the mind a state dream-like – how best to explain it? I begin to feel I no longer exist as a *person* in any sense. I am not of God or Adam's image. I am a collection of wasting organ and rebel impulse and skin parched of sun. What I am is not human, and deserves not a name. Life does not exist, either, with the words by which we give the experience name and weight now empty of meaning, now blunted by banging against this thick entire darkness: day, night, rain, down, up, walk, nothing, nothing. Rebecca melts. I am able to flourish like this. My person, so frail and as yet indeterminate, shimmies out from beneath the tyrant's boot like a voile; my mind, already so fractional in its operations, had no use for the conformities now stripped away. No. I have no wish to stay – if the turnkey left the door standing open, I would flee in a blink. But it suits me, more or less. In another life I might have been an anchorite, or perhaps a martyr. Or like Saint Simeon the Stylite shut away behind circling walls on his fifteen-foot pillar. I am pleased, at last, to be peculiar – at my emptiness I invite the Devil to nurse, for I would be known well.

I speak little and listen much. I am listening on the thirty-sixth night of our captivity, when we have snuffed out our sullen candle and retired to our shared bed of rags. Margaret Moone's snoring, Mother Clarke's muttering, and a new sound over the moaning of the fever-stricken prisoners held above. I hear footsteps, and I hear the scrape of spurs on the stairs. I flinch at the sudden skewer of lantern light as the door is cracked open.

'Miss West,' Hopkins calls, his face invisible, his voice unmistakable, 'come with me.'

22

Chapel

At first I do not know if I am able to trust the withered muscles of my legs to carry me further than the threshold of the cell. But they do. Out of the cell, up the stairs and down the corridor, my eyes stung by the lavish flame of the Witchfinder's lantern, its brilliance almost divine-seeming after my long month locked away in obscurity. The other prisoners moan and shift in their fevered sleep as we pass. Hopkins walks quickly, and does not look behind to ensure I keep pace. He keeps his kerchief pressed tightly over his mouth. Curiously, I no longer mind the smell, which must be ripe, must be morbid. I have been inured to stench through long and close acquaintance.

I barely remember these corridors from when we were brought here, and I am surprised to find we emerge at the gatehouse. Here, he produces a set of heavy iron keys and begins to remove my manacles, silent and businesslike. He stands close to me to do this. I can smell summer rain on his clothes, and the fields too, fresh. He wears corselet and tassets now, of polished metal – why? Have the roads become so dangerous, or has witchfinding? – beneath his black coat. The same broad-brimmed black hat and collar of sable beneath the same thin, raptor face.

'You are to stand hard by me, Miss West,' he instructs. I rub at my wrists, stunned to be suddenly relieved of the burden of manacles. It is a queer feeling – like my hands, so light now, might simply pop from my wrists and float up to the ceiling. He moves closer and secures a heavy cloak and hood at my throat. A mixture of excitement and terror churns the paltry content of my stomach.

'We are not going far,' he says.

It occurs to me that perhaps I am being taken somewhere I will not come back from. He takes my arm, but I stay right where I am. 'Sir – will I be returned? My mother . . .'

He peers down at me, piqued. 'You will be returned here,' he says.

The night is of a deep, enchanted blue. A big moon glazes the rooftops beyond the castle wall. And stars. Stars! My breath catches in my throat at the freshness of it all, tender *all* almost forgotten, so many stars clustering and wandering, small and large, dim and unfeeling and legion. Hopkins, watching me, makes a nearly amused sound. 'Sometimes beauty is the only argument He has any need of,' he says, his hand on my shoulder.

I look at Hopkins, who is still looking at me. I am surprised to hear a man like Hopkins express his faith in terms so graceful.

'I had forgot it,' I say.

He waits, then – he gives me some minutes with the stars before he grasps peremptorily at my arm and leads me away from the glowering bulk of the castle, toward an arched entryway in the thick walls of the grounds. From there to a narrow side street, lined with slumping houses and boarded shops that stand silent; it must be late indeed. Or very early. There is no other soul abroad, it seems, except the two guardsmen who have followed us at a distance from the castle, their helmets gleaming in the moonlight. I suppose they are here in case the Devil deigns to lend me his teeth that I might tear

Hopkins' throat out. Carefully, I pick my way barefoot across the slimy cobbles. Rain drips from the gutters, and somewhere nearby I hear the quiet whickering of stabled horses, dreaming their horse dreams. Smell them, too. They smell better, more wholesome, than I do. At the end of the side street is a squat, square building of mottled stone, with a high, vaulted window on the north-facing wall. Hopkins pushes open the heavy door and draws me inside. It is a chapel. Or was. Now it is a bare stone chamber with an empty altar table and torn hangings, the walls scribbled over with profane arabesques of graffiti. It smells of stale piss.

Hopkins removes his hat and sets the lantern down on the altar table. 'What know you of Saint Helena?' he asks, drawing over an upturned stool and an empty crate from the corner. 'Sit,' he commands, waving me toward it.

Saints. It is a test.

'I know nothing of a Saint Helena, sir. The scriptures make no mention of her, sir, to my memory.' I sit down obediently on the crate, by the altar table. It is cold in the chapel, and the vaulted stone throws my voice's mocking twin back to me – *I know nothing of a Saint Helena, sir.* I find that without meaning to, I am grasping at my wrists, so accustomed to the manacles have I grown. I feel denuded without them, now the Witchfinder has brought his gaze to rest on my dirty face.

'She was the mother of an emperor – the first emperor to abandon the pagan faith of his forebears and embrace the one true God,' he explains, brightly, and – curiously – not as though he imagines I am very stupid. 'Some say she built this very chapel. I thought – perhaps – you might wish to pray, while we are here?'

Another test. I look about at the rough stonework and peeling plaster, and shrug. 'I need not visit a chapel or a church to pray, sir,' I answer, tartly. 'God lives everywhere.'

Hopkins' mouth curls into the customary rictus. 'Quite so,' he answers. 'Victuals, then?' He produces an oily packet of brown paper from the inside of his cloak and opens it out upon the altar table. Blushing cold cuts of ham, thickly sliced, and a wedge of cheese. I feel my parched mouth flood with spittle just at the smell of it and fall hungrily on this repast, tearing at it with my bare, dirty fingertips. I must look half-wolf, but I am too hungry to care. Hopkins watches with remote interest. Watches my fingers move in and around my mouth, I notice. O defilement.

'I feared you had come to take me to trial, sir,' I say, swallowing.

'Trial? No,' Hopkins answers. 'You are not to be tried until the summer assizes.'

It was late in March when we were arrested and bound over. It must now be nearly June. The summer assizes must be soon indeed – a matter of days, even. I feel a sudden rush of nausea that is stymied by Hopkins speaking again: '. . . *next* summer's assizes.'

So we are to wait a year or more. 'And we are to be kept at the castle?' I ask, my voice edged with indignation, for all my efforts to remain temperate, to appear obedient.

He peers at me. He nods. He takes a little leather-bound log book and pencil from his cloak and sets them out on the altar table. So that is it. Those with the authority to pass judgement upon the matter, and thereby close it, have other priorities. The witches of Manningtree are beneath the notice of such lofty persons – and so, by implication, is Matthew Hopkins, minor country gentleman. It galls him, I can tell.

I wipe my lips on the back of my hand. 'It is very long to be bound over, sir,' I say. 'There is gaol fever above, and Mother Clarke is already ailing in her—'

He holds up a hand for silence, in that way he has. He restores his smile. 'Perhaps you are truly blessed, in your bondage,' he says, 'for such hardships bring us closer to God, in his infinite mercy. Removed from all temptation, one might more readily beseech Him for knowledge of your sins and, with ready mind, perform your penance. Truly,' he continues, 'I do not think there be man or woman alive whose soul would not benefit by so . . . concentrated a period of reflection. For the Lord is the Spirit, and where the Spirit of the Lord is, there is freedom.'

I watch him as he says all this and I can find nothing there. Where does he keep himself? What is Matthew Hopkins, truly? Did he have a mother? Is she alive, and does she know her son? What makes him laugh? Did angels come in the night with knives of silver glass to pluck out his squirming mortal heart and carry it away? 'Yes,' I say. 'I will entreat God.'

He presses his pencil to the blank page of the log book. 'Now,' he says. 'At the house you share with your mother, there was a cat. Large and yellow in colour.'

'Vinegar Tom.' A flash of loose body, limp paw, red fur. We had a cat once. A cat in a house, curled up by a fire. How little I appreciated the quaint nicenesses of it, that being-a-*person* business.

'Vinegar Tom,' Hopkins repeats, noting it down in cramped shorthand. Shorthand – for the first time in so many weeks John Edes wanders into my waking mind, in his fetching blue doublet, with his battered leather portfolio tucked under his arm. 'And did your mother christen this cat?' Hopkins asks, 'or otherwise anoint it with oils?'

'I do not think Tom would have borne *anointing*, sir.'

'From whence came the cat?' he asks, his mouth set straight as the London road.

I say I know not. That we had Tom from since he was kitling. For as long as I can remember. Hopkins' pencil loops to a sudden halt and he raises his eyes to my face. 'As long as you can remember, say you? Unusual longevity for a cat, do you not think?'

'A – it was a turn of words, sir,' I shrug. I lack the strength for these games. 'You think him an imp, sir – a familiar, as you call them. But he was just a cat. A good mouser, in point of fact. Liked to curl in a nice sun-spot, as cats are wont.'

Hopkins cants his head as if to say *perhaps – or perhaps not*, then smartly turns a page and rummages in the satchel he carries. This time, he produces two most peculiar objects and lays them side by side on the table, on the greasy ham wrappings. They are two dollies, manikins about the length of a palm, one in likeness to a woman and one a man, in miniature hats and gown, faces scratched from nubs of wax. A skein of yellow horsehair sticks from beneath the tiny cap of the girl-dummy, and a sewing needle is impaled through her ribboned waist. He studies my face as he sets them out. 'Do you recognise these?' he asks.

I do not, I tell him. But my stomach tightens, because these images were not made without purpose – and they were not made far from Manningtree, either, if Hopkins is showing them to me. 'Have they resemblance to any particular person, to your eyes?' he asks.

I look back down at the manikins with their obscene, bloodless little smiles. They remind me of England – and therefore death. 'They resemble everyone,' I say.

'And what of this one, in particular?' He takes the girl-doll up in his gloved hand and holds it out before me, teasing at the blunt fuzz of yellow horsehair with his thumb.

'Judith has red hair,' I say.

His smile widens, and I cannot immediately think why. And then I realise I have given it away. His face says I have, and that it works to his benefit. The cold cuts, his gentle politesse, and he made me forget I am swimming with black snakes. As punishment, I twist my fingers sharply at the tender skin of my wrist. It was Master Edes who told me of Judith Moone's bewitchment, on the very night it was supposedly made manifest. Edes, Stearne and Hopkins – who else would have known? No one. And now I have told Hopkins that *I* know. And he himself did not tell me, and neither did Stearne, and so it is only a matter of time before he might surmise who did, and that to tell me Edes must have seen me – and what we did when he saw me—

'Judith Moone? No,' he sets the dummy back down by her stiff brother. 'No.' Pause. 'Though it is interesting that you mention her. No. It was Goody Hart I meant. Goody Hart was with child when you were last in Manningtree . . .' He remembers to flatten his smile just in time, remembers to pretend he is not enjoying himself. 'She was miscarried of her babe, not two weeks hence. A son.'

'Oh,' I say. 'I pray that the Lord will comfort her, in her loss.'

Hopkins peers into my flat face. I peer back, mild and inexpressive. He moistens his lips. 'Goody Hart has said that you long held her to be your very great enemy,' he ventures.

'That is untrue, sir,' I answer. I tell him that though Goody Hart and myself were not companions, I never wished nor spoke any ill upon her.

Hopkins dips his chin. 'You will remember she was in very robust health when you left Manningtree,' he says. He keeps saying it like that: *left Manningtree, when you were last in Manningtree*, as though I have chosen to take up residence in the Colchester gaol on account of the serviceable appurtenances.

I shrug again. It begins to wear upon me, this back-and-forth, this circumvention. I tease at a string of pork gristle caught between my teeth to show him he no longer warrants even my pretence of rustic good manners. 'If you mean to say, sir, that it was by some curse her baby was lost, then it cannot have been I who worked the conjuring. We have been kept at Colchester a month or more.'

'A witch,' he smiles, 'may easily be in two places at once, by way of her compact with the Devil – distance is irrelevant to the efficacy of her black arts.'

Then what, possibly, can I say to exonerate myself? Does he even hear what it is he says, a man of learning? 'One might think, sir,' I snap back, unwisely, 'that being so, we might be more trouble to imprison.' *We*. Why did I say *we*?

'These manikins were found in the home of Mistress Godwin,' he says. 'In a scuttle.'

So Mistress Godwin has been making images and sticking pins in them. Making images, sticking pins in them, then hiding them at the bottom of a coal scuttle. It is not the sort of thing for which an innocent explanation can be found, if Hopkins speaks true. I remain resolutely silent, now. My noises serve no purpose. I am just a dog yapping at the end of the rope. I look at the manikins again, with their scratchy wax faces, in their little suits of rag. You would think things used to do evil would have a greater smell of evil about them. Hopkins himself does.

He takes a long, deep breath. 'Look at me,' he orders.

Dutifully, I raise my eyes. His voice is soft now, almost gentle, as he reaches out to take my hands in his own. The dark leather of his gloves feels soft and expensive. I realise I have never seen his hands uncovered. 'Whatever sin weighs on you, Rebecca,' he says, 'God will forgive, if you only give it name. I wish to *help* you, not harm you. You have been like unto Daniel in the den of the lion, your soul imperilled . . .'

I find I am gulping back tears – of frustration, though who knows what Hopkins might think engenders them. 'Whether my soul be imperilled or not, sir,' I say, 'I cannot tell you what I do not know.'

Hopkins inhales sharply through that beatific mask he has fixed over his face. His grasp of my hands tightens. 'There are witches who have offered their babes up to the Devil fresh from their bodies and still glistening with the mucus of their wombs,' he pants, 'who consign their progeny to Hell ere they have so much as named them. Does he come to you, Rebecca? Does your mother bring him to your bedside?' His tongue twitches at the corner of his mouth. 'Do you whore yourself to him?'

There it is again – the excitement. The thrill nested secret in the black of his eye. I take my hands away and his gloved fingers close on the air. Perhaps, I think, remembering the man in black my mother spoke of, I ought to entertain the possibility that he is correct. I feel empty all of the time. The Devil's claws might account for it; a once-long-ago scrape made at me, so the fiend might seed his malice there. I have sinful thoughts, always. I have done sinful things, now and then. I press the flat of my hand to my hot cheek, and realise my breath is held—

'Anne West, your mother,' Hopkins continues, his voice constricted, 'has confessed before witnesses to the conjuring of storms by the aid of the Devil. You are complicit in *maleficium*, Rebecca – unless,' his voice tapers to a mere sibilance, the better to insinuate itself into the cracks that begin to patulate on my aching skull, 'unless you were compelled to it.'

And there it is. The bargain is proffered, the terms are set out: my life, for my mother's. He cannot put it any more clearly without compromising his Godly posturing. What Hopkins wants is the anguished testimony of a once-chaste maid forced to Sathan's concubinage by her own nefarious mother – what magistrate would not take pity on the former? Or fail to condemn the latter?

'I know nothing of the Devil,' I find myself saying, 'nor of conjuring, nor familiars, sir.'

His mouth twists petulantly. 'Tell me, Rebecca – have you your maidenhead?'

In one instant that breaks up to multiplicity as it courses along the channels of my mind before crumpling inward and collapsing back upon itself – picture a flock of starlings that twist in the sky, each bird a sensation – I feel it all again: the wet cotton clinging to my back, the heaviness of John Edes on top of me, the prickling of his beard a fire at my neck. I flush red – I can feel that as well, in the here and now, where I sit in a ruined chapel on an upturned crate and Hopkins' eyes bore into my face. I should not have to tell him. Has he even the right to ask? I am forced to conclude, *probably*. My voice quivers as I perjure myself: 'I am unmarried, sir, and have my virtue still.' Sin breedeth sin.

Hopkins sniffs. Hopkins softens. He snaps his log book closed and returns Godwin's dummies to his satchel. I will be taken back to the castle, to the wide grave of that cell. No more light. Now my return is imminent I feel I would do anything to remain here, above ground, where people move their arms and look up at the stars whenever they are of a mind to. All reason dissolves in a black, welling despair. I could do it now, confess. It is so easy to say words, and words are all he wants from me, no more. He waits expectantly, one beat, three, and yet I have said nothing. Then he rises from his seat. 'I am bound for Aldeburgh,' he tells me, lifting the storm lantern.

'Aldeburgh,' I repeat, for no particular reason but to prolong my relative liberty.

'Indeed,' he sighs. 'Unchallenged, the Devil's confederacy has proliferated amply. I beseech you, Rebecca,' he says, taking me by the shoulder as I rise from my seat, 'to consider what I have said. To consider your soul. I will return when I am able.'

The guardsmen lead me back to the castle, manacles creaking

at my wrists again. They are frightened of me, their faces kept deep in their collars to evade my Evil Eye – but they need not bother themselves. The clouds have cleared at dawn's approach, and I keep my gaze lifted to the fulsome morning stars like a thirsty man at a fount, all thoughts of Hell and Hopkins in those moments flensed by the bright distant light. I will spend tomorrow in the dark again.

23

Witchfinder

May becomes June becomes July, but how might anyone know? The rain is relentless, insistent, subsuming all in its cinereous element, beating out a death fugue on the rooftops and on the fields where men lie blown to pieces. It beats on the meadow in Huntingdon, where on a sodden afternoon the Witchfinder orders men to dig, eventually unearthing a mouldering effigy of straw, man-shaped: drawing the iron nail from the poppet's trunk, Hopkins effects the miraculous recovery of a local landowner's convulsive daughter, and three more witches are led away in chains. They meet a woman in Skeith who keeps a great fat bee that drinks blood from the tip of her thumb. Word spreads. *Why was a spotted cat seen to jump in at your window? Why do your sweetpeas thrive so, battered by the storms?* These questions matter, now. A parson's wife in Rattlesden is found halfway out the dairy window when Hopkins' party arrive, her ankles flailing in the air. Up go her skirts so that her fundament might be inspected for teats right then and there, by which she giveth the Devil suck. Matthew Hopkins, Witchfinder General, is a name known. And women know to fear it, and know to hide their fear.

The Justices and Guildsmen and Ministers are his *most humble servants*, they write. They want him. They send letters entreating him to come, to Shotley, Tattingstone, Witham – as far away as Northamptonshire. They offer money. Not so much that it might offend the sensibilities of a Puritan ascetic, but enough. Enough to make him rich-ish once his horse is shod and stabled, his mutton dressed, and a few shillings have been pressed into the prickers' sticky hands. Enough and a little more again to make the long nights of watching and the bumpy rides down flooded country lanes worthwhile. But he'd do it for free, of course. He'd persist in God's work if a whole army stood in his way. Fortunately, no one does. Or no one of consequence, at least.

It is clear there is no time left for modesty, if the Devil's muster is to be stymied. God's warriors can ill afford to wait at a discreet distance while suspects kick and flail beneath the needles. Often, now, they are resisting, and they must be held down for the pricking. Bodies. Women's bodies, so many. Thin and fat, old and young, in all their fleshy actualness. The strange parts, the birthmarks, the dark spots on their necks, the warts and blebs, the breasts veined like fine blue cheese. He observes all this with a clinical detachment. None of it arouses him, which he also finds interesting. An aspect of the Devil's unnatural power, he supposes. Or are the elect immune even to sins of the mind? He pictures reaching out a hand to touch a bared breast or the underside of a thigh, and in his mind he sees the flesh wrinkle at the barest graze of his fingertip and a thousand black spiders burst from that point of contact, flicking ichor from their hairy legs. Yes – these are not women, but bags of spiders in women's skin. Tissue filled with dark stuff. God. It is horrid. It is fascinating. He dreams of caves. He fasts frequently and severely. He dreams of Rebecca, gets hard again. It is not her body, it is something else. Her soul? She moves him. Why? Big eyes, like a woodland creature. He thinks of touching her shoulder, back in the chapel. He will save her, she is not like these. *Get behind me, Sathan.*

And what is Mister John Stearne doing? Whatever Hopkins tells him to. He's the soft power in their partnership, the one who warms the magistrates and brings the provincial constables to heel, who serves a sop of jocularity with Hopkins' caustic wash. He drinks the good port pressed into their hands by the bottleful by grateful, Godly townsmen. He buys a slashed-sleeve jacket lined with chartreuse silk. It belonged to a dead man, but what does that matter? He may be the least-cursed man in all of England, near-pneumatic, irascibly perky, practically coin-operated. At the inn in Yarmouth he is deep in his cups, and won't shut up about Agnes, *his dear Agnes, the sweetest creature in all God's creation, I swear it*, whom he loves twice as much now as he did when he married her. Hopkins knows his Proverbs very well – wine is a mocker, strong drink is raging: and whosoever is deceived thereby is not wise. Hopkins also thinks, quite ungenerously, *I hope you are being cuckolded. I hope your sweet Agnes is inviting the baker's boy into your marriage bed as we speak, John Stearne.* Then his own cruelty frightens him, and he worries the Devil's taint has spread to him like a pox from witch-flesh, though he touched it only with his eyes. He fasts again, for three days this time, taking only bread and water.

Thirty-six women, then thirty-seven women – and two men, as well – fill the town jails. Almost all of them are poor. Some are vagrants, reduced to sucking milk raw from the teats of cows put out to pasture unattended. Food – its lack, its necessity – the prevailing preoccupation. For England is now gripped by famine. The fields go unplanted because the planters are soldiers now, and what harvest there might have been rots in the fields. The wheat is freckled blue with ergot, and makes men mad, makes them see things – in the sky, in their wives' eyes. The soldiers who were planters drive away the herds and plunder cellars out of spite, or for shits and giggles. Baptise horses. Rape. Children are whipped for feeding cheese to dogs, then for feeding the dogs anything at all, and then for refusing to eat the dogs themselves, when there is nothing else left to make a meal of. Imps are sent to steal pork-crackling and cakes cooling on windowsills. No one is quite sure when it happened, but a threshold has been crossed. Strain your ear to the roll of summer thunder, and hear a door swinging closed behind. It is an upside-down time. If the herring and trout were to rise from the waterways and take flight like birds it would surprise no one, for surely God's Day of Judgement is near at hand, and in that time hail and fire will be mingled with blood, and locusts will fall upon the fields in breastplates of iron and with the faces of men.

The Witchfinder General is not the only son of East Anglia who rides the ensorcelled wind into the annals of history in this year of 1644. The hero of Marston Moor is the Earl of Manchester's Lieutenant General, one Oliver Cromwell. He is well beloved by women because he is known to love his own mother well. Like Hopkins, he says he went to Cambridge (unlike Hopkins, he is telling the truth). Like Hopkins, he would be handsome, *if*. His deep-set eyes gaze up from shrivelled broadsides across the country. A good face he has, sturdy and sober-looking, if lacking in refinement. Plangent, stoical, a holy mount of nose. Puts you in mind of Proverbs: *counsel in the heart of man is like deep water*, etc. And where else do we hang our hopes? The Medici Queen is fled to France, and that is something. The Godly folk of London strip themselves of lucre to offer up to Parliament, carts full of pewter plate and bushels of good cloth pulled past the crystal husk of Whitehall. Burn and salt the earth, for He cometh; raze all this unholy Albion. It is madness, delightless and hot.

By September Hopkins and Stearne, our two holy itinerants, are in Sudbury, Suffolk, where a local witch has sent her dog-familiar to rock the crib of her neighbour's newborn son with such wicked enthusiasm that the babe fell out on the flagstones and broke his neck, among other sundry mischiefs. The gobber-toothed old dame in question freely admits to being given the sandy dog by a gentleman in a fine black suit with silk points, who told her, quite brazen, to name the beast Sathan. The prickers can draw no blood from a mark by the woman's left armpit, and gamely she utters maledictions and curses upon everyone in the room as she is needled and walked before the hearth. All in all, an easy twenty shillings. And yet Hopkins seems inexplicably melancholic as he sits down to dinner with Stearne that evening.

He stabs his fork at a hunk of brawn. Their conversation is limping, sporadic – but turns, eventually, to the Manningtree women, who languish in gaol at Colchester. 'It will all be for naught,' Hopkins says, 'if the Manningtree women be not convicted. The whole enterprise.' He cringes involuntarily at the word *enterprise*. The wrong word, conjuring images of receipt notes and scales and accounting books. And yet the word that sprang first to his mind.

Stearne has no doubt they will be convicted. He counts the arguments out on his fingers: two confessions, Godwin's manikins and enough extraordinary swellings upon their bodies to cook a pie of. 'Besides,' he adds, with a mercurial grin, 'half the Godly folk in town have grievance against them, and will happily testify.'

Hopkins swirls a nub of gristle around in his gravy, and grunts that he will not have himself made the instrument for the vengeance of a vexatious fishwife.

Stearne shrugs, not much caring what he is, provided it is not hungry. 'What does it matter, when the end is the same?' he asks. 'The malefactors are removed and the good, God-fearing folk—'

'—are free of the Devil's predations,' Hopkins sighs. 'For the time being.' This is how they talk – like they are heroes. Perhaps one of them believes it.

Stearne smiles. 'Our duty done.'

Hopkins slumps back into his seat, with a weary look. 'The Prince of Air is cunning indeed,' he breathes, rubbing at his eyelids. 'In the smallest motes of inconsequence he frames havoc... from paltry stones builds his hateful palace. The girl,' he says, 'Rebecca West.'

'Trough-eyed little thing with the nice...?' Stearne's fork clatters to the edge of his plate as he makes a squeezy-squeezy motion with his hands.

Hopkins ignores him. 'I must secure her confession.'

Stearne sits back as well, picking at his tombstone teeth with a dirk. 'A confession – a display of contrition – would recommend her to the Justices,' he says, between stabs. 'But her mother...'

'Now the brother shall betray the brother to death, and the father the son; and children shall rise up against their parents, and shall cause them to be put to death. So saith Mark.' Hopkins knits his fingers in an attitude of prayer.

Stearne jests, chuckling, that the Lord himself can scarcely know the Gospels as well as the Witchfinder. Hopkins stares holes into his blasphemous associate's head. Time to change the subject. Master Edes – have they had any luck in tracking down their erstwhile secretary? Stearne rummages in his jacket pocket for pipe and tobacco pouch. Agnes has heard word from Bicks, the innkeeper, that Master Edes sent for his possessions.

Hopkins blinks and waits for further explication. Working with Mister Stearne is often an excruciating affair. 'And where,' he eventually asks, 'did Master Edes ask that they be sent?'

'Oh,' belches Stearne, 'Harwich.'

Hopkins allows his hands to fall to the tabletop, his taut mouth relaxing into a smile. 'I see. Thank you, Stearne.' He drums his thumb against the tabletop and peers out of the window at the leaden night. 'Master Edes gave her lessons, you know,' he adds. 'The West girl.'

'I should like to give her *lessons*,' says Stearne.

His clay pipe scuds across the floorboards as he falls from his seat and onto his side from the force of the blow. Then the toe of Hopkins' boot collides with the hard cartilage of his throat, and he brings his arms down over his head with a whimper. Through the hard rasp of blood in his eardrums he can hear Hopkins, hear him saying *sinful, thou degenerate, thou slime, neckless fat* – and Hopkins kicks him again hard, in the belly, and blood spackles the backs of Stearne's teeth and he tastes bile and brawn in his mouth, the black beating like a rope tightening around the throat – *mercy, Matthew, mercy*—

And it stops. Stearne, arms still clenched down protectively over his head, spits blood on the dusty boards and on the sleeve of his jacket (the new one, lined with chartreuse silk). He blinks up at Hopkins with a look of astonishment, as though he is only just now understanding his body's capacity for pain.

Hopkins stands over him, long and dark, shuddering with the vehemence of his own anger. His pupils have contracted into spots on the whites of his popping eyes. *Good*, he thinks. *Good. Feel it. Be wounded at last.* He breathes, slowly composing himself. He reminds Stearne that he is a married man. He reminds him that they are God's warriors. All this he says reluctantly, resentfully, like a wronged child making an appeal to a hated father's authority. He knows he still needs Stearne and his mercury-manners. He knows their association cannot be broken yet.

But there is something inside of Hopkins. He feels it, the Devil's hand tightening around the stem of his brain, the Devil's fists beating at the inside of his ribs. He imagines his extremities – his toes and fingertips – turning black as though frostbitten, or leprous. If he was scratched, smoke would come screaming from his flesh, or thorns, or horns. It is an intolerable feeling. He wants to throw himself on a pike. He wants to fuck something to death, probably the world. He saw the Devil once, cloven feet trampling the bluebirds on his mother's Turkey rug – how could it all be so *wrong*—

The innkeeper's wife appears at the doorway, roused by the noise, and claps a hand over her mouth. Without apology or explanation, the Witchfinder grabs up his hat and cloak, pushes past her, and flees.

24

Lonely Men

The port of Harwich is where England bares her rump to the continent. The ships come in from the curling spit of land called the Hoek van Holland, ships laden with fine linens and Flanders lace and, anecdotally, Papists. It is early evening when Hopkins arrives and stables his horse at the inn, where he feels fortunate to go unrecognised. He cleans himself up, takes a glass of good port, and walks over toward the foreshore in the fading light of day.

Little sloops and caravels dip in the docks, their sails furled. A few seamen linger about the harbour, smoking and playing cards. Dutch, for the most part. They pay little mind to the Witchfinder, this dark stranger who falls to his knees at the jetty to pray. They have fought their own lowland wars over God, and they know how peculiar it can make men, to see the High Father coming staggering home, his white beard speckled with blood or shorn by dogma. A few look on Hopkins sympathetically as they unload the last of their cargo, as an individual clearly fraught by spiritual crisis. Sailors are sensitive people. They know such men are best left alone.

Hopkins looks out over the placid grey sea, hears it suck against the planks beneath his bent knees. The rain, the endless rain. There is something about rain over the sea, something stately in its utter drab superfluousness. It makes the world seem a mausoleum. The

Witchfinder's prayer goes something like this: *God, Father, guide me now, for I have erred. I look around and all I see is chaos – and for a moment, I allowed myself to be swallowed, lost to confusion and sin. I am thy instrument. Guide me to thy will, use me to fulfil it, then strike me down, if you must. Only let me serve you, before you give me over to the Devil entire.* He opens his eyes to look out over the ceremental horizon and feels out his body from the inside, rarefied and refined by hunger and insomnolence. This is the way he likes himself, keen as a whetted blade, secretly suffering. How could it be anything but providential, that in that very moment he hears the tender resonance of church bells a short way off, calling the faithful to evening prayer? And how could he do anything but answer that mellow summons?

He finds himself in a small church – little more than a seaman's chapel. A single high window of clear glass over the altar aluminises the dusty chamber, unadorned but for a faded mural on the far wall depicting the Genesis, and the Fall: fawns and lions cavort ill-proportioned through pockmarked Edenic splendour, and a fat serpent coils himself about the waist of a pale, pink-nippled Eve. There she stands, poised blithe forever at the moment of lapse, beneath a smiling sun of many rays. Hopkins positions himself by a pillar close to the door, and removes his hat. The pews are empty but for a few old dockhands with sunburned necks who smoke continually, even as the careworn minister ascends to the pulpit and begins his preaching (an insipid remonstrance against the episcopacy that Hopkins recognises as plagiarised, for the most part, from the writings of John Bastwick). The door opens and closes behind him, and a latecomer hustles into the back pew. Hopkins knows with inexplicable certitude that this latecomer is Master John Edes, so much so that he waits until the preacher bids them lower their heads in silent prayer to peer over his shoulder and check. His patience is rewarded. There, indeed, pressing his hat to his chest, stands John Edes. Hopkins is afforded the opportunity to study him at length. He appears a different man to the one Hopkins sent from the Thorn that chill March evening to fetch the pricker-women: his shoulders are narrow and hunched, his hair now cropped close in the Roundhead style. Hopkins notices that his reddish beard is flecked with grey. Nevertheless, John Edes: the last piece, the keystone.

The sun has set by the time the sermon ends, and the rain clouds, half-disgorged, have turned a roiling plum. Hopkins follows Edes down the narrow streets of Harwich, until, passing under the flaking sign of an alehouse, he sees his chance, and, stepping forward, he grasps for the arm of his former associate. Edes wheels on the spot, and stares, surprised, into Hopkins' smiling face.

'Sirrah!' Hopkins exclaims, with a false and somewhat threatening good cheer. 'Master John Edes. I had not thought to see you here.'

'Hopkins,' Edes replies, on the edge of an inhalation. His eyes skid up and down the narrow street.

Hopkins tightens his grip on Edes' arm. 'It has been too long. How do you fare, my good man?'

'Did the magistrates summon you here? I heard nothing of...' Edes trails off.

'Nay, nay,' Hopkins replies. 'An unexpected digression.'

'I see.'

Hopkins flourishes a hand in the direction of the squalid alehouse called the Stingray, and insists they enter to raise a glass to Cromwell, *for old times' sake*. Master Edes at first protests, but Hopkins is insistent, and the reluctant Edes soon finds himself impelled toward the narrow door.

A single poky room with a sawdust floor. The alehouse is deserted except for two hooded men at the bar conversing intently in French, and the innkeeper, a shifty-eyed little man with tufts of white hair at his nostrils. Hopkins presses Edes toward a sticky corner table, out of sight of the door. Edes still seems dazed by his associate's sudden reappearance. He moves slowly, carefully, like a man navigating the deck of a listing ship, his world suddenly aslant. They take their seats. The innkeeper comes, wholly unbidden, and scrubs a wet rag around the table between them. He steals covert glances at Hopkins, whom he recognises by reputation. His interest is irritating. 'Bring beer,' Hopkins orders. 'Then leave us.'

Two mugs of ale are set down between them. Edes drinks. He wipes his moustache on the back of his hand, a nerve jumping in his jaw. Hopkins knows John Edes will be an easy mark, as all agreeable people are. The man cannot bear silence. Even now, confronted with a void, he rushes to fill it. 'You have made the London news-sheets,' he says, finally. 'You and Stearne. You are fortunate men indeed, to be so called upon by God. "Witchfinder General"...' He lets out a nervous chuckle.

Hopkins smiles. 'A more... ostentatious sobriquet than I would like – but if I might better serve God, being so called...'

'Such purpose,' Edes mumbles, inwardly, stroking his thumb against the side of his tankard. 'A lucky planet, you must have been born under.' He is warming up already, Hopkins observes. Falling into his ease. He has had only a few gulps of beer, so it cannot be that. Perhaps he has been lonely, sequestered away by the sea. Edes peers up into Hopkins' face at last, his blue eyes tired and dim. 'It seemed a bad business to me, back in Manningtree, Matthew. The devilry, choking—' He massages a hand over his throat, '—like smoke from wet kindling. I was...'

'You were frightened,' Hopkins suggests.

'Frightened. Yes. But...' Hopkins watches John Edes search for words. John Edes – this big, winsome man-thing he must baby to the correct conclusions, to the proper names for his mistakes. 'The Manningtree women,' Edes says, carefully, 'are bound over for trial?'

Hopkins nods. He explains that Anne West and Elizabeth Clarke have confessed to the most horrible villainies, and are unrepentant. That the widows Leech and Moone were consorting with all manner of infernal spirits, making images stuck with dressmaker's pins. He watches Edes carefully as he speaks, notices the incremental tightening of the fingers around his beer mug. 'We may never have the full measure of the mischief they wrought at the Devil's behest,' Hopkins sighs.

'And what – what of Rebecca?' Edes asks, as Hopkins knew he would.

'She denies every particular.'

Edes exhales and nods his head, relieved. Hopkins allows him this moment of reprieve to take a deep gulp of beer, before he produces, from inside his cloak, a hat. John Edes' hat, with the square brass buckle. This he places wordlessly on the table between them, and Edes stiffens in his seat. '*I*—' he sputters, uselessly, and, '*That*—'

'Do not perjure yourself by false explanation.' Hopkins smiles. 'Your own sin concerns me not. Rebecca West's, however . . .' He turns his hands palm-upward on the table, as if to show Edes the girl's soul dancing on his dark glove. 'God has bid me extirpate the scourge of sorcery . . . and return to him the lost. Rebecca West must confess. Only by confession can she be redeemed. You know this.'

'What must I do?' asks Edes, his lips trembling.

Hopkins tells him he must testify at the summer assizes. Edes' eyes dart feverishly around the dingy room, like those of a cornered animal. Testify to *what*? he asks, mind bent on the preservation of his own reputation above all else. 'I taught her letters – her catechism – we never – witchcraft, nor the Devil, never . . .' He labours to straighten his face, to click the mismatched halves of it, the frantic brow and the stolid mouth, into place beside each other.

Hopkins was never allowed to hunt – his mother forbade him to ride out to the woods with his elder brothers on account of his weak constitution. But now he feels a little of what they must have felt – the stippled red pelt, the racket of hounds, the scent of blood. 'The Devil's servants disguise their malevolence well,' mutters Hopkins, leaning forward. 'If you cast your mind back to the hours you spent with Miss West, I am certain you will recall instances when her true nature – subtle, devious – was made apparent to you. *Laid bare*,' he adds. 'So to speak.'

Edes' eyes narrow as he listens to Hopkins. He snorts mirthlessly and draws himself back up to his full height. 'You,' he says, shaking his head. 'The *Witchfinder General*. You say you hate the Devil but I think you are very like him. Coming by night in your tall black hat, with your insinuations. All these souls under your power . . . you make of them your play-things.'

Hopkins' lips twitch. He went too far too quickly, questioning the man's honour. He must give him some slack before he reels him in again. 'Happy is he that condemneth not himself in that thing which he alloweth,' he says, taking a sip of beer.

Edes laughs at that. 'You seem a *very happy* man indeed.'

'Rebecca West is the Devil's handmaiden,' Hopkins continues, coolly. 'A cunning wanton. Like to Salome, shaped by her master to draw men into sin. I know it well, John, for she has practised her charms against me too, come cooing and lecherous even as I pleaded with her to forsake the Old Deluder and find her salvation in God.'

'Stop,' says Edes, cheeks reddening, 'you slander her—'

'I do not.' Hopkins' hand stiffens at the edge of the tabletop. 'The Devil hath inflamed her mind and had use of her body. You know it. You know her to be a terrible fornicatress. Swear to it, and ease your soul.'

Edes' defiance wavers. He tugs at his hair. There is some fright in his look, the big white teeth half-bared. Of the fornication, at least, Hopkins is not wrong. Edes feels himself to be no longer special. His sin – and the passion that precipitated it – was not unique, exceptional and therefore forgivable, but *sin*, true and cheap as bad mutton. Slattern. Wanton. Whore. There must be some way to purge it. Some way to wipe himself clean. *Ease your soul.*

'All this,' sighs Hopkins, reaching out to grasp Edes' wrist, 'all your suffering will be ended. Help me. Help me, John, to cut away their rot. Then all will be peace. Do you see? It must begin with us. It must begin with men. We were set above them to guide – to nourish. And to punish.'

He does see. Shame itself a kind of bewitchment. Edes' mind is ruction and tumult beneath his furrowed, reddening brow. *Peace.* Peace is all he wants now – to slough off his guilt and slither away to be left alone in silence. Perhaps saying will lead to believing, he thinks. It wasn't him, it was her, all her, *cooing and lecherous even as he pleaded* – just as Hopkins says – flesh bedizened with sin and raindrops, eyes and skin – some exquisite spell like soft black candy on her tongue—

'For she sitteth at the door of her house,' Hopkins says, quietly, his head bent low over his mug, 'and as for him that wanted understanding, she saith to him that stolen waters are sweet, and bread eaten in secret is pleasant. But he knoweth not that the dead are there, and that her guests feast in the depths of Hell.'

Edes balls his hands into fists and presses them hard against the table, his knuckles livid. 'I will do it,' he says, hoarse and hasty. 'I will testify.'

That easy. Hopkins draws back and takes a long, hard look at the broken man sitting across the table, pretending not to be a broken man as best he might. Edes looks as though he is trying not to weep. There it is again, that seething black powerful feeling. Only this time, it is good. Potent yet conformable, like hard, shining glass over his insides. *Here I sit*, he thinks, *the son of a minister from Wenham, Suffolk – and yet God-like.* He recognises this thought as his first gleeful blasphemy.

Edes' shoulders quiver as he takes a long, resonant sniff, and begins to slowly rise from his seat. The two men look one another in the face. 'Deuteronomy sets the price of lying with a virgin maid at fifty silver coins,' says Edes, with a bleak, ironical smile. He lifts the hat from the table, and turns it in his hands. 'It seems I will pay a higher one.'

'I do not ask you to impute any dishonour to yourself.'

'Nay,' Edes replies, sucking the inside of his cheek. 'You do not. A mercy indeed.'

'I entreat you to remember, sir,' Hopkins murmurs, surprised – perhaps a touch unnerved – by Edes' sudden sanguinity, 'her soul is at stake.'

'I do not think it is her *soul* that so preoccupies you, Matthew.' Edes drains his beer mug.

The Witchfinder's nasty smile inspissates on his mouth. 'You know, a curious thing about the Manningtree case,' he remarks, his tone stringently casual, 'is that seven women – by all accounts simple illiterate folk possessed, at best, of a low animal cunning – were able to achieve by confederacy all that they did. Often, in similar cases, there is a supervisory masculine presence at hand, an attendant conjuror or wizard who serves to mediate between Sathan and his servants, much as a Minister does for good Christian folk.' He watches Edes, poised and pointed. He doesn't need to say it, but he wants to. Edes may be an impulsive wretch, a people-pleaser, but he is no fool. Hopkins wants Edes to see how powerful he is. He wants to show someone who might fully comprehend what he can do.

Master Edes claps his hat back on his head with a little laugh. 'You, Matthew Hopkins,' he says, smiling, top lip despair and bottom spite, 'are the most twisted villain and rogue in all of England. I look forward to reading of your death in the London news-sheets, and knowing at that very moment the Devil is dragging you down to Hell. I do not think it will be like the Hell of your imagining. I think it will be far worse.' He turns on his heel and strides away.

'I will send to you when the time comes, John,' Hopkins calls after him. Edes waves a dismissive hand over his head to show that he has heard, before slamming the door closed at his back. Hopkins drains the dregs of his beer and sits alone, seething. The two Frenchmen by the bar peer silently over their shoulders at him. The only sound is the sputter of the rain against the windows, the plangent squeak of the innkeeper's rag in a dirty tankard.

'Il a l'air solitaire,' one Frenchman remarks, prompting a throaty chuckle from his associate.

He looks lonely.

1645

'Observe these generation of Witches, if they be at any time abused by being called Whore, Theefe, &c, by any where they live, they are the readiest to cry and wring their hands, and shed tears in abundance & run with full and right sorrowful acclamations to some Justice of the Peace, and with many teares make their complaints: but now behold their stupidity; nature or the elements reflection from them, when they are accused for this horrible and damnable sin of Witchcraft, they never alter or change their countenance nor let one teare fall.'

Matthew Hopkins, *The Discovery of Witches*, 1647

It is February when he next sees her. True winter refuses to leave, tantrums, threatens to scatter abjection all over the country again. Dark clouds flex and leer above the cursed cities and empty fields with a renewed sense of commitment to pathetic fallacy. Riding high. The world seems his; he thought it would feel better than it does.

She is wearing a threadbare prisoner's habit now – a straight tunic of grey stuff. Her feet are bare, her hair disordered and filthy, her face like a tissue stretched over the bone. Hopkins finds her inanition shocking. Then he finds it alluring. There is something cold and pure in the vacancy of her huge eyes. He thinks of a painting he saw in Paris, of the Mother Mary draped in cloth of gold, closing her hand around her own breast, which was pale and perfect as a shell. He thinks of falcons, their *qui vive* beauty, their tiny crushable pittering frightened hearts.

25

Cadaver

My manacles are taken off, and then the gaoler leaves. I look around the chamber. I see nowhere I can be meant to sit, nothing I can be intended to look at or remark upon. A storeroom, it seems to be, the walls lined with crates and sacks spilling grain on the dirty flagstones where the rats have got to them, shapeless bulks draped over with dust sheets. It smells odd, unpleasant. I have a high tolerance, now, for odd smells – but this is a special one, full-bodied, a sourness sinister in its proximity to sweetness. And there is the Witchfinder standing before me in his tall hat and long cloak. Everything beyond the four walls of our cell seems unreal to me – something in the manner of a waking dream, ripe with grotesque potential.

He asks me how I fare, knitting his hands behind his back. As though he is a country husbandman passing the brewer's wife on the road to the market. What new game is this? My first thought is that he has brought me to this secluded place to kill me. Or to hurt me, at the very least. I am surprised to find this thought precipitates very little by way of terror. Just a feeling of drear curiosity. He has brought me here to lie with me, is another. But then I remember my matted hair and unwashed body, my lousy scalp and broken nails. Do men not mind that? I cannot rightly say. The gaoler does not seem to, when he takes Helen away. Hopkins clears his throat. 'Miss West?'

Of course. The world remains the world, and in the world there are answers required of me, even to foolish questions. I tell him I am well enough, but that the cold has held from winter longer than we had prayed it might.

'Have the gaoler bring blankets,' he says, as if we would not have thought of it. *Just like a man*, my mother would say to that. Just like a man to suggest the most obvious thing in the world as though it might be revelation to a woman's cottony mind. When it seems to me all the *most obvious things* in the world must be done by women, or else they wouldn't get done.

'We cannot afford to, sir. Our debt in victuals already runs to more than we could ever—'

'I will pay,' he interrupts, scratching at his nostril. Even his kindness seems somehow vindictive. An ugly, expensive accessory. Still, blankets.

'Thank you, sir,' I say. I gaze resolutely at – and shuffle – my dirty feet, and the feeling of his eyes on me seems somehow worse than the lice. I remember, then, when I first met him, that parched Sunday two summers ago. I remember how ashamed I felt of my muddy shoes and fraying stays. How frivolous, now, that feeling seems.

Next, he asks if we are well fed.

I shrug. What is this he is trying to have with me? A conversation, it seems. Very well. I ask if Parliament are victorious yet. The gaoler will not tell us. I do not think the gaoler rightly knows there is a war occurring.

'The Covenanters have taken Newcastle, so soon we will have coal again,' he answers. 'And Queen Mary is fled to France, with all her heretic retinue.'

'And the King?'

'They say he is determined to remain in England and crush the rebellion.'

'For rebellion is as the sin of witchcraft,' I say, and I cannot help but smile.

'And stubbornness is as iniquity and idolatry,' he answers, his voice hardening. I walked into that one. He asks if I have considered what we spoke of when last he came.

'I have little else to do but consider it, sir,' I say. I intend, at first, to stop there, but find I cannot. 'It seems to me that my position is an impossible one,' I continue. 'If a man is accused of murder, let us say, but he can prove that he was at home and in his bed at the hour of the murder, would any Justice not conclude that it was impossible the man might have committed it?'

The Witchfinder cocks his dark head, but does not answer.

'But if a witch can be in two places at once, as you say, then I cannot prove my innocence by those same means. Nor, it seems to me, by any other. I can say again and again, a thousand times, sir, that I am not a witch, and have no traffic with the Devil nor his spirits, and it will account for nothing. But if I say once that I *am*, then it will account for everything.'

I can tell by the way that he looks at me, then, that he has never heard a woman reason a thing out before. Certainly not a woman like me, anyway. And then he laughs. 'You are a clever girl,' he says, and takes a step toward me. 'Do you know why you are here? Why it is you, and not Prudence Hart, or Goody Miller, who is here?' He motions his arms toward the damp cellar walls.

I step backward as he steps forward, and try as best I can to meet his look. 'I am here because my mother is a woman of ill-report and loose tongue. And Prudence Hart and Goody Miller have husbands who might shield them against such slander.'

'No,' he says, his voice soft. Sympathetic, even. 'You are here because you stink of sin, Rebecca. Sin, hot and foul. The Devil has marked you hideously, and every man who sets his eyes on you sees it. How could anyone believe you to be anything but utterly defiled . . .' And then he lifts a hand as if to touch my cheek, and I draw back still further, and I say *no, no.*

He clears his throat. He drops the hand. He tells me he visited with an old friend of ours. Mister John Edes. He parts his lips. He is about to ask one thing, but then at the last moment decides to ask another. 'Do you love John Edes, Rebecca?'

I intend not to answer, to remain silent. But instead I find myself saying, 'I do not know. I thought I did, once.'

'He is to testify at the assizes, Rebecca. He is to testify against you.'

There is a strange squeezing at my chest. The trial – I had not properly considered it before. It will entail those whom I am alleged to have wronged appearing before me. Master Edes, now. Doubtless Prudence Hart, Richard Edwards, Priscilla Briggs. I will have to look into their faces, and hear myself explained, condemned. How I came to be here in the first place is not something I can properly untangle in my mind, who said or did what to whom. There is no neat exchange of action for consequence. I know that I suffer, and that suffering is attendant on sin, so I suppose I must have sinned. I sinned with Master Edes. Does Master Edes suffer, too? I hope so, which I suppose means that I never really loved him. That sweet rank smell is overpowering.

Hopkins says my name. He bids me look at him. He asks me again to confess. Confess, or accept eternal damnation. 'His Day of Judgement is near at hand, and on that day you may yet stand among the righteous, Rebecca. You may yet be saved.' He speaks with a solicitous urgency, his arm outstretched as though to usher my almost-carcass into an embrace, and I am almost tired enough to believe in him, and to want it. *I can no longer stand alone – the Lord will uphold me. Matthew.* It is for the good of my soul he speaks. And yet. The power to deny him remains to me. I feel faint. I say 'Sir—' and I reach out to grasp the wall of the cellar, to support myself, but my fingers graze uselessly over smooth, cold stone. 'Sir. I cannot confess to a sin I have never committed. If it means I will hang – so be it. The Minister will shrive me for what sins I have.' Bile burns my throat.

'You look unwell,' he says, with gentlemanly concern.

An understatement. It is the stench. The rot, I tell him. I ask him, What is it, that *smell*?

'Ah – of course.' I hear only half, then, of what he says of *an experiment. In many matters for you see continental authorities concur with our domestic experts on the virulence of image-magicks, the significance of the sorceress' ministrations to her imp as outlined in the Magia Adamica* – the flickering sound of his lantern passing behind me through the darkness. *And they present other theories I have not yet had the opportunity to test – for instance* – a movement in the dark, a rustling of cloth – *a shrewd token by which a sorceress can be known is that she will cause a corpse to bleed by her touch.*

And though my mind reels I intuit all at once that there is a cadaver in the room, hidden behind the door, and that Hopkins is now leaving through this door, and means to lock it behind himself. I turn on the spot, and in the last gasp of lamplight before the bolt slides home I see a flash of white, dead meat slumped in the corner, greasy tangled hair, and I fall to my knees and I cry out for him to have mercy, beating my fists against the door as he turns the key in the lock. I cry and I keep to crying, until the sliver of light from the corridor vanishes, and his footsteps quieten. Silence. Then I stop crying, because it will achieve nothing, and there is so little left in my body I ought to take care not to waste even my tears.

I see what is happening. The rich boy thinks that if he cannot fright me, the dead might. And he is wrong. I had a dead little brother and sister both, whose downy heads, apple-size, I was made to kiss before they were buried still smelling of my mother's inside. I wipe away my eyes on the collar of my shift, and chide myself for thinking that the Witchfinder might be moved by wailing. If he will not be moved, then neither will I. I press my back against the cold wall and reach out through the darkness toward my cell mate. I feel his dead hand in mine, cold and thin.

I must sleep there, in that dank little storeroom, because I dream. I dream light again – light that slants down upon me, brilliant and in many variations of rose. I open my eyes to find myself sitting in a high-backed pew, with a vaulted ceiling above me. It is St Mary's church. I feel at peace. There is a sweet, luxuriant smell, as of incense, in the air. I rise to my feet and walk the aisle.

I see that the boarded windows have been glazed again, and the sun streams through the opulent folds of saints' red and purple robes. No – not saints. Witches. In the high window of the nave is Old Mother Clarke, her peg leg a pillar of flame emerging from her singed skirts, shears held aloft like a sword. She is flanked by my mother and Helen Clarke, both in gowns of brilliant crimson and wearing crowns of hemlock. My mother pours wine from a shining pitcher. Liz Godwin carries a wax manikin in her hand as a Bishop would his crozier. The Widows Moone and Leech carry a paring knife, a cleaver. They look down at me, gorgeous and beneficent, thick-thighed angels. The sun-spots fall onto the stone floor through their bright frocks, making a flower bed of every corner.

There is a voice from the front pew, a man's voice. 'Ah,' he says, 'you have awoken, at last.'

In the first pew before the altar sit Judith Moone, the Cavalier from my first night at the castle, in his jacket tipped with silver lace, poor Vinegar Tom, and the Devil himself. They make a jolly-looking sort of a party. It is the Devil who bids me good day, and I find myself returning his greeting with a smile and a dip of the head. It feels the correct thing to do. I say to the Devil, 'This is the very last place I expected to see you,' and he laughs.

I look to the others. Judith appears just as she did when I saw her last, in white smock and cap trimmed with ribbon, short-chinned and grinny. Vinegar Tom looks in very fine health indeed, smoking a long bone pipe – he dips his furred chin to me in generous greeting. He is the size of a man now, and wears a handsome waistcoat of bottle green velvet. Lastly there is the Cavalier, his face pale and his long hair hanging ragged and unkempt about his shoulders. In his lap sits a white rabbit with red eyes, small and bright as coral beads.

'Are you dead?' I ask them. Then, 'Am I dead?' It seems a distinct possibility.

'Certainly not – and mind your manners,' Judith laughs.

'I am,' says Vinegar Tom, his ringed tail flicking in his lap.

'And I, alas,' replies the Cavalier, with a lackadaisical smile.

'To be as alive as I am would kill any man,' says the Devil. 'Or woman.' He winks.

'I suppose I will need to choose what I will be, soon enough,' I sigh.

'It is already chosen,' says the Devil. 'There is no shame in enjoying one's own company.'

'But I do not know what to tell them, what to say,' I protest.

'Just scream,' says the Devil.

I do not think his advice very helpful, but I lower my head in deference, nonetheless – he is the Devil, after all, and some respect is due. The Cavalier scratches at the rabbit's ears with his thumb.

'I have seen that rabbit before,' I say.

The Cavalier nods. 'You have,' he says. 'And next time you see him, it will be the time to do it. And then you will be led back to yourself. Do not be afraid, nor ashamed. Now go.'

I turn to walk back down the aisle, toward the heavy doors. I think it is what I am meant to do. I pause, and turn to call over my shoulder: 'There is no Hell after all, sir, is there? Or is this it?'

The Devil smiles indulgently. He is lemon-scented. 'I know this will sound strange coming from me,' he says, 'but there are some things it is better not to know. That is Eve's lesson. Regardless, Miss West. You have places to be.' And with that, he flaps his hand, and I find myself knocked from my feet and blown down the aisle by a great warm gust, my hair torn loose from my cap and swirling all about me. The doors of St Mary's groan open, and out I fly into a blinding brightness, elated in my heart, light as a spark, though I could not begin to explain why.

I wake to the squeal of key in lock. It is the gaoler, come to collect me, because I am alive. I rise, cold and aching, because I am alive, and allow him to fix the manacles back on my wrists. In the light of the turnkey's lamp I can see the face of my night's companion, and what I already suspected is confirmed: it was the Cavalier I slept beside, though he now looks like nothing so much as the sort of creature sometimes found frozen to death beneath a hayrick, his bloated face half-obscured by matted hair. A turquoise still sparkles on the cadaver's stiff, blackened finger. I see the gaoler notice it too, and wonder how much he will sell it for. It probably belonged to a woman, once. His sweetheart, perhaps. *Cadaver*, I notice, is a very pretty sort of word.

I am led down corridor on corridor, then another corridor, the enforced briskness of the walk soon restoring the feeling to my heavy legs. We pass narrow windows and the pale red of dawn is coming in strings of fire across the old stone of the walls, it is touching my skin as I pass by. The kind of morning light that carries within it the qualities of heat and frost both. Spring will come soon – and then summer, and the summer assizes. I am alive.

They are sleeping in an animal pile, a tangle of slack undifferentiated limbs, and in the moment it takes my eyes to grow used again to the utter dark of the cell, I wonder if I could do it: if I could damn them all to save myself, to walk out into the beautiful blue-gold promise of the morning. The first face I discern through the murk is my mother's. She is awake, and she is looking at me where I stand at the cell door. Slowly, she disentangles herself from the others and rises to her feet, coming to embrace me and – yes – pet my cheek, and press my face into her shoulder. 'Oh, Beck,' she murmurs, 'oh, Rabbit. I was afraid they had taken you away for good.' And I believe she truly did think me gone for good, and truly was afraid. Better late, as they say, than never. She moves back to look me over, but of course cannot see an inch of me – not bruise nor bone – for the darkness of the cell. 'Beck?'

My hands, clasped in hers, are trembling.

'Where did he take you?' she asks, meaning the turnkey. 'Was harm done?'

I shake my head. What can I say?

She takes me to the corner of the cell, where we huddle together around the meagre light of a candle stub. The others sigh and stir on their mean bed of straw, but do not wake. She asks again where I was taken, stroking at my hair. I tell her to a cellar, somewhere below. The cadaver and the dream I keep for myself.

'With Hopkins?' she asks.

I nod.

'And he urged you to confess?'

I nod again. She looks at me, expectantly, and I see that she thinks I already have. I bubble with resentment at her presumption. 'He did,' I say – 'and I will not,' I lie.

She grabs at my shoulders then, and looks into my eyes, and tells me not to be a tender imbecile. 'Do it,' she hisses. 'And do it now, before they wake.'

I say that I will not, and remind her that she is innocent of that of which she is accused and that she ought to cleave to this innocence. She spits on this – quite literally, spits onto the floor – and fixes me with a glare, and asks can I not see that there is far greater dignity in being villain than victim?

And I ask her, 'What of *my* dignity, Mother?' I remind her she asks me to lie, which is a great sin.

'Chickenshit,' she says. 'You are too young to be much concerned with *dignity*, my girl. Dignity is an old woman's game. What of your life?' She grabs up my hand and squeezes it tightly, and gives me a nod. Everything is happening too fast for this to be a moment of very great acknowledged tenderness between us, but it is all we will have. I squeeze back.

I lean toward her. The nightsweat of her neck sticky on my brow. 'I would know, Mother,' I ask, 'how Bess Clarke came to lose her leg?'

She blinks at me uncomprehendingly, and then she does comprehend – that I will not have another chance to ask, and if I do not, then there will be none who know how Bess Clarke came to lose her leg. 'Dog ate it,' says Mother. She grins, and grabs at the back of my neck and pulls me in to kiss my brow fiercely. 'I wish I knew to tell you, Beck,' she says. Then, 'Do it. Do it now, girl.'

So I do. It happens just as the Devil said it would – I begin to scream. The gaoler's boy rushes down to find me clawing desperately at the door of the cell, so hard that two of my nails break from their beds. I thrash and wail on the dirty floor (to affect a frenzy is surprisingly easy, once one has begun – you are carried forward on your own crazed momentum, like a pig on fire rolling down a hill). I tell the gaoler's boy that he must fetch his master at once, for I can no longer bear to be among Sathan's own brides, whose very dormant sighs at that moment choke me, set me all aflame, and that if he will not take me from this accursed cell he shall find me a dead woman by noon. I demand to be taken to Hopkins – to the Witchfinder – at once. And all the while Mother sits in the corner of the cell where the slender glow of his candle will not reach, and cackles like a mad woman (which she may well be). She did not think to say it, but I know that she loves me, and that she would see me flourish.

The others begin to stir from their sleep and gaze bleary-eyed around, confused by the tumult. Only Helen Clarke realises what is happening as it happens, and as the gaoler and his boy hook their arms around me and move to haul me up out of the cell, she spits at my blistered feet and says I shall burn in Hell if I think to break faith with them, which is the very least that I deserve.

26

Confession

I can tell that he is frightened of me now that I am obeying him. He was not before. Is it because he thinks I have *chosen* to obey him? That every curtsey, every *yes Mister Hopkins*, puts him in mind of the young woman's heart as a slanting wild red place, inhospitable to reason? Men like to keep women under their power by force. A clever woman can help a man to forget what he is, and both of them are the better for it. Unless he wakes of a sudden one morning in a cold sweat and remembers, the truth of himself sinking in and spreading its damage outward like a bullet. No. I would rather be a woman. We understand our abjection before God, because we understand our abjection before man. And we get to laugh behind their backs.

I am kept on the upper storeys of the castle, now, with a washstand and little barred window all my own, from which I see the pewter sky, the dirt-coloured wall, a swatch of green grass. I am to testify before the Justices today. The Justices in question are an Earl, a Baronet and a Knight. Mister Hopkins brings me a fresh gown, and a looking glass. A looking glass, as though it were the most ordinary thing in the world. I try to hide my excitement. I think it is a very plain and usual sort of looking glass – a few oily fingerprints in the top corner – but it seems to me no less than sorcery. I have been told before that a mirror is like a picture writ with light itself, but it looks more real than that – as real as a doorway one could step through to join one's other, mirror-self as easy as a *good morrow and god bless*. In truth I am grateful I never had a glass before, for my time in gaol must have changed my looks for ill, but never having seen more than the general shapes of my self, I shall never know how I have been marred. I move forward and backward before the mirror. I tilt my chin, open my mouth wide, inspect the sallow meat of my cheeks, my own little teeth. I am entirely delighted with myself, this first Rebecca West. I am clean again. My hair has been clipped to my shoulders and put away beneath a new white cap. The gown has a high collar and is of a very sober grey wool. Butter wouldn't melt, as they say.

Sat down before the Justices, I feel rather less impressed with myself. The Earl of Warwick is tall and sharp-nosed and fast-talking, and wears voluminous sleeves of washed gold silk. His hair creeps back from the dome of his head as though his speedy progress through our sad little world has blown it half away. He owns ships and African slaves and a good part of Massachusetts Bay, but looking at him sitting there and scratching at the back of his hand I cannot conceive of how one man is able to do all of that, and yet remain what could be called a man. There is the Baronet, Sir Harbottle Grimston, deputy lieutenant of Essex, whose hair falls in waves from a black velvet cap like a spaniel's ears. It was this very Baronet, I know, who first issued the warrant for Mother Clarke's arrest. I do not like the insinuating way he talks – like Mister Hopkins, he thinks he is a very clever man, but I do not think he is so clever as Mister Hopkins, even, sitting there darkly, a toad of satins. Then there is Sir Thomas Bowes, the Knight, whose face is a pretty, pale snowdrop above his marvellous collar of lace. It is clear that Sir Thomas is unsure exactly how awed it would befit his station to be, in the presence of the Earl and Baronet, and as a consequence he quivers between *not at all* and *very* awed with such a quickness one fears his dainty neck might snap clean in two. A dull spring morning of rainy, watered light, and not a one of them wants to be here at the castle listening to the prattle of a peasant girl beneath a borrowed cap.

This is the story I tell.

I tell of a Shrovetide evening, when I was not yet seventeen, on which my mother bid me make haste about my work, for she wished me to join her in a visit before sundown. Two women walking through the fields, the dewfall of evening on their shoes. There, I say, my mother gave me great charge never to speak of what I should hear or see, and faithfully I promised I would not (for the benefit of my noble audience, I lower my eyes and muster a blush). 'Ere long we came to a house, but I know not to whom it belonged, and never saw it before or thereafter, and within were Mother Clarke and Liz Godwin (I people my invention only with those whom I know already to be damned). Liz Godwin produced a book with a red cover and from it we read a prayer that I no longer remember, and thereupon the imps, in their deep unrelenting shapes and pristine noise, like the jingle of shells worn on the coat of a Lord of Misrule, did appear. I tell how Mother Clarke's skirts were filled to overflowing with them in the shapes of blue-eyed kittens about a week old, and how Mother Clarke kissed each and said that they were her children, had by as handsome a man as any there was in England, and the creatures delighted me. I tell how Mother Clarke turned one hoary eye upon me, her face thin and leathern as Methuselah's own snapsack, and asked if I would keep counsel of what I had seen, or else suffer greater tortures and pains than those of Hell. I speak of a Covenant and Oath wherewith to renounce the blessings of Christ our Lord and all merit of his passion; I speak of a little black dog that jumped into my lap and kissed me thrice, kisses I felt to be very cold (Hopkins notes that witches commonly testify the Devil's touch to be unnatural cold, and how by that token they surely know him to be their master). And then I stop, and I wait for the hard look of God to clatter down from the sky and through my back like a fiery lance, because I am a liar. But nothing comes.

The Justices listen, grave. The Baronet looks gravest of all – I think he has already come to regret his part in this whole sorry affair. He has the face of a man who has come off his horse after riding through a storm, and slid directly into a cowpat. 'Miss West,' he addresses me, 'you have been bound over for near a year – why is it only now that you come to confess?'

I say that I very much wished to discover all I knew as soon as we were taken to gaol, but that I was put to fear by the promise I had made and Mother Clarke's insistence that any who betrayed our infernal league, the Devil would pull apart with pincers (this last part comes to me even as I speak, delivered whole into my mind). I say I found myself bound in horrible extremities of torture that agonised my body worse than the rack, whenever I thought to confess. I say that when I looked down at my body I saw it wreathed in tongues of flame. But now these tortures have ceased, I explain, because the witches have once more been brought under the law of God and man, and I think myself the happiest creature in all the world, that I might sit before them and disburden my conscience of its horrible tonnage.

'Miss West,' asks the Earl, 'do you know your commandments, my dear?'

'Your honour,' I answer, 'I know my commandments. And my letters. I can read, and write some little, as well.'

The three noblemen exchange looks. They are surprised. 'And

see what use she put this education to,' breathes Sir Thomas Bowes, with a shake of the head.

'Indeed,' sighs the Baronet. 'A sad prognostic of the consequences attendant on female literacy, I fear.'

They have other questions. Does the Devil speak plain English, and has he any accent when he speaks it? Can the Devil take any shape he chooses from among all those of beasts and men, and thereby appear to the unwary in righteous costume? Did I – and their carefully primped gentility will not serve to mask their hunger – have carnal copulation with the Devil? What shape did he take when we copulated – the shape of man, or beast? (Another deep blush kindles in my cheeks.) When they are done, they thank me. The Earl of Warwick says he will pray to God to forgive me my very grievous sins, and I wonder if an Earl's prayers have more weight than those of other men, if God gets round to listening to them more speedily. I have never seen lacework as fine as what the Earl has on his collar, splashed all over with roses almost as big as my hands. Just one of those big slatternly flowers must have taken a week to stitch. And now I am to be honoured with a place in his prayers. A black speck clinging on the shiny skirts of his eligible daughters.

'You did well, Rebecca,' Hopkins tells me, as we stand outside my cell. I can tell he is surprised, and elated, by my account. His fingers twitch at his belt in readiness to set my recollections down on paper. So much of what has gone before has been like the tracking of a whistle through fog, but here I stand at last; real, and telling him he is right, that the Devil lieth heavy upon me, and that I wish to be saved.

Even I, with my very small knowledge of men, think it quite likely that Hopkins will fall in love with me now. I begin to see he thinks he has already. He bows, awkward and uncouth, like a drunk man pretending he is not. He says he will not see me again until the assizes, but he hopes I shall keep well until then. 'Do not fear, Rebecca,' he says, gently taking my fingers in his, 'you shall be provided for. I will find a place for you, once this business is over. A place where you might nourish your soul in quiet, and in the pious despair of contrition.' He kisses the back of my hand. I take no pride in this inadvertent seduction. The *pious despair of contrition*, indeed.

Time passes. I spend most of it in my cell, watching the world warm through the window in this, my twenty-first summer of life. Sometimes I am allowed to walk in the grounds of the castle, under guard, and I listen to the clattering of carts and oyster sellers' cries from the town beyond the walls. Watch the crows bask in their sun-blanched nests in gullies of stone. They look safe, sure of themselves, apparelled in black for the New Jerusalem. I am here because my obedience is plausible, my body strong and fit to be put to work again. I think often of my mother and the others, and hope they keep well – except for Elizabeth Clarke, who is so very old, and whom I hope it would please God to take by gentler means than those Hopkins and the Justices might devise. At night I lie dry-eyed on my little bed and turn my head to and fro to catch sight of one little star by one little star along the tail of Hydra, and think *you are alive, you survive. Is this not what you wanted?*

27

Trial

There are to be fifteen witches tried in Chelmsford on this, the 23rd of July 1645 – and it can only be the start, for near one hundred more are held bound over across Essex and Suffolk, awaiting judgement. The sky is headlong, cloudless blue, and the square outside the courthouse filled with a clamouring multitude. Those who have arrived early and been fortunate enough to have secured spots by the windows have brought victuals and pots of beer, and will not move all day. They'd piss their own shoes before losing these coveted situations. Stories are passed through the crowd of the witches' myriad villainies, but also of the Witchfinders' infallible and wonderful power in discovering them. There is also a moderating dose of cynicism – the cultivated suburbanites of deep-inland west Essex, where the hills roll dry and golden, laugh heartily to hear that their neighbours from fen and salty tide-wash can find nothing better to do with their time than tip cows and ride one another to Sathan's black masses by means of enchanted bridles. They would not be surprised to learn that all of this nonsense was the result of nothing more sinister than simple rustic folk baking mottlegill into pies. Then there are the countryfolk themselves, scrubbed and primped as though for church, anxious of pickpockets. Some – Goody Parsley and Minister Long among them – have come down from Manningtree to bear witness to the testimony. Some – Misters Rawbood and Edwards among them – have come to give it.

The women wait in the courthouse cellar, lined shoulder to shoulder on benches, chained at wrists and ankles, behind bars. It is cool and earthy-smelling here, underground. They are frightened, quiet; but for many who have been kept long in provincial jails, there is a relief that something, at last, is happening. Some are even hopeful – assize judges are invariably learned men, and learned men give short shrift to country superstition, or the local grievance and prattle wont to shape it into nooses. So their quiet, nervy talk goes. The Widow Moone is weeping, great big silent tears that sit on her face undisturbed, like seed-pearls. 'There, now. Take it on the chin, Mag,' says Helen Clarke, who is shackled up beside her. This prompts Liz Godwin to comment that it ought to be easy for the Widow Moone to take things on the chin, having so many to choose from, which causes the Beldam West and Widow Leech and Mother Clarke to fall to furtive cackling.

Hopkins paces the boards in the courthouse directly above. He saw the women arrive that morning, women by the cartload. A happy morning. They are so dirty and narrowed by inanition that it is hard to differentiate them from one another at all, now. An assortment of sour shapes in rags. More like dried-up seed cases than women, paltry things the earth pushed up, that the wind could blow away. He remembers certain names, those which had a homespun poetry about them – Fogg, Greenleaf, the Stowmarket woman with the gall to be called nothing less than 'Dorothy Magicke' – and particular countenances, but cannot, in his memory, now unite the one properly with the other. It is *so* hot. He adjusts his collar, pushes back his hat. Today is a day to make account. He hopes he looks well for it. What did he do, really?

For what can he be held responsible? Not for the law, not for that. He went only where he was invited. He took just what money was offered. He gave nothing more than the benefit of his learning. He is a true servant of God. True servant of God. True servant of God.

Our Father, who art in Heaven, hallowed be thy name. Thy kingdom come. Thy will be done, on Earth as it is – as it is in Heaven. Give us this day our daily bread and forgive us our trespasses – as—

See she cannot the witch cannot say it the witch the word of God sticks in her craw the good word why are her eyes like that un-wholesome like something baked in its own skin in the sun imagine licking a rotten – where they ripen and fall in secret – rotten in a mouth—

Forgive us our trespasses as—

There must be signification it is not difficult after all a child knows it my daughter my four-year-old can count upon their hands are rings of gold click her fingers and turn the fleet to frothing blood—

Our Father, who art in Heaven, hallowed be thy—

And why singest thou Psalms my love when thou knows't thyself to be a damned creature – and just like that a handsome face a jag-ged hoof set on the edge of the milk-pail it cannot be ignored and neither would you – you would take it in your mouth – the truth is he likes girls and women. Truly. They are steeped in story, and also violets – a sweet life song—

Our Father, who art in Heaven, hallowed be thy name. Thy kingdom come – for ever and ever—

And the truth is was different last night seemed to want it more spirited avid jagged what was she thinking about damned if I know never – says she dreamed of walking through the white gardens of Heaven when she came by a harp resting on an outcrop of cloud and pushed it having within her a strange and sudden urge to destroy to see it topple – down through the sky like a morning star – which is after all the meaning of that name, the meaning of the name *Lucifer—*

The Baronet leans forward to look at Old Mother Clarke (who was born in Clacton Port the very hour Michelangelo died in Rome, though she does not know it). 'You cannot say,' he sneers, voice swelling with incredulity, 'our Lord's prayer, madam?'

'I can say it,' she says in a small voice, her liver-spotted hands resting on the bar. 'I know it.'

'But you do not say it, madam.'

Was she not affrighted, asks the Earl of Warwick, to have so many little devils about her skirts?

Old Mother Clarke smiles at that. 'Why,' she asks, 'would I be frightened of mine own children?'

For killing by *maleficium* of cattle belonging to Richard Edwards of Manningtree, valued at £10, Mother Clarke is sentenced to death by hanging.

Richard Edwards demands financial recompense for his lost cattle, but who will pay? Mother Clarke has no estate to seize. 'Does the fool propose I descend to Tartarus and ask the Beast himself for ten English pounds?' remarks Earl to Baronet, behind his hand.

Helen Clarke claims she is with child. The Baronet adjusts his eyeglasses, peering between his notes and the dirty girl in the dock before him, with her rascal smile, and prison shift slipping from her shoulder. 'You have a husband, yes?' he asks. 'One Thomas Clarke, who fights with the Eastern Association, a Parliament man?'

She nods.

'I – you were among those bound over at Colchester Castle, yes? For more than a year?' This is a deeply embarrassing situation for the Baronet. He appears to hope that if he simply states and restates the supposed facts of the situation in a tone of increasing disbelief, someone might come to his aid by pointing out the glaring inconsistency they collide about.

She nods again.

The Baronet ushers over his steward, and asks who the gaoler at Colchester is, and if he might be counted a respectable man (the Baronet assumes that all the men in England of a class below his own must be somehow acquainted with one another. Surely there is some school or other they all attended?) The Baronet and his steward converse in hushed tones for quite some time, the latter flapping up his hands helplessly. The Baronet eventually sighs, and dismisses him.

Sir Thomas Bowes raises a satin finger – he can, he believes, cut to the heart of the matter. 'Does not Aquinas speculate,' he begins, drawing the digit thoughtfully to his lips, 'that offspring could be born of a union between woman and demon, if the demon first collected seed from a man – and—' He begins to look less sure of himself here, '—and, of course, given the demon were able to find means for keeping the seed . . . *warm*, in his ethereal passage between man and . . .' Here he indicates Helen, surly in the dock, '. . . and woman.'

The Baronet and the Earl of Warwick look down the bench at Sir Thomas. Mister Hopkins clears his throat. He notes that Aquinas did indeed speculate this, yes – but given none present are theologians in the strictest sense, it would perhaps be desirable to skirt this demonological quagmire, and have Helen Clarke sent back below pending further investigation, so that the business of the day might be properly proceeded with. The Justices agree that this would be best, and a jeer goes up from the crowd massed round the windows as she is led below again, grinning with triumph, her hands around her swollen belly.

Helen Clarke is granted temporary stay of execution.

It is hot in the courthouse, baking in the streets. Beer is passed about and sloshed over reddening cheeks. There is shouting. The shouting is so loud that sometimes the indicted women cannot properly hear the charges that are laid against them, and the Justices cannot hear how the women plead. Conclusions are both foregone and seemingly impossible to arrive at. Each must be held partially responsible for the crimes of the others. Margaret Moone will do naught but weep as the teats found about her fundament are described meticulously by Abigail Hobbs. Thomas Hart raises in his balled fist the bloodied sheet upon which his wife miscarried, like a battle pennant. Hopkins lays the manikins found in Liz Godwin's scuttle out before her, and at first she says she knows not what they are. When Hopkins turns down his lips in mock surprise, and says, 'Are you certain, madam? They were found upon thy husband's property, after all,' she concedes, *yes, she does know what they are she has seen them before but sir it is not what you think they are but innocent a remedy for* – and her protestations dissolve in bitter weeping as she realises it is over, she is done (and that knowing what is good for him her husband, Edward Godwin, did not come). Anne Leech is accused of laying a curse on one Elizabeth Kirk, who refused to give to her a much-coveted bonnet. The bonnet in question is laid down before her at the bar by Elizabeth Kirk's father Robert, white with thrills of rose-coloured ribbon, and the Widow Leech laughs that being accused a witch would be slander enough, but the suggestion she would wish to put that giddy-looking coif anywhere near her head is aspersion almost too great to bear (with the utmost of respect to Miss Kirk, God rest her soul, whom she is sure the bonnet did well become). Robert Kirk cries out that the witches will burn with the Devil for what they have done, his *sweet Eliza gone*, and he must be restrained, and is led weeping from the courtroom.

For killing by *maleficium* of a mule belonging to Robert Taylor of Manningtree, valued at £1, and causing by *maleficium* Goodwife Hart of Manningtree to miscarry of a son, Elizabeth Godwin is sentenced to death by hanging.

For the killing by *maleficium* of Elizabeth Kirk of Manningtree, Anne Leech and Margaret Moone are sentenced to death by hanging.

And then up comes the Beldam West, the one who sank an entire hoy and drowned every man aboard for no other reason than she felt like it. She wished to. It entertained her. She peers around the courthouse, into each and every jeering face, with a look that says, *this entertains me too.*

And there is a dignity to her villainy. She stands at the bar, gorging on the wails of the multitude as happy as Lilith might, ramrod straight as time unspools around her along with the sweaty curls of the gentry women gazing nervously down from the courthouse balcony at this thing, this worst-of-all, this Hecate. She does not answer a single question put to her, which agitates the crowd. But she does not hear their bawling. She hears instead the sound of waves, of breakers on a beach. She thinks of her daughter. Her daughter will be carried over waves, away.

For the wrecking by *maleficium* of the *Oliver*, carrying cargo valued at £35, and the drowning of all souls aboard, the Beldam Anne West is sentenced to death by hanging.

*

When Master Edes mounts the witness box I see that, to begin with, he dare not look up from his hands for fear of seeing me. Then he does look up, but he does not see me, by a door at the back behind the blinking scribes. I had almost forgotten what he looks like. I am not fond of his short hair. It makes him look older, and meaner, and more like other men do. I suppose it is fortunate the sight of him precipitates no great rush of love within me. It was not meant for me. He was not.

He speaks coldly. I cannot hear most of what he says above the noise of the crowd, but can piece together an ugly enough story from the scraps I glean: *familiarity, Devil, gave entertainment, seven year, one Thomas Hart of Lawford, whose wife being with child. She conceived the Devil could do as God.* He is accusing me of blasphemy. A slow nod, a thumbing of his cuff, the thoughtful consideration of a question posed by the Baronet: 'He lay with her as a man,' he says.

Yes, Master Edes, I think, *you did.* I watch his mouth alone, moving, slandering me, and think how strange that it has also touched my skin, and fitted itself kindly round my name. I realise he believes what he says. He has traded places in his mind with the Devil. It is easier for him that way. It is easier for him to believe his own untruths. Man and woman, we have each only one body. Very often we wish to forget where it has been, and what it has done, and who it loved. I do.

The Information of John Edes, Clarke,
taken upon oath before the said Justices, 1645

This informant saith, that Rebecca West confessed unto him, that
about seven years since, she began to have familiarity with the Devil,
by the instigation of her mother Anne West; who hath appeared
unto the said Rebecca at several times, in diverse shapes: at one time
in the likeness of a proper young man, who desired of her, that he
might have the same familiarity with her, that others that appeared
unto her before had had: promising that if she would, he would then
do for the said Rebecca what she desired, and avenge her on her
enemies; but required further, that she would deny God, and rely
upon him.

28

Execution

The sky has crammed full with low cloud overnight, and yet the weather remains torrid and hot. A closeness and stickiness oppresses the throng that moves slowly through the streets, from courthouse to scaffold. Cheering and drums. Women hawking hot buns, stingo and oysters, flies everywhere thicking the warm, wet air. The kind of day that wants to be shaken open by a storm. I hope it is. I want them frightened by lightning and thunder, this gap-wit multitude. I see their jaunty faces and wish I could spit in every one. I see that a good many have brought their children. Children on their shoulders, clinging to their skirts. For the righteous shall rejoice in the workings of the Lord.

How often does the Devil put a curse in your head? When I stop to take account of my thoughts, I sometimes find I am full up with cruelty, ungodliness, with the wish to wrong those by whom I have been wronged. I hate their faces and their grins and the loudness of their voices. The hate catches like a fire, and spreads to bystanders, who have not wronged me yet but who might, if they were given the chance. Their bodies disgust me. Their grievances are childish. My head like a closet of clean, sweetened linens that dirty grey mice have nosed their way all about. Today the fire has caught and I hate everyone, man and woman and child. And yet there I stand behind

Mister Hopkins at the base of the scaffold, hands meekly folded, blessed by God's forgiveness, apparently, and Parliament's reprieve. A free woman, except that there is no such thing. I peer over my shoulder and see the faces of those closest to us bent toward me, their hands raised to hide whispering mouths. I suppose a confessed witch must make herself used to whispers.

I turn back to the scaffold. How will it work, the execution? There is nobody for me to ask. One by one they are brought up onto the platform, women unknown to me in drab prison gowns with dirty hair. Old Mother Clarke is the last of them. She must be helped up the stairs to the scaffold by a guard, who holds her by her shoulders before the noose as the others arrange themselves. The women are speaking quietly to one another, reaching out to join hands, and speaking to the executioner as well, as though they are all old friends – but the band are still playing, and I cannot hear what they say over the trilling of the pipes. Perhaps offering him their forgiveness, or coin for a clean drop. One yellow-haired woman with a pock-marked face staggers into position as though drunk, which she may be, for the damned are given ale to soothe their spirits. Their calmness surprises me. But I suppose it would not do to panic. At least not before time. But for their poor apparel and their filthiness they could be eight women milling in the market square, so composed they seem. It is when the music stops and the warrant for death is read – as a Minister comes forward to shrive them – that their faces ossify into looks of fright, or slacken with bewilderment. The executioner starts with the left-most. He asks her something, but she shakes her grey head, and peers out over the crowd as if she is searching for someone. The executioner comes with a hood, and she cries out, 'Glory be to God!' before he puts it over her face. There are jeers, some *amens* as well. Then the noose is put over the hood, tightened at the back of her neck. Then he guides her the three steps up onto the ladder, then the squeal of rope as he kicks the ladder out from under – *I do here in the name of Christ Jesus and His Church deliver you up to Sathan and his power and his working.* I do not want to watch her twitching. I look to Mother Clarke, who stands with her eyes closed, the guard propping her on her one good foot, and I hope she has no proper understanding of where she is, of what is happening. Away, away, on the faded meadow. Please God.

The executioner moves down to the next in line. Some of those on the scaffold are maids who must never have seen a hanging. Others are old country women, who might have seen one but can scarce remember what it was like. If you are on the right end of the scaffold, do you watch those to the left of you twist, do you watch them die attentively, so as to better understand what is to happen to you? Or is it best not to? It was nearly me – so nearly. This second woman I remember from the courthouse – Goody Wyatt, a Minister's wife, and she yowls like a cat and her face is swollen and wet with tears from the blubbering that began when the pipes died. She must be held by the executioner, she fights hood and noose, stick-like arms flailing, but eventually – she wails *forgive me God, forgive me* – and then comes the *I do here in the name of Christ Jesus and His Church deliver you up to Sathan and his power and his working.* Altogether a graceless performance, for all it matters what I think.

I would have one shout out her hate, drop her vengeance into the gawking multitude like a meteor. Scatter their limbs and drive them screaming from the square. My mother would. My mother will. But my mother is not here today. My mother is to be hung in our hometown, in Manningtree, to serve as an example.

Everything dirty and hideous, the low grey of the sky near-suffocating. I watch a fat gleaming fly pick his way across Hopkins' shoulder. I think, *kill him,* a thought directed nowhere and at no one in particular, just there and baby-kicking at the back of my heart. On Mister Hopkins' shoulder, by the fly, there are tiny flecking raindrops now, the beginning of a mizzen like the letters of a secret inscription, and a few of the least reverent in the crowd sigh in their banal way that it is going to rain, that they came all this way and it is going to rain and their sport will be spoiled thereby, and the alehouses will be too busy and besides the staff cannot be found these days – what a world, I think, and how do any of us face up to the fact of our living in it? *Glory be to God my strength*, shouts the next as she is kicked from her ladder, a mere girl, the noose biting at the slenderness of her neck. *I do here in the name of Christ Jesus and His Church deliver you up to Sathan and his power and his working.* In the distance, beyond the trembling rope, there is the cathedral tower. *On the fourth of the eight already*, a man says, *and the first not yet dead* – and his neighbour comments, with an expert air, that it is because the women are half starved, too thin, and have not the bulk to them proper for the use of such long ropes. *A very poor showing indeed, Mister Witboro*, he says, and asks if this Mister Witboro will be going to the cockfight later—

Hopkins coughs. It seems to pain him, the cough. He cringes his face into his kerchief. I see him draw the cloth from his mouth and look furtively at the pink stain there before he stuffs it away again in his right breast pocket. There is nothing in his face but casual discomfort. The rain has brought a chill and the executioner moves to the last-but-one, the last-but-Mother-Clarke, I must be ready, *creak thump twist – I do here in the name of Christ Jesus and His Church deliver you up to Sathan and his power and his working.* Water is dripping from their skirts, piss, like rotten fruits they hang there voided, a true hag-tree. Old Mother Clarke nods and they lift her to the ladder. By now some in the crowd are wincing, and have resolved not to watch. She is the smallest and most frail of all of them, and it will be a long choking, *not right, is it, whate'er she might have did,* says the man behind, not Mister Witboro, *be she a Minister of Sathan or—*

Now. I do what I know I must. I wonder what Mother Clarke hears and feels in this moment – I hope it is nothing – I wonder if she hears Hopkins call my name, hears *Rebecca* shouted in reproof, and my bonnet perhaps flashing whitely through the guards' crossed pikes through the dimness of her cataracts, a bother and commotion I am causing, this is the work of mercy worked. There is a gasp of legitimate astonishment going up from the crowd, the stalled beating of a drum and a shout, another shout, as I have passed Hopkins too fast and am there at the scaffold, and I move to leap up and grasp at her. I wrap my arms around her body at the ankle at first but it is not enough so then at the hips, and I can smell her more than I can feel her, so slight she is, like catching up at an angel in the ascent, there is that little of her, my cheek pushed to the sagging flesh of her belly. I add my weight to her nothing and pull down, down – feel a warmth against my head and my cap is pushed aside, the front of my gown wet – she is dead, saying no words and making no sounds, neck broken and leg hanging limp, the light of thy countenance leaves her.

When it is done, their bodies are cut down from the scaffold and dragged away for burial in an unmarked trench, all together, piled up. Much as we slept beneath the castle. The rabble crowd in to grab at their hair and tear away handfuls of their shifts, so that they will be buried near-naked. The collar of a witch is worth more than a twin-baby's caul, to the right buyer, for use in charms.

1647

'A woman spoke true of the men in her life.
Cold lies the dew.
She spoke with a truth some mistook for delight.
Cold lies the dew.'

Amy Key & Rebecca Perry, Insect & Lilac, 2019

29

Foreknowledge

An August afternoon in the victualler's shop. Stacked in crates there are apples green and pink, plums and damsons, gem-hard and ripe and very good-looking against clean brown paper. Redcurrants and dark cherries, too, and speckled eggs stuck with soft gluey wisps of down, and warm loaves, and black rhubarb, and pickles and jams. So the worst of the war is over, and the curses of every witch have slid from the rooftops like sun-loosened snow.

Little Ruth Miller in her tidy black frock and pressed apron, standing on her tiptoes. Her mother holds her right hand, and with the left, she reaches out to take an apple gleaming on the very top of Master Taylor's carefully arranged stack. I see what will happen all in a blink before it does, before the gleaming apple on the very top of the stack teeters and falls, rolls lazy across the boards and comes to rest against my shoe. Pale green apple, little round speck of bruise, black buckled shoe. I bend to pick it up, I offer it out to her. Ruth Miller looks at me warily with her hands pushed together over her apron. A few blonde hairs stick skew under the edge of her laced cap. I smile, and hold the apple out to her. I see it – little hand – I see it happen all in a blink before it does. This is the day I will kill a man.

Ruth Miller is reaching out to take the apple, but Goody Miller grabs a hold of the girl's shoulders and moves her away from me, and says *no*, loudly, *no, Ruth*. Ruth Miller pulls back her hand as though it has been scalded. Goody Miller looks at me with a face full of spite and begins to drive her daughter out of the shop, her repugnance so fulsome she leaves behind her butter, her redcurrants. I am well accustomed to these acrimonious encounters. Master Taylor being out of sight in the back room, I slip the apple into the pocket of my dress, and the redcurrants too, for good measure. Sin breedeth sin.

My walk back to the Thorn at Mistley takes me over the green. It was here, by the old oak, on an August afternoon a little short of two years ago, that my mother hung. Mother, Liz Godwin, Margaret Moone and Anne Leech, all together, a flock of queer ducks. I could never discover what happened to Helen Clarke, or her baby, that supposed Devil's spawn. I did not attend the hanging, which occurred during my period of great melancholy, when Mister Hopkins thought it best to confine me to my room. But most of Manningtree did. I suppose it is often spoken of still, among certain circles – our very own gibbet, and of women, as well – though no one has ever been so unkind as to speak of it in front of me. So I do not know how it passed. But this is how I have pictured it.

A glowing afternoon, with a coolness moving in to cover over the heat of the day. I invoke a breeze to ruffle the leaves of the old oak. I give them a low tide, as well, to look at – the kind of day when the river drains out and the mud plains catch the pretty colours in the sky. I have my mother standing on the scaffold looking northward through the noose. She is not looking for my face among the faces of our neighbours. She knows I will not come, that I would not want to see it. Instead, she is looking down the narrow street to the banks of flowers and the shimmering flats, and she is imagining running across that splashing field of fire, then over the rolling hills beyond, and from thence, who can say – to Hell, if it is what she wishes. Perhaps she was a witch, and it is where she would be happiest. I suppose now I will never know, for certain.

I give her a sombre audience, too: respectfully quiet, their hearts bit by doubt as to the rightness of what it is they are about to witness. I sometimes give my mother things to say and do – curses to utter – but I know these are never as good as what she *did* say, which was exactly nothing to Minister Long who was shriving her, or attempting to, and to Mister Hopkins only that he would choke on his own blood, again. And I have no wish to imagine any further. I do not know where she is buried, either, all together with the Widows Moone and Leech and Liz Godwin. No doubt it is a very noisome sort of grave, and many ugly bright cantankerous flowers will rise up nourished by the bickering of their skulls. I wish I had more or better knowledge of my mother that I could give you. Or knowledge of her that I could hold to myself, secret. She was born in the Port of Clacton in the Year of Our Lord 1600, she had one daughter, she caused much vexation, she died.

So here I am. The orphan girl Rebecca West, confessed witch, walking along the banks of the Stour, where the loosestrife sways, a stolen apple in my pocket. Before I kill a man I will kill a bird, for supper.

30

Contrition

The Thorn is not so much an inn these days, as the ghost of one. Who would want to drown his sorrows beneath the creeping feet of a witch, or the leery eye of her Godly keeper? Poor Matthew, poor Rebecca, washed back up where we started, brittle and insipid as driftwood. The common room is wide and empty, the stoups and pewterware furred with dust.

He kept the promise made to me in Colchester, that I would be taken care of. He brought me to the Thorn to work as housegirl, but it was a long time until I could remember how to be useful again. I languished for many months in my little upstairs room with the curtains drawn tight around so that there was nothing but darkness, and imagined myself back in the gaol, with the bodies of the others – my mother, my friends – warm around me, beneath me. I would screw my eyes shut and hope that when I opened them again I would see tallow-light and chains, Helen Clarke picking at the sore that grew above her lip. But it was no use. The feather bed was too soft. In those first weeks Mister Hopkins would sometimes come into the room and draw a chair up to my bedside, where he would sit and read scripture aloud, but he never dared part the curtains to look in on me. His words would lumber solemn through the hangings and flop with impertinent majesty on to my waking dreams of cells and lice and empty, griping bellies. He would read from the Book of Job, from Genesis. Daniel in the den of the lions, of course. *My God hath sent his angel, and hath shut the lions' mouths.* It was there I did the needful dying. And then very slowly, I climbed upright again.

I had to learn all over how to be. I had to learn what Manningtree was for me, now that the constant points of light by which I had plotted my life had shifted, or else been snuffed out. My mother dead. Master John Edes gone away and joined, they said, the New Model. I could not picture him in one of those red coats the New Model men wear, for red would not be his colour. I could imagine him killing a man well enough, though, or being killed by one. The latter thought pleased me, in fact, and I was no longer surprised by my own vindictiveness. Judith Moone had vanished from the town about the time of our arrest – slipped away, no doubt, in fear for her life. See how everyone knew it best to be a coward, but me? Perhaps I am, in the end, my mother's daughter. Hopkins' household consisted of Goody Briggs – now Widow Briggs – whom he had taken on as housekeeper (and who had strong reason to resent me), and a boy and girl named Samuel Tapp and Verity Cate. All felt me worse than an imposition – they felt me a poison. An adder brought to their home by our master's misplaced tenderness. Still, they were at least frightened of me, meaning their hatred was expressed through looks and wagging tongues, and gossip had already done the worst to me that it might to any woman. I no longer cared a groat for wagging tongues.

Hopkins himself came and went. It worked like this: he would receive a letter from the citizens of some little town or hamlet beset by misery without seeming pattern nor remedy; he would read to me from the letters, sighing and shaking his head over the cruel subjections visited by the Devil on the innocent all over England (as if there be any such creature as an innocent Englishman). Such obscene pictures. Children retching out awls and heavy petting in the streets, slender men seen dancing on the rooftops by the light of a full moon. The town would levy a tax by which to provide for his keep, if he would visit. *Please come forthwith, Mister Hopkins. Please come and tell us what to do, and who to blame. Our butter has turned stubborn, will not churn.* And Hopkins would fetch Mister Stearne and the Widow Briggs and off they would ride. A celebrated man, a warrior of God. Something like a prophet, I suppose, of the New Jerusalem said to gleam beyond the cold mist of tomorrow morning. A good, clean country of good, clean folk where psalms might be heard sung at every hearth, and every woman would be kept to her right place, beneath a man, one flesh. Tomorrow it would come – then the next day. Then the next.

When he was gone, these were the periods of my relative contentment. I read very much. Probably I was not meant to. Hopkins was a Godly man, but there was nothing Godly about his library. There in his study I would set down my dusting rag and find myself floating in some strange corner of the heavens, with a wise stranger as my guide. I learned of the Doctor Dee, who by means of a polished stone and ancient alphabet had effected conversation with God's own angels. I learned of that extraordinary prodigy, the three blazing suns, that had appeared in the sky over London on the nineteenth day of November 1644, which was the birthday of His Majesty King Charles, and which the astrologer Mister Lilly thought to bode extremely ill for our benighted sovereign. I learned that long ago there had been many Gods, and maiden-Gods and woman-Gods too, and some Gods that were horned, and that these Gods would put on all manner of disguise to walk among the simple folk of that time, and even have children by them. I know these tales are thought by most to be no more than pretty heretic superstition, but they do not seem to me very different from our own talk that puts the Devil at a widow's door, leery in a pedlar's coat. In short, I learned that the world is full of wonders. I cannot pretend I understand very much of them.

When Hopkins was gone we would do our work, have our simple meals of pottage at the kitchen table and retire early to bed, where I would lie in the dark and listen for the hooves of the big black horse that bore a Witchfinder, stepping in cold and excitable from a long journey, calling me from my chamber to unlace his boots and listen as he told me of the old man who sank fishing boats by a clap of his hand, or the woman who was driven to the Devil's work because the fiend told her he had the souls of her three departed children, and would shred them like flax if she did not give herself over, body and soul, to Hell. I saw he took almost a housewife's pleasure in it: he loved the mess. He liked to be presented with a filth, a tangle, a nasty something to sweep up. Aldeburgh, Ipswich, Northampton – he would cut away the rot, give them a good drubbing, leave them looking after him as he rode away with faces clean and gleaming like children ready for morning school. Our father, who art in Mistley.

When he was at the Thorn he took great pleasure in my obedience. I would join him in fasts – three days, four days, a week with nothing but cheat bread and water, perhaps a little warm milk. If he came in from town with his greyhound (newly acquired – Mister Stearne called it 'a gentry affectation') to find me scrubbing the scullery floor he would seem surprised to see me there, sometimes, and all of a sudden declare that I must go to my chamber and make hearty supplication to God for forgiveness of my many mortal sins. Lock the door behind me. What I ate, what I wore, was his, and was therefore – it occurred to me one day as I crossed the garden to empty the slop-pail – bought by blood. He did not like me going into town or even walking up by the woods, where

I could see the trees changing through their many fantastic reds and yellows from the window of my second-floor chamber. I could feel his uncertainty around me. The indeterminacy of his intention. Something between pet-witch and prisoner-witch, held in the house on the dark, rain-swept cleft. In some ways he had as good as wed me to him. And I did hear by way of Verity Cate that some of Manningtree's more romantical souls suspected it was his intention to formalise our strange union; that having delivered me from the lion's den he would offer me a husband's protection, ere long. This was the wholesome version, no doubt. I can hear the unwholesome, in the voice of a Moses Stepkin or a Richard Edwards: *there's no saucier bedfellow than one the Devil's tasted. Just ask our Matthew.* I could be his little taste of red milk. I see it in his eyes and around his mouth, when I bring him his port or sit down to do my darning while he reads the gospel aloud to me. Sometimes I wished he would, if only because it would make everything easier. The whore, after all, has her throne.

A year of this, a year and a half, and the world had changed beneath him and he took no note of it, his eyes being fixed so resolutely upon the heavens. It began at Bury St Edmunds, where he had gone to rout a coving of supposed witches. There a preacher spoke out against him, they said, and he had to leave very soon after he had arrived, on account of this souring of local feeling. Another town that had had their own Minister led away for conjuring began to gripe that it was not right, what had happened, and that surely the Witchfinder had been mistaken, and had himself been led astray by the Devil. This, you see, is part of the service a Witchfinder provides – when a town calls him it has already decided who it wants gone. But if they change their minds after the fact, then they have the Witchfinder to blame. Every prophet ends up a pariah.

There were learned men in London, too, who spoke and wrote

of the Witchfinder General, as he was known. One said that Mister Hopkins and others like him are wont to inflame the base superstition of the country folk, who hold the power of the Witchfinders – for he had many imitators – in greater faith than that of Christ or God or the gospel preached. Others said that Hopkins' special innovations, the walking and pricking, were close enough to unlawful tortures so that they ought not to be condoned, and that the whole blood-soaked affair had begun to look quite French. Or worse, Spanish. And then at the Norfolk assizes these learned men delivered their queries to the judges who were to preside over the trial of several women Hopkins had had a hand in indicting. The women were pardoned. The women were freed. A very public humiliation. And so, ordained by God or no, he quit the work of witchfinding summarily. He gave it all up before the wind could properly change, and came back to Mistley with one last fat purse of silver to be Matthew Hopkins, country squire. He is rich enough to live well, but a man like Hopkins does not know how to live well. Or even, really, how to live.

He is restless, resentful. He is twenty-six years old, and has nobody to love him. There is also the matter of his health. He is prone to violent coughing fits. He wheezes. Perhaps he has spent too long in the fetid air of county jail cells and cunning women's nasty hovels; perhaps the curses lain upon him by old widows all over Essex have finally accreted into a blackness that rests on his chest and chokes the life out; or perhaps it is no more than the ague, which creeps in with the wetland fog. But Mister Hopkins' constitution is failing. He shuts himself up in his study with the tobacco pipe the physick recommended as remedy for his weakened lungs. He writes.

Which brings us to this afternoon in August.

31

The Book

I sit at the back-door stoop. From here I can look up out over the hills, the fine blue sky, striped with the last tender veins of fading day. It is a little cold, but a fire blazes in the kitchen, warming my back, and it is pleasant to sit there. I have wrung the neck of a chicken for Mister Hopkins' supper. Now I pluck. Rough handfuls of white feathers. Peace. I listen to the birds trilling sweet and sad out in the yard, as though in mourning for the fat hen in my lap. The master's bitch lolls by the fence, sniffing the first acerbs of winter in the air. I sniff winter in the air as well, and think it will be a long one and a dull one, trapped here at the Thorn, and without even the jollity of Christmastide to leaven the dark season, given that my master is Puritan and Puritans think it blasphemy to throw birthday parties for Our Lord Jesus Christ. But far be it from me to complain of boredom.

I know someone has come into the kitchen because the dog turns to peer at the open door where I sit. It is Mister Hopkins that calls my name. He stands by the kitchen table, Lazarene in his housecoat and damask headwrap, dark circles under his eyes. With one hand, he squeezes a stained handkerchief – I find these handkerchiefs scattered everywhere in the house as I go about my work, red and white and lace-trimmed, like savaged brides. In the other he holds a book. 'Rebecca,' he says, 'I have something to show you.'

As I move to set aside my work and rinse my hands clean in the bucket, he comes to where I sit at the open door. 'It is a fine evening,' he observes, looking out over the haze on the fields, his voice quiet and touched with wist. A sigh rattles in his throat.

Because he is so close to me, I fall still with the chicken sodden in my lap, and say nothing. He brings his fingertips to rest on the nape of my neck, just below my cap, and they twine about the short locks below where my hair is tied. I feel them there, cool and unaccustomed and affectionate. Him. He probably calls the sky the *firmament*. The fingers creep round to rest on my shoulder, and then my cheek, and he compels me to rest my head against the side of his leg. This – this is certainly *a moment*. Anyone who saw us would think it a tender one. 'Perhaps we might take the air after supper?' he suggests. 'A walk by the water? I think it would do me good.'

This is entirely unheard of. 'If you wish, Mister Hopkins,' I say.

'Good,' he replies, and releases his hold on me then. 'Come here.'

I shake the dander from my apron and follow him to the table. 'It was delivered from the printers down in London today,' he says. 'I thought you would like to see it.'

A slim volume neatly bound in black calfskin. He moistens his thumb and flicks this open to the title page – *The Discovery of Witches: In Answer to severall queries, lately Delivered to the Judges of Assize for the County of Norfolk. And now published by Matthew Hopkins, Witch-finder, for the Benefit of the whole Kingdom* (and beneath, Exodus 22:18: Thou shalt not suffer a witch to live). What lies before me is no less than his personal vindication. I understand then that he feels his climacteric to have passed. He believes he will soon die. I feel him looking at me. I see him smile. God's elect are wont to welcome death with rejoicing. 'And it all began with thee,

Rebecca,' he says. 'It all began—' And here he turns the title page over and brings his thin finger to the frontispiece, '—here.'

There is an engraving, and pictured in it are Old Bess Clarke and my mother, two hooded women sitting hunched in their chairs. Around them dance all manner of strange beasts: a black rabbit, a white thing half-cow-half-hound with a long curling tail, a horrid dog creature with the face of a baby. And the women speak, and gesture. Bess Clarke and my mother sit and name these beasts. They name them Newes, Holt, Grizzel, Greedigut, Peck in the Crown, Jarmara, Sacke and Sugar, Vinegar Tom. He has taken Vinegar Tom's name. And in the centre of it all, with a countenance graven in a look of tired and steadfast nobility, stands the Witchfinder, in his tall black hat and keen spurs, unmistakable, one hand pressed to his breast in a gesture of horror braced to unflagging resolve. I do not know what to say. The vanity of it is almost amusing – that he must have told whatever artist sat and carved the block that made this picture, somewhere in a cellar shop in London, how he ought to be dressed in it. *I wear a tall black hat*, he would have written, or said. *Boots above the knee. My hair curls.* I look between the Witchfinder General there on the page and the thin, spent man swaying at the table beside me in his dirty gown, a tideline of blood on his lips. I do not know what he wants from me. The wise thing would be to say what he wants me to, but for the first time in a year I do not know what that thing might be. Sentimental? So I say, 'I had a dream once that you kissed me upon my neck.'

He looks at me, curiously, and I am glad I said it, because now the shoe is on the other foot, and it is him who knows not what to say. He moistens his mouth. 'Really,' he replies, a word that can be spoken in both reproof and curiosity, and if said in a certain voice commits the speaker to neither mode. The fire crackles in the grate as we stand there at the table, face to face. The dog comes in to whine and nose at the hem of her master's housecoat. A spayed hound kept in the house drives ghosts away, they say.

I look at the engraving again. A black rabbit in the corner, Sacke and Sugar. 'Rabbit is what my mother would call me, sometimes,' I tell him. I do not know why I tell him it. He has a way, I think – or a way with me. Broken knows broken. And to who else am I to tell myself?

'Your mother was damned, and you would do well to forget her.' He closes the book.

'Is yours dead, too?' I ask.

He peers across at me, as if I am myself a haunting. 'No,' he says, slowly. But then he says, 'She was a very virtuous woman. Dutch.' *Was*. And that is all I will have of him, for he orders me back to my work, and snatches up the book before turning to sway down the hall, toward his study.

I finish plucking the chicken, scrub, stuff, tie the legs with string. Then I sit back down at the stoop to enjoy watching the day perish, in my quiet way, and the dog comes to rest her muzzle across my knees. *Yes*, I mutter to her, softly. *Yes, you poor thing. Your master is dying, and you will be alone in the world*. Her eyes are watery and sad. But then, they always were. Poor hounds, of countenance forever tragical. And Hopkins never gave her a name. *His bitch. My bitch*, is all he calls her.

32

Consumption

At Briggs' bidding, I knock at the door of Mister Hopkins' study. There is no answer. I call his name. Still nothing. But as my mother would say, a man is never so old he won't sulk given the chance. 'Supper, sir,' I say. I knock again. Still no answer. I try the handle, cautious. The door is unlocked.

The grey evening light comes in low at the window, and no fire burns in the hearth – all is shady, shapes of things like bone in deep water: the desk, the mantel, the books piled about on the carpet, and a pale figure recumbent on the settle, a man (or so he seems now), his palms upturned on either side. Silence but for the feeble cooing of the pigeons that have nested in the chimney breast. Again I say his name. He is inert, head tipped back, floating on the stagnant gloom. 'Mister Hopkins? Matthew?' He remains motionless.

A dark stain glistens across the front of his nightshirt. I nearly cry out, because it looks like blood. I find myself on my knees beside the settle grasping at his shoulders. I feel a wetness soaking through my skirts at the knees. I can smell it, too – not blood, but wine. A bottle rolls down by the side of the settle and clinks against a drained glass. It must have slipped from his grasp. A dark pool of it smothers the roses at the hem of the Turkey rug. Is he dead? A curious thing, to find a man dead. *Cadaver*, that pretty word again. I take the bottle and move to stand when I hear something, a scrabbling noise, coming from somewhere in the room, and see it from the corner of my eye, see Him again – a flash, grim and a little golden, like jewels stuffed quick in the thief's pocket, a hot breath on the side of my neck. Aloud I hear myself say, 'Thank you,' then, 'I did not think you would—' and then I do scream, I scream very loudly as a sticky hand closes tight about my wrist.

Hopkins' eyes half-open in the half-dark. He tries to say something, but I can't make out the words through the catch of blood in his throat. The blood spatters out his throat and over the breast of his housecoat as another fit of coughing racks his body. I haul him up by the shoulders so that he might breathe better, and dab the corner of my apron at the threads of reddish spittle coming from his mouth. He is very light in my arms. Mother Clarke was very light in my arms.

'What have you done?' Goody Briggs is standing in the doorway. She must have heard my scream. Her right hand – pink from the laundry pail – claps to her cheek.

'Nothing!' I shout back. Did she hear me speaking aloud to Him? 'Nothing—' I say again, and I make a great effort to compose myself. 'Mister Hopkins is gravely ill. The physick must be fetched at once. He cannot breathe, mistress . . .'

I tip Hopkins' head back and hear him breathe at last, breathe the stale air. It seems to calm him. His hand loosens at my wrist but his eyes remain wide and feverish and fixed on my face above his. Priscilla runs to find Samuel, leaving us alone. There I kneel by the settle, bent over Hopkins to hold him in that posture, where it seems he can breathe. He looks surprised. Maybe surprised that I am helping him – but I suppose death must be surprising as well, when it alights all of a sudden at your shoulder like a grim bird. I feel his body tremble in my arms, smooth his hair off his slickened brow. I suppose I should say some words of comfort to him, or sing a psalm, perhaps, but I find my mind is empty of all tenderness. I lower my mouth to his ear, and I ask him, as he once asked me, if he has his virtue, still. His eyes roll to my face as I pull away, and he wheezes, and I smile. 'Because I do not,' I say. 'Your Godly friend Master Edes saw to it. But then, I think you already knew. It must be vexing, I think – to deny oneself those earthly pleasures, thinking that privation common – and then to learn one's fellows only pretend to it. But of course, God knows the truth in every man's heart. The quality of his intention.' Cruel. But if I'm not now, the change may never present itself again.

His nostrils flare and another blood-glazed bubble swells at the corner of his mouth. I pat it away with my apron. I see his *Discovery of Witches* down by my feet at the side of the settle, the lovely new calfskin marred by a splash of port. 'I shall read your little book,' I tell him. 'I shall read it after you are dead. Are you afraid of Hell?' I ask, and feel his body shake below me, and hear the blood simmering in his gullet, and it is answer enough. I do feel something like tenderness then. Not for him, but for everyone else, all the other men and women. All the fright and confusion, the world piling its terror and abundant beauty up high on our broken backs. I do not forgive him, but I embrace him. I tell him that I do not think it is to Hell nor Heaven that we go, but nowhere – and nowhere is not so bad. I know because I have been there before.

Doctor Croke rinses his hands and pulls the counterpane up over Hopkins' bared chest, moist and quivering in the reed-light. Hairless, I am surprised to learn. Hopkins' mouth is cleared of the crusted blood. His breathing has eased – but it remains laboured, sawing.

'You are prepared to minister to him, Rebecca?' the physick asks. 'It would be unwise for a whole multitude to be tramping in and out of the sick-room. Your master's condition is catching. Strictly—' He shakes a finger in my face, '—no visitors.' *As if any left in Manningtree would choose to visit this boneyard.* But I nod. The doctor must think me the most disposable member of the household, to confer this responsibility on me – and he is not wrong to. He snaps his little leather bag shut and stands, flicking out his coat-tails.

I follow him into the corridor and down to the empty common room. 'Oh!' he ejects, lifting a dusty bottle from a half-empty shelf by the bar. 'Claret. May I?' he asks, tipping the bottle back and forth in his hand with a boyish grin. So that rumour is true.

I shrug, which he takes as permission enough, and finds two glasses beneath the bar. 'What must I do?' I ask him, as he dusts them gamely on his lacy cuff.

Doctor Croke shrugs, pouring the wine. 'The consumption is very advanced . . .' he sighs, tapping his fingers on the neck of the bottle. 'There is really very little that can be done. Unless you have a king handy to administer the touch? Although if you did I might suggest selling him to Parliament, instead,' he chuckles, taking a sip of wine. 'We could split the lucre.' His teeth are small and brown like acorns. I stare blankly at the physick, until he gets bored and concedes to my wish that I be taken seriously. 'Very well,' he says. 'Warm wine thrice daily. A good fire. Keep his mouth clear of blood. And pray, I suppose. He might have anything from mere days, to, well . . . God's power is great, his mercy infinite.'

I sit down at a table and he sets a glass before me. He returns to leaning against the bar. I fold my hands in my lap, and feel the Doctor considering me. He takes a sip of wine. 'Have you any kin remaining, in the country hereabouts?' he asks, carefully.

I shake my head.

'I see.' He tips his glass back and forth in his hand, thoughtfully. 'Your position is . . . well. You may wish to consider what alternatives might be available to you in the way of, ah, employment. In the event that your master – in the event that your master is to . . .'

'Die,' I offer.

He nods, with a simpering smile.

'I do not think there is any other in Manningtree who would take me on, given that I have – that I am a—'

'Witch,' he offers, in his turn.

I nod. I was going to say 'felon', but why bother. 'And I have no money to speak of with which to leave. So . . .' I take a sip of wine. It is woody and bitter in my mouth, a little flensing to the tongue.

Doctor Croke rubs the side of his nose and arranges the front of his doublet. 'That is unless you were to, ah—' He stands straight, clearing his throat, '—unless you were to marry, Miss West?'

'I think a reputation for sorcery might preclude happy matrimony much as it does gainful employment, sir.'

'You could marry me, Miss West.'

I struggle to swallow my wine. Just how much has he had to drink? Doctor Croke, with his horse-piss smell and his little leather bag and his coat of dark purple with the crimson trim (which Mister Hopkins might be able to carry, but the Doctor decidedly cannot). I raise my eyes to his face, and see that he is wholly serious, even keen. I take him in. Round-bellied and hale. In his late fifties, perhaps. He has kindly eyes, which I like. A thatch of white hair over a red face. A witch and a recusant – stranger things have happened, doubtless. They have happened to me, in fact.

He takes another gulp of wine and begins to speak again, words dribbing all in a great heap at my shy turned-in feet: *of course I am old enough to be thy father after my Margaret died you see God never blessed us with children but of course the marriage bed I would not expect you to unless but you are still a young woman of course I would not expect unless you wanted you might after all want but I am comfortably off fine house of great moral rectitude my faith is not I know people say that but I am not my work means I am* – until I raise my hand to stop him. I tell him that, respectfully, I must decline. Why do I decline? I can think of no reason more compelling for me to deny him than that I do not want to marry him. And this will have to suffice because I have done it now. There – flap – one future eaten up like a moth drowsed too close to flame.

'Oh,' he murmurs, and slumps back against the bar, scratching a finger under the brim of his hat. He does not look so very crestfallen, I think.

'But perhaps – Mistress Briggs would like to, sir?' I offer. 'Now that she is widowed.'

He peers up at me and purses his lips. 'Mistress Briggs? Hm.' He gulps down the rest of his claret and begins to move toward the door to the stable yard. 'Mistress Briggs. A hard hand, that woman has been dealt. A hard hand.' He repeats this quite a few times – *a hard hand* – as though the only way he might possibly justify his desire to marry again is that it would serve the community to remove some ill-starred destitute from the parish dole rolls. But I think he ought to, if it pleases him. It surprises me to find that I wish Goody Briggs no ill whatsoever.

I open the door for him, and dip my head. 'Have you any other calls to make tonight?' I enquire.

'Mistress Briggs,' he repeats, stroking his thin beard.

I nod again.

'No, no other calls.' He wanders distractedly across the yard to where his little piebald pony is stabled. 'Why?' he chuckles, narrowing his eyes at me across the court, playful-like. 'Not planning to throw any little charms out on the night, I hope?' He wiggles his fingers. I think he is quite drunk.

I smile, despite myself. 'No, sir.'

'Good, very good,' he hiccups, climbing shakily onto the pony and balancing his case in his lap. 'You take care of yourself, now, Miss West,' he says, grabbing hold of the reins and looking blearily toward where I stand in the doorway.

'I will, sir.' I dip in another curtsey.

'I mean it,' now kicking the pony on, 'look after *yourself*, Miss West.'

I stand at the door and watch as the pony's white rump and swishing tail disappear beyond the wagon yard and into the shadow and I think, it cannot be true what people say about Papists. Doctor Croke is a bad physick, but he is a good man. Good enough, at least. I take a deep, grateful breath of the cold night air before bolting the door and heading back inside. I find the greater part of the bottle of claret in the common room. It cannot be far from midnight. The inn sleeps. Yet how queerly alive I am.

I take the wine and return to my kitchen stoop, wrapped in a shawl. The wine must already be shambling about with my head, because I think, almost aloud, *good kitchen stoop, good friend kitchen stoop* as I sit down, setting a candle at my elbow. I sit there for a long while, and I *drink*. Myriad moths and longlegs flit about my small light. I watch them, brown and gold, like dirt brought alive. And that is when I see it – the white rabbit, just a flash of it, with the coral-bead eyes, the knife ears. His leg bends just within the glow of my candle before he sees me, and scutters away across the yard. Bead eyes and knife ears. I slide on my pattens and move to follow him.

I am halfway up the hill behind the Thorn before I think to wonder what it is that I am doing. The dew splashes cold on my ankles and up and up I climb, the bottle bouncing against my leg. When I reach the crest of the hill I stop and turn on the spot. Darkness, no moon-of-rabbit but real moon, huge and shot through with spears of cloud like a sacred heart. I can see all of Mistley behind me, and

Manningtree too, huddled at the waist of the river. Little bracelet of lights flickering on the water. The sounds rise to meet me: the clop of an axe on a log in a dark yard; a child laughing; dog bark, dog bark two, in answer. The fires of the shipyards, the smell of love. How terrible, how beautiful, all these people dreaming in their beds and fucking there as well, and marrying and dying and hanging their washing out to dry. There were towns like this – and larger – all over England, sacked and burnt to ashes now. Washerwomen. Books. I think to myself, *I am drunk*. I remember what I have left to do, what has been left for me to do.

33

Felon

I stand at the end of my master's bed, and consider his sleeping face. Matthew Hopkins, Witchfinder General. Matthew. I wonder if he had – or has – brothers and sisters. If he had brothers, were they, too, named for Apostles? *Witchfinder* is as it sounds, I suppose because there is no need to add further complication to an already complicated matter by the use of troublesome terminology. A Witchfinder, he who finds witches. Note, that is all he claims to do – find them. What happens to those witches once they have been found is someone else's responsibility, this name seems to intimate. The 'General' appellation was added I know not when and by I know not whom. Probably by Hopkins himself, like a dyed plume to a hat. 'General' as in common, and being appropriate to all things? Or 'General' as in a warrior, one who leads men? I could not say. I have never thought to ask.

The spring of my sixteenth year, the Glascocks' outhouse burned down. A rain-shower quenched the flames overnight, but I remember the look of it the next morning, the thatch bent in on the softened, steaming beams. That is what Hopkins' face reminds me of now, his *handsome-if* features mollied and diminished as though the bone itself has poached beneath his feverish skin. I take his face apart in my mind. I itemise. His beard has grown long, and gives him a wolfish look – a sick wolfish look, the look of some poor whining thing that has eaten aconite. His eyes roll and twitch beneath the lids. He has long, thick eyelashes, like a boy-child's. I had never noticed them before. His black hair sprawls about on the pillow.

Then his body. His chest, hairless and convex, quivers under the quilt like the dry skin of a drum. His hands, thin and delicate, are folded over his bosom on the counterpane, each finger ending with a long, broken nail. There is blood under those long, broken fingernails. His blood. I think, should I clip his nails, and file them? Should I make him look presentable for what is to come? His mouth is open. His breath – the rasping. The bed-drapes are of purple damask. The sleep of the rich comes so beautifully wrapped.

He opens his eyes a crack. 'Rebecca?' he says (or a sound like *Rebecca*).

'It is I.'

He asks, has the doctor left? It hurts to hear him try to speak.

'Yes,' I say. 'I have warmed a little wine for you, sir.' I move to his bedside and he turns his head toward me. I try to help him sit up, but he shakes his head, *no*.

'Doctor Croke instructed me to—'

He interrupts with a wheeze. 'It matters not,' he manages, eventually.

'Come now, Mister Hopkins,' I say, gently, and feel it to be obscene that I am chivvying him like a mother, even as I fluff his pillows and draw him up upon them, even as I splash a little of the warm wine over his lips. 'Doctor Croke has said your condition may very well improve, if you will only consent to rest,' I burble, like a happy idiot, 'and he reminds me – the power of God is great.'

Hopkins swallows down the wine and forms words, both with difficulty. 'Doctor Croke is an imbecile.'

'Aye, he must be, because he asked me to marry him.' Probably the wine has loosened my tongue, but it is too outlandish, too amusing a thing to sit upon.

Hopkins rolls his bloodshot eyes toward me in an attempt at an expression.

I laugh. 'I denied him.'

He watches me curiously as I raise the glass to my own lips, then grunts and settles his head back against the pillows. 'Perhaps,' he mutters, the wine-fumes seeming to have loosened the snarls in his throat, 'he is . . . he is correct. It might be – merely the chill on the air. The chill of the lengthening nights.'

'It may well be so.'

'Read to me,' he coughs. 'John. The Gospel of John.'

A Bible rests by his bedside, the spine worn and cracked. *In the beginning was the Word, and the Word was with God, and the Word was God.* He listens, silent but for his hacking breath, until I reach verse twenty-nine, when the Lord Jesus comes to John, and John bids him Behold the Lamb of God, which taketh away the sin of the world, and there I stop. Hopkins turns to look at me. His eyes are wet. He reaches out his hand to clasp mine, our fingers entwining against the open book.

'I have never . . . properly thanked you, Rebecca,' he says. 'For your part in helping me to – to drive out the darkness.' His colourless lips curl in a smile almost fond. He means this. It comes from his heart, wherever that hard facility might be. 'Your truth spoken like a bright bolt from Heaven. You gave me my sword, my armour.' His fingers twitch against mine.

'I lied,' I say. 'And you knew it.'

He is still. He lets out a rattling sigh. 'For the greater good,' he says. 'The will of God . . .' He trails off. Even he is tired of *the will of God*, that everyman's sop. We cannot all know it. We cannot all have it. We cannot continue to pluck the limbs off one another until we finally decide who does.

I feel my teeth set hard against each other in my mouth. 'You made me a sinner.'

He rolls his bloodshot eyes and turns his head away. 'You made yourself a sinner.'

I shake my head. My voice is shaking. 'But that is not your doctrine. Your doctrine is that we can make of *ourselves* nothing. There are damned and saved, and the saved climb over the bodies of the damned to reach Heaven. Do you believe it? Do you see yourself—' my voice is full of rage, it surprises me, '—shining?'

'The world is stained,' he mutters. 'Black with the filth of sin. Filth like—'

'Like me?' I laugh. 'Aye, and the filth you like to play in. Like to get just close enough to smell. Like to touch then wash your hands of—' And it is a thing a child would do but I do it – I pull my hand away from his and slam the heavy Bible shut on his thin fingers, and he lets out a cry. I think he realises then, because he tries to push the covers away and to stumble up out of the bed. He is frightened, for it follows that if the saved are beyond reproach then the damned have nothing to lose, and he knows it – and I throw it, I throw the Bible because it is in my hands and it is heavy and it hits him square between the shoulder blades as he rises wobbling to his feet. He falls forward and against the wall, slithers to the floor, the counterpane wrapped about his legs, sticking to the sweat of his sickness. I am upon him then, a black horned feeling then quickly white hot, white, thought and intent very clear like a black horse standing in a field of gold, I picture it and it makes me steadfast – a black horse in a field of gold. He scratches at my throat and breasts and hands, and my hands have something else in them, a pillow, and I put it over his face and feel him struggle, he struggles and thrashes between me, between us – my thighs – a thin and slackening body, life a slit of light swallowed by the cloud. He is so weak now, like a baby, and dying. I am strong. I am also drunk. And that helps. And it stops. He stops moving.

What I next know is that I am huddled beside a cabinet, my back against the wall with my head on my knees, breathing, breathing into my bunched apron. And he is not breathing. Mister Matthew Hopkins is not breathing. *Take care of yourself, Rebecca.* I can see his limp, bare feet before me, a little tuft of wiry black hair on the big toe. Still. Will never move again, his feet, his spurs that clink. There is thinking to be done, along with the breathing. Fleeing too, certainly. Who was in the house and what was there to hear? My throat stings, web of scratches – *beat and claw the witch until I fetch blood of her*. Stop. I am alone in the room. It was me, not Him. Do the needful thinking. There is no one to help.

First, I take the pillow from his face. I do not look at his face. It feels important I do not look at the face. There is blood on the underside of the pillow. I put the pillow back blood-down upon the bed, fluff it, *good girl*. I will not be able to move him easily, to lift him back into the bed, to shape the body into a semblance of serenity, to make it look as though he passed in his sleep. No. It would take too long. Bible returned to the bedside, with a swift prayer of gratitude to Saint John. Take the key from the drawer, where he keeps it. Kept it. It is the only key, and it is now mine. Stand, killer. *Quandary the first*: do I use the key to lock the door to Hopkins' chamber from the outside? They would have to knock it down, pick the lock – it could buy me time until he is discovered. But immediately it would raise suspicion, for the door to be locked, and from the outside, and no answer coming from within. I decide I will not lock the door. Downstairs to his study, light on my stockinged feet, careful not to knock the wine glass still rolling by the settle, disturb the books stacked in the shadowy corners. I creep. The desk. He keeps his money there. I take his money, velvet purse of money, twelve pounds at least, no time to count, but I see at a glance there is enough, and a bit more again, to pay for all of Richard Edwards' damnable bewitched cattle. I take his book, an old riding cloak, lace my boots. Pray the hour is early enough that I will not be seen. *Quandary the second*: how will my own disappearance be accounted for, except by the assumption I had a hand in my master's death? There is an irony there, how I have made myself matter at the very time I would most wish not to. Perhaps, if I am lucky, they will think the Devil, having used me as the instrument of his vengeance, has finally made away with me. Perhaps, if I am lucky, Doctor Croke will prove himself as good a man as I hope him to be, and will stall on my behalf. And so it is I find myself trudging through the gloaming, empty streets of Manningtree, and see not a soul, and no soul sees me, praise be to God.

Past the White Hart, the quay wall, and then I follow the winding Stour. Lord, let this damned place forget me. Let it let me go. The sky lightens until I can see soft wrinkles of blue on the slow-flowing water, through tall reeds crowned with blonde cotton-stuff, where godwits and wild fowl and nesting geese make their secret conventicles. I must be careful where I put my feet, for the ground is marshy, soft in places. My body aches with tiredness, but I do not allow myself to feel it. My mind is glittering like a coin set on its side to spin. I see the dawn rise across the fields, behind the fat tower of Dedham church.

In the last hours of the moon, I find myself walking in the half-light of Dedham High Street, where the houses are larger, set back from the cobbled road, clothed prettily in ivy. The shops are yet to open, but I find a carter bound for Ipswich, who lets me sit up among the boxes. I do sit at first, restless and upright, my hands cramping around Hopkins' velvet purse, but our swaying progress through the waterlogged fields soon lulls me to sleep. The carter takes no liberties, asks very few questions, and wakes me gently when we arrive. I am slumped on my left side and covered by the cloak, but he must see the scratches at my throat. He will not let me pay him, which I take as a good indication that I must look either very ill indeed, or very well indeed.

In the busy streets of Ipswich I am apart from all, men and women, listening for the word, the name, the *Witchfinder* – but I hear nothing. No hew and cry raised at my back. Vegetables and fruits and fresh-cut flowers soup their smells together in a sunny market square. Smiling faces. I picture the afternoon light – for it is now a very fine day – spilling through the window of Hopkins' chamber to gild his limp undiscovered feet, and his sallow undiscovered cheeks. A tinsel in his hair. It makes me feel peaceful. Cocky, even, for at a rag and bone cart I buy a little scarlet jacket with a trim of black ribbon and trade my cap for a white lace kerchief worked with a design of rosemary sprigs (rosemary stands for remembrance). And I no longer look like Rebecca West, or do for the first time look like Rebecca West. But the name I give myself is Rebecca Waters.

I also buy some oysters and cherries and a pot of beer and find a seat at the bank of the river, where I make a tidy feast of it. Two passing women carrying baskets look at me quite strangely when I find myself laughing aloud, thinking how I threw a Bible at him. It was an accident, really. I could remember it as an accident, if I chose. As Master Edes chose to remember me.

34

London

From Ipswich another cart, and this the eighty-and-some-spare miles to London, where I think it unwise to linger. But I do see Saint Paul's, which I think very dirty and grey, with vagrants sleeping heaped in the passages, and I do stand upon the bridge, London Bridge, where I watch the boatmen try to shoot under at high tide like caddisflies on a stream, seeming to make a sport of it, which appears to me most perilous and unwise. Mind, it seems unwise they have only one bridge for all of these people. I see many poor men and many rich men but am frightened of neither, for in my small years I have already been held in a gaol with nothing but the slip on my back and lied most perniciously to the Earl of Warwick, which must make me a woman of the world, all told.

I gather up snatches of conversation, apprentices' grievances (and there are many, apprentices and grievances for them to hold) or preachers' kindling or the trollop-talk of whatever young buck in a marvellous lemon-yellow coat might pass me on the street, but never once do I hear news of home, or of the Witchfinder. The talk is of Cromwell and Pym and Colonel Rainsborough, and many other names that I feel ought to be familiar to me, Rebecca Waters, woman of the world and Citizen of the New Republic. I feel, for the first time, the enchantment of money. With eleven pounds weighty as a pig's heart at my hip, anything I want can be mine, and is: candied apples; mauve ribbon and a handful of small silk daisies I want to sew on a bonnet I do not own; a little book of poems I buy from the stalls at Saint Paul's for nothing other than the beauty of its marbled end-papers. Really 'freedom' means 'money', and if anyone tells you otherwise it's a good bet they've plenty of both already.

Then south of the river. The ships moored at Deptford are bigger than any I have seen before, painted in black and gilded at the ribs and points, pennants shivering just half visible through the thickness of tar smoke and wrights' fires and God knows what other harbour bubble. Dog-meat. Kickshaws. Their front parts loom thrilling up over me, over the dock, like the great bellies of dragons, crusted with barnacles and cornice-work and beautiful women with long blue hair, and I love each and every one – the *Diamond*, the *Antelope*, the *Laurel* – entire, from crow's nest to keel. I press through the throng unheeded and hear many tongues spoken, French and Dutch and others I could not name if you held my feet over a fire.

On to one great galleon men in chains are being led. I stop to watch, because I know that there are men brought from Africa to the New World as slaves, but these men look no different from those in Essex or London or those that might be found anywhere else in England, for all I know, except dirtier (though not by much). Long hair hangs ragged about their shoulders and they are half-dressed, some in shirts of good cloth, though stained and ripped. Two men smoking their pipes under the eaves of a storehouse must see me looking, for one says, laughingly, *Chevalier – king-men, king-men* – and his fellow laughs more when I flinch and move away from them. He tells me they are soldiers from the King's army, and our Parliament sends them to the sugar plantations in Barbados, sells them. He laughs again, showing me his tiny yellow teeth, like a dog's. I feel somehow dubious then, as though I have seen something that I ought not to have, dog-teeth and chained men both; but it is happening there quite openly at the busy dock, and people are sparing no more than a second glance for that sad processional. In some way I am glad to see it, for it strengthens my resolve to leave England as soon as I might, England where Christian men sell other Christian men to other Christian men.

I do not know what a sober captain or an honest fare might look like, so I find myself following the Puritan folk about the harbour, reasoning that they probably have a shrewd nose for both. There are many of them, in that familiar drab costume: anxious, austere husbands dragging wives dragging sons and daughters through the gaily-hued crowd, luggage boxes squeezed under their arms, over-burdened with cauldrons and spinning wheels, bound for Boston, Maine, Virginia, Massachusetts Bay – a *new* New Jerusalem, that one that was so recently declared in London having already failed to meet their Godly expectations. There are so many ships, after all, that one must surely be bound for Paradise. 'Rockport' seems an unlikely name for Paradise to go by, but that is the destination I eventually settle upon, for no other reason than that I admire its honesty. I know what a rock is, I know what a port is; there can be no surprises in a Rockport. Even fewer, for Rockport is in 'Essex County'. For a moment, lining at the gangplank, I envision my arrival, eight weeks hence, at Manningtree's strange double, every detail arranged identical across the ocean by God's own meticulous hand; the same rusted bell in the port; the same dirty swans circling the bay; the same sagging rooftops and chimney stacks. But it was not God that named that part of the New World 'Essex County'; it was man. Or men. Trying to make it feel like home, I suppose, except it is the Agawam who are putting torch to storehouse and stable, instead of one's brother Christians.

The Captain of this ship, the *Myrmidon*, is a handsome Scot called Scanlan, with a ruddy face and eyes of a very bright elemental blue, as though they became that way through too long spent staring at sea and sky. He looks twice at my red jacket and laughs, which makes me shy of myself, and takes four pounds fare and board, which frightens me, being likely more than my mother's whole house and all within it might have fetched, back in Manningtree. But I pay it. He says if anyone gives me bother to come to him directly, and bows deep like a gentleman, which is the surest sign he is not one.

There is much bother and activity as the ship glides from the port and out onto the Thames. Deptford becomes a muddled thread of colour and smoke across the water, and the westerly light falls on the palace at Greenwich, making the stone glow like a chip off an angel's leg. Then the green hills of Kent rolling southward into the dusk, and the world of the dead, England, beneath. The deck empties as the evening light dwindles. The Puritans go below to find their bunks, but I stay above to feel the wind and watch the water widen, the banks thin, the gulls argue in the cloud, and say *goodbye goodbye I will not miss you*. There is another woman standing alone by the prow, who seems to be saying her own inside goodbyes. She is short and slight, wearing a jacket of grey wool. Her red hair is uncovered and arranged into an artful burst of coils in front of her ears. Red hair – and then I see that this woman is Judith, Judith Moone, the upturn of her sharp nose against the haze of the evening sky as known to me as Proverbs. I think it cannot be, but nonetheless I call her name, immediately, unthinkingly. She turns and looks me full in the face, her eyes widen, and then she turns again, hitches her skirts up, and walks off welcher-quick toward the prow. So I call her name again and follow after. This continues for quite some time, Judith dashing about the deck with myself in hot pursuit and half the sailors watching bemused, until at last I throw up my arms and call out to ask where it is she thinks that she might go – with our being on a boat, of all things – that I cannot follow. She stops, spins on the spot and narrows her eyes. She hustles over and grabs my arm, drawing me to the taffrail: 'I thought you were dead,' she tells me. To which I dip in an ironical curtsey and say it is a mighty pleasure to see her too.

She softens and releases my arm, sweeping her eyes up and down over me. 'Sorry,' she says, grudgingly. 'But what – I cannot – how is it that you are here?' And I can tell she truly *did* think me dead, and that a part of her still does, so staggered she seems by my sudden appearance.

I sweep my eyes, too. Her apparel is poor and sad, made sadder by the flourishes of gaiety: a lilac kerchief around her grimy neck, two circles of rouge on her cheeks, green stockings sagging at her ankles. It has been four years since we last saw one another – four years since she left Manningtree. I do not think those years have been very kind to her. Maybe not so downright spiteful as they were to me, but. Suffering is suffering. 'I left Manningtree,' is all I can think to say. 'A week.'

'The others?' she asks, her big eyes suddenly wet, shifting side to side. She raises a hand to tug at her kerchief. *The others*, by which she means her mother. She knows what she did, but not what came of it. Telling her will have to be revenge enough, I suppose.

I shake my head, which she understands to mean, *dead*. 'Well,' I add, with a weak smile, 'apart from Helen. I do not know what became of her. But we have not been below, yet, so perhaps—'

It is a bad joke. One ought probably not to make any sort of joke to a person who has just learned they are an orphan. Judith looks suddenly sick, and turns away from me to place her hands on the rail, head slumped. Hesitantly, I lay my fingers on top of hers. She does not withdraw, and we stand for a while in silence like that. The wind snaps about the rigging. 'I thought,' she sighs, eventually, rubbing at her eyes with the corner of her kerchief. 'I heard four were hung in Manningtree, but not the names. I had a man read me the news-sheets. There were no names. I knew, anyway. You know—' She rests the point of her chin on her hand and looks over the water, '—I didn't realise how *funny* mother was, until I was in the company of men. They were *funny*. Whether they meant to be or not. We had laughter, if shit all else. But that is no small thing.'

A man? All right then. I glance around the deck. 'You travel alone?' I ask.

She nods, she sniffs. She smiles slant at me. 'Aye. And a little further than Ipswich.' *Side by side on her bed in our smocks, white smocks.*

I edge in a little closer, so that we might not be heard. 'Where did you go?'

'London. I was at the playhouses. In the chorus. I wore a crown of flowers in *Timon*,' she says, with a fleeting smug cant of her smudged chin, 'and then Parliament closed the playhouses.' And then she was something else, I glean. She straightens and draws her threadbare shawl tighter around her shoulders, for the wind is biting out on the opening water. 'You are not angry with me?'

'No.' I think for a moment. 'I was angry I did not think to do what you did first.'

'Your neck . . .' she says, and reaches out to touch my throat, and the scratches there.

My own hand leaps to bat her fingers away and rearrange my neck-tie. 'Your face,' I say back.

She grins broadly. 'Look at us. Being uncivil to one another – but on a big old ship.'

'If they could see us now...'

Judith loops her arm through mine and we promenade toward the forecastle, gulls wheeling above our empty old heads, and I am glad to have found a friend again. Especially one with whom I might laugh at death, which tried to close in around us, and very nearly managed.

35

The Devil

Judith and I share a bunk in the hold below, and I am even more glad of her, because it is deathly cold and we are permitted no fire bigger than a lantern-light. It is also frightening – or uncanny, at the very least, the air close with the smells and the whispering of strangers, the timbers heaving and straining all about. The sort of thing you need to get accustomed to. We lie face to face and speak quietly of the things we did – and the things that were done to us.

Judith did not stay long at the Thorn. The very next night after her arrival, with the town thrown into tumult by Old Mother Clarke's arrest, she stuffed a pair of Hopkins' silver candlesticks beneath her dress and slipped out the back door, which he had neglected to lock (perhaps not yet fully appreciating the banal cunning of the impecunious country maid). She cut across the Vale of Dedham, much as I had, and made it as far as Sudbury sleeping in hedgerows, before she found a carter who would take her to Brentford, and then another who would take her from there to London – or to Poplar, at least. Every carter in the fens must have a panicked maid lolling atop his freight these days.

She tells me she found work as a domestic in the lodgings of one Dame Pearson, work she was precisely as ill-suited to as I had predicted. She tells me she drank too much – or too strong, at least. She tells me of her short and unhappy marriage to a Godly brewer named Dalton, who liked to impose frequent and severe fasts upon their household, needing no more excuse than the immanence of a Sunday. He eventually decided, instead, upon an altogether quicker route to God's right hand, flinging himself from a bridge one night and leaving her penniless. She tells me of the baby they had, a boy, and how it died. She tells me of the playhouses and the brothels and the places which were both by turns, where Earls consorted with pickpockets and the sailors drank a strange cordial, like milk with black seeds, which made their eyes as big as their ideas. She tells me of visiting the palace at Whitehall, where the glass domes stand broken open to the rain, and seeing the King's own nightshirts there, which were very fine. She did not see a camel, for all the beasts that were kept there had long since died, but she did see a drawing that was made of one.

So now she is Judith Dalton, and I am Rebecca Waters, and I do not know what I ought to tell her back. I tell her of how they came to take me from our house on Lawford hill, where the rosehip grew by the kitchen window, and of how proud the Constable was that he had killed our cat. I tell her there is no longer a market cross at Market Cross, just a nub of pale stone, so I suppose they will call it Market Nub now. I tell her that the windows at St Mary's remain boarded up. I tell her that Prudence Hart miscarried her baby, which she is much cheered by. I tell her of John Edes. I tell her what we did in the wood, I tell her how he ran away and left me, I tell her how he is a soldier in the New Model now ('Good,' she says, 'I hope Prince Rupert's Boy eats his prig face right off then shits it out in a ditch'). I tell her of Hopkins. I tell her he is dead – I do not tell her how. I do not tell her I saw the Devil. I tell her that the Widow Moone, her mother, spoke often of her, and kindly, because lying comes easily to me now, and as lies go I do not feel it to be an especially sinful one.

We talk until the goodwife in the neighbouring bunk rolls on her side and huffs at us to cease our prattle so that she might sleep. Judith mutters out of the corner of her mouth that our wearied interlocutor is a *curd-faced old bag*, but nonetheless leans across to bid me goodnight, presses a kiss to my brow, then turns away to face the timbers. Above the blanket, I can see the little bones of her spine pressing against her freckled skin. I count the freckles, *one two thirteen twenty*, over and over by the low light, but find I cannot sleep. Instead, I observe the queer listing movements of the lantern that casts light over the cabin, listen to the soft snoring of my fellow passengers, and wonder how deep the water is beneath my back and what strange creatures swim in it. And that last thought is a sure way to frighten oneself aboard a ship, buried in all the sea's great yearning and shuddering, which it is written shall one day engender the end of this very sad world, gulp all men and women down to salt. We must still be close to England's coast, and yet my mind makes fathom on fathom of darkness to sink through, darkness where serpents weave their bodies together, and at the bottom of it all the human bones that ever were lying strewn about, and with no thought at all for what body they once belonged to, or what doctrine it held. Carefully, so as not to wake Judith, I come out from under the blankets and drop to the cabin floor. I fetch my cloak and pick my way toward the ladder, through the sleeping passengers and their scattered luggage. Frying pans and three-string guitars and spindles, the sad inventory of the lost.

Up on the deck I am doused in cold, clean air, and the sea seems a good thing again. A near-full moon hangs high over the shuddering water, and stars so thick they are a white pith around it. The Atlantic – the Great Sea. I have not been there long, standing by the starboard rail, when Captain Scanlan arrives at my elbow, dipping his hat. 'A calm night,' he says, like a father gazing proud at a sleeping babe, almost, 'let us pray it continues.'

'I think I ought rather to pray yourself and your sailors are able to win us through if it does not, Captain Scanlan, sir,' I reply.

He laughs at that, Scottishly. 'Have you ever sailed before, Miss . . . ?'

'Waters,' I tell him, after a longer pause for thought than I would like. 'No, I have not.'

He nods and looks out over the short waves. 'Aye. Then I shall endeavour to ensure you fall in love with it, Miss Waters. There is nothing else in all the world that is the like of it.'

Nothing else in all the world that is the like of it? Please. Those are words he has practised many times, and to many maids before me. 'And what? Become a sailor, in the New World?' I sally. I realise I am playing the coquette. Rebecca Waters is an unpredictable character indeed.

'Why not? All things are possible in the New World, Miss Waters. And you have the name for it. A sailor, a whaler, or perhaps,' he turns to look at me with a greedy grin, and there is a flash of gold in his mouth, a gold tooth, 'or perhaps a sailor's wife?'

I feel a strange wringing feeling in my guts, because that was what my mother was. A sailor's wife – although I never thought of her that way, never asked how and where it was that she met my father, her husband, God rest. I look at Captain Scanlan, handsome and weathered with his thick neck and his gold tooth and his merry soul, and think, *yes, I see.* Did it go something like this? I hold my cloak tight at my throat and smile over my hand, and say: 'I thought sailors were meant to be married to the sea?' And I could picture my mother saying it, too. *Apple never rots far from the tree.* That's another thing they say. Hag-tree.

He laughs again. He is a laughing man, which is better than a smiling man, I think. 'Aye, they do say that. A sailor's mistress, then?'

I click my tongue. 'I think I might do better, sir.'

He smiles and lowers his head so that his smile, glittering tooth and all, is visible below his hat's tilted brim – a gesture tenderly choreographed. The wisp of hair that licks at his beard in the sea-wind, a felicitous addition. 'I expect you will, Miss Waters,' he says, and bids me goodnight, striding back toward the forecastle. He whistles as he goes, which is just as well, because whether smiling or laughing, I cannot abide a man who whistles.

I stand there with the moon and the pithy stars a while longer, soothed by the gentle sway of the boat and the look of the waves' naked backs as they catch the night-glow, then release it, then swell up again, bucking and foaming, seeming to have fun in the moonlit dark, to enjoy themselves, to humour our tiny ship with mercy. At last I turn to head below, and catch sight of a shape in the prow; a dark shape, a man in black, wearing a long coat like a presbyter and a high-crowned hat. He turns his head. He smiles at me over his shoulder. There is a wind in his long black coat, and the same wind is in my hair, the wind of many seas, it feels like. So I loose my hair, I loose it for him. And I find I am no longer looking at the man in black, but looking back at myself, death-dealer, her white cap balled in her fist, hair blown like a rose in the wind of many seas.

Afterword

John Stearne and Matthew Hopkins – the self-appointed Witch-finder General – were active across East Anglia and the Home Counties of England in the middle years of the 1640s, during which time they are estimated to have had a hand in the execution for witchcraft of anything from one hundred to three hundred women and men (Stearne, in his *Confirmation and Discovery of Witchcraft*, first published in 1648, puts the number at two hundred). The so-called Witch Craze of the English Civil War was an apparently unprecedented period of persecution, which historians have accounted for by citing myriad social, religious, economic and local factors: the vacuum of authority and the widespread famine engendered by the war (which also interfered with normal legal procedure); virulent anti-Catholicism; growing Puritan radicalism in the south of England; the growth of the merchant class and shifting attitudes toward poverty and vagrancy (belief in a providential God rather sours one's opinion of a needy neighbour – there is no such thing as hard luck, just the Lord's ire). The impact of Hopkins' own personal charisma and undoubted animus against witches is, in this fraught context, hard to properly judge, as are his true motives.

Matthew Hopkins, a Minister's son from Greater Wenham, Suffolk, was born around 1620 and died in Mistley in 1647, apparently of tuberculosis. Conflicting contemporaneous accounts of who he was and where he came from combine with later conjecture and Gothic mystification to create an impression of a man who seems at best to have been a serial bullshitter, at worst a compulsive liar. Certainly, he died very young. He may have been a craven opportunist and arch manipulator; or he may sincerely have believed in his cause, subscribing to the Puritan dogma of damnation and Biblical literalism that demanded the extirpation of witches. We will never know. But I had fun weighing the possibilities. I hope readers will, as well – but my real interest was in the persecuted, not the persecutor. The accounts of the Essex witches' trials offer an invaluable – and deeply moving, I think – insight into the fears, hopes, desires and insecurities of the women who scratched out their existence on the very edges of society, and who have otherwise gone voiceless, or else been muted by victimhood. I hope I have done justice to their character, humour and pride, which radiates from the records of their lives and deaths even after four hundred years.

All trial scenes were excerpted from contemporaneous accounts of the Manningtree witches' arraignment and Rebecca West's confession, first published in 1645, and easily accessed online. These I transcribed to modern English, and sometimes edited for brevity. Timelines have been condensed, some characters have been relocated (the Moones actually lived in Thorpe-le-Soken, not Manningtree) or had their roles expanded (John Edes, Priscilla Briggs, Prudence Hart, Minister Long), and some are wholly invented (Thomas Briggs, Leah Miller, Doctor Croke). But I have endeavoured to remain as close as I could to the facts, as they have been presented to us, in doubtless sensationalised form, of the life of Rebecca West, described to us only as 'a young maid, daughter to Anne West', and of her direct associates, who – with the exception of Elizabeth

Clarke, who died in Chelmsford – were executed in Manningtree in 1645. Rebecca disappears from the record around this time.

Witch-hunts – which involved the brutal torture and execution of thousands of women and men in Europe in the sixteenth and seventeenth centuries – are not a relic of the past in many parts of the world. We exported them. In recent years, alleged witches have been murdered by the Islamic State, as well as in Tanzania, in India, and in other countries dealing with the brutal legacy of colonialism. I would recommend the work of Silvia Federici to anyone seeking to learn more about the witch-hunt as an ongoing social and economic phenomenon. I am also indebted to the work of historians including Keith Thomas, James Sharpe, Diane Purkiss, Malcolm Gaskill and Stacy Schiff.

Acknowledgements

First and largest thanks to my agent, Zoe Ross, and my editor at Granta, Ka Bradley, whose insight and creativity were instrumental in shaping this story. The manuscript was undergoing its final stages of editing and production during the Covid-19 pandemic of 2020, and I am profoundly grateful to everyone at Granta Books for their diligent work in bringing this book to publication in these unprecedented circumstances: Christine Lo, Mandy Woods, Sam Fulton, Sarah Wasley and Jo Walker, who designed the beautiful cover of this edition.

I was only able to complete this book because I had reached, for the first time in my adult life, a position of relative financial security. I am grateful to the Society of Authors for a small work-in-progress grant I received, and to the Ledbury Poetry Festival for the Forte Prize for Best Second Collection (awarded for my poetry collection *Fondue*) which, at the risk of sounding trite, changed everything for me. Thanks also to Luke Constable and Michael Williams for the unglamorous but indispensable bestowal of corporate latitude.

I am fortunate to have so many people in my life whose friendship and work has nourished my own. Eternal love and abiding gratitude to Kate Duckney, Amy Key, Jessica St. James, Rebecca Tamás,

Eli Goldstone, Sophie Collins, Rebecca Perry, Alex McDonald, Richard Scott, Jane Yeh, Helen Charman, Bryony White, Martha Sprackland, George Vaisey, Mark Abirached and Louis Doyle. And to my logical family, Katrina Buchanan, Robert & Kezia Herzog.

Finally, to my long-suffering Virgo, Edward Caddy. My grandmother, Sheila Blakemore, and my father, Paul Blakemore, (my first and best reader, honorary Manningtree Witch).